"Yes. We are interes[   ] will buy it. Him."

Eadward's laughter choked off. "Rowena! You cannot be serious."

Rowena gritted her teeth. She did not take orders from anyone any more. Not even a king's thane. She would never let anyone make decisions for her again.

"I am. I thought it might be amusing." She smiled. "Twelve mancuses. I will send my steward," she said to the trader across Eadward's sudden silence.

Her feet crunched on the gravel path. She would not look back over her shoulder.

But she did.

They unchained him. He scarce seemed to notice it. She could read neither relief nor apprehension in his expression, only a fiercely controlled attention that would have drawn the secrets out of a runestone. It spoke of a will that was unrelenting.

She turned away from all the disturbing power she had just purchased.

Behind her, she could feel the clear gaze of the slave, like a knife in her back.

What in heaven's name had she done?

Helen Kirkman's love affair with Anglo-Saxon and Viking history began when, as a schoolgirl, she stood on the mysterious grassy remains of a hill fort and dreamed of what might have been. Other school projects, a degree in languages and various jobs intervened, but when the opportunity came to write in a way that combined history with romance, it proved irresistible.

Born in Cheshire, she now lives in New Zealand in a house by the sea shared with her husband, two sons and a word processor. Her desire to write was encouraged by Romance Writers of New Zealand and, in 2001, she won the Clendon Award for Best Romance Manuscript.

A recent novel by the same author:

A MOMENT'S MADNESS

Look for her next novel

EMBERS

Coming soon

FORBIDDEN

Helen Kirkman

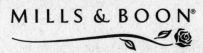

MILLS & BOON®

*First published in Great Britain 2005
by Harlequin Mills & Boon Limited,
Eton House, 18-24 Paradise Road, Richmond, Surrey TW9 1SR*

© Helen Kirkman 2004

ISBN 0 263 84518 4

153-0705

*Printed and bound in Spain
by Litografia Rosés S.A., Barcelona*

For Iris, Arthur and Margery, with thanks.

CHAPTER ONE

Wessex, England 716 A.D.

"THEY WILL KILL HIM."

"What?" Cold shock jolted Rowena's thoughts.

"Why not?" asked Eadward, the King's Reeve. "He is only a slave and untameable, they say. If they cannot sell him, why should they bother to go on feeding him?"

"But—" She could not show that she cared. Caring about the fate of some low-born bondsman would be a sign of weakness that Eadward would leap on.

Rowena's gaze moved from the handsome elegance of her companion to the line of slaves for sale in this corner of the market, chained at the neck so they could not escape, paupers, prisoners, debtors, criminals, those born to the life. But it could not be right that...

She should not care.

"You mean the one at the end?" Sun glinted on smoothly turned skin, polished, lethally thick with muscle. That was trouble. That was exactly what trouble looked like.

And it was going to be killed.

The man's hair was indecently long. It was the colour of…she did not know what colour it was. Moonlight on shadows. Dreams.

"Beren's bones, Rowena, if you could see your own face. You are soft-hearted as a child. It is quite engaging, really."

Anger—frustrated, hidden, appalling in its latent strength—stiffened every muscle in her body. She was no one's child. Not anymore, and you could not break a heart twice. She was no longer a trusting fool to be manipulated. Eadward should know that.

"You mistake," said the new Lady Rowena. "It is nothing to me what happens to a slave. We will find you someone, some*thing* more suitable to buy." She looked away from the broad shoulders of the man marked for death, glancing down at her fine dark blue skirts instead, twitching the embroidered hem out of the dust.

But just as she fixed her attention on this most necessary task, someone jostled her from behind in an effort to get past her to the honey stall. She stumbled forward, unbalanced, her veil swinging across her face. Blinded, she grabbed for Eadward's arm. Caught onto it. Managed to stop herself from falling. Just. She had got mud on the hem of her gown.

"You might help me," she snapped.

He was sulking over the coldness of her tone. He… was no longer wearing his tunic.

Her hand was on naked skin. Her stomach clenched.

The folds of her veil fell aside and she was staring at alien, unclothed flesh, caught under her fingers.

"What an eye the Lady has. That is the best one in stock." A hearty voice with an accent. Cajoling. And underneath, sharp with eagerness.

The slave trader.

The best one in stock…she risked half a glance. The naked arm snaked upward in the bright sunlight, strong, solid and endless. Somewhere in the distance it was attached to a gleaming shoulder, a mind-numbingly broad back. A neck enclosed in a wide band of iron. There were chains hanging off it, thick, heavy. Cruel.

She realised what she was clutching.

The thrall at the end of the row. The one that was untameable. The one they were going to kill.

"Ah, she cannot let go. I can see the beautiful Lady…and the Lord—" across her head, the trader threw an assessing look at the well-clad figure stand-ing at its ease beside her "—both know how to drive a hard bargain."

"Be sure we…*I* shall. If I buy," said Eadward with the disdainful glance of a moody thane confronted by a second-rate merchant. Rowena could see the trader's face harden. His narrow eyes, cunning, soulless, sur-veyed his stock, his human stock, as though they were not people at all. He was a large man and strong-looking, like most Frisians, but then not, perhaps, so large as the ungovernable slave.

All at once, she became aware of the warmth of the

human flesh under her hand. It should not be so warm. It was dead flesh. Or would be soon enough. The thought made her shiver. She set her teeth. No weakness over such things. That was no longer for her.

"Look at the muscle on that," began the trader with a wary glance at the warrior thane. "You could plough two acres a day with that. Three. Lift the revenue from your estate in no time." The man's eyes seemed to assess every last ounce of silver, every glimpse of finery that decorated Eadward's impressive person. And hers. She watched as everything was valued, from the bracelets at her wrists, the twisted gold fillet fastening her veil, to the silk embroidery on the now muddied hem of her soft blue gown.

"You will not go wrong. Best one you will find this year. Ten mancuses."

"Ten?" sneered Eadward. "It is not even worth a pound. I would give you six…"

They haggled. Eadward was exceptionally good with money. But then he was King Ine's Reeve and collecting revenue was his duty.

Rowena tried not to think about the strength of Eadward's attachment to riches and the dark path down which that had led him. If the nightmares that plagued her most vulnerable moments were true, Eadward was a murderer.

She intended to find out.

"…strong as an ox. A bargain…"

She examined the arm left lying in her hands.

Such fine skin. Turned gold by the summer now

almost at its end, but so fair and…this one was actually clean. It really must be the trader's showpiece. The bronzed skin had been anointed with oil to flatten the body hair and show off the muscle. She twisted it experimentally and the tight muscles moved under the fine skin like corded rope.

St Beren's bones! You could do more than plough two acres a day with that. You could do anything.

Anything…

The ghost of the most reckless, the most unlikely idea she had ever had began to shape itself in the back of her mind. Her body tensed with it. The arm stayed in her hand. It could have moved. She would not have been able to stop it. But it did not. The idea trembled on the edge of existence.

Her gaze raked along the length of the arm. It was so solid, like a thing fashioned solely for strength. There was no shred of compromise in that seamless arrangement of bone and muscle, only power, a power without limit. It lay quite passively against her hand, but she knew what she held. It was dangerous.

Dangerous…and fascinating.

Trouble. Untameable. The words beat in her head.

Her fingers were nothing against it. But it stayed, even though it was stronger than anything. Stronger than Eadward? She did not have a man's strength. She needed it, and suddenly, out of the blue, it was under her hand: like the advent of some hero from a story, appearing out of nowhere, at need, a champion come to right wrongs and restore the blighted land.

"Look at that." The trader's voice bellowed, shocking her. "The beautiful Lady can see quality. She will tell you."

But the spell of what might be was so powerful that she could not even turn her head. She could not tear her eyes away from the sight of her slender fingers on that strong limb.

"You will not find better. Two acres a day. What do you say? Do not take my word for it. Go ahead. Just try the strength in that."

She felt the muscle under her fingers contract at the slave trader's words. Alive. No, more than alive. The strength the trader was talking about seemed to spark through the tight skin with a force that could not be contained by anything as ordinary as flesh and bone. A force that seemed to vibrate into her own flesh, to have its own fierce life. Life. For how long? It did not seem possible such a force could be extinguished.

Her hand tightened and her breath quickened. Perhaps she could prevent it. Perhaps... The strange something stirred in the pit of her stomach. Her hand smoothed out and curved round that other flesh, testing its strength. She felt the living warmth of it, rich and enticing, flowing up through her fingers, seeping deep inside her in a dark surge of excitement. Possibilities, thoughts—chaotic frightening thoughts—jostled inside her head.

She moistened her lips.

"The lady is a discerning buyer. She can see value. What about the depth in that then?" The trader yanked on the arm she was holding. Turning its owner towards the light. Rowena's throat closed.

He was half-naked. The slaves, all of them, had been stripped to the waist to show off whatever they had. But all she could see was the dead man standing in the sunlight at the end of the row. The one she was holding.

Her eyes took in the smooth powerful line of his naked chest, the dark gold hairs flattened into the gleaming skin, the thick ridges of muscle, the entrancing male shape; the strange excitement seemed to swell inside her, making her dizzy with it so that she could neither move nor let go of her grip on the golden flesh.

''Well?'' demanded the Frisian.

Her moistened lips moved. But no sound would come out.

''Not shy, are we, Rowena?'' mocked Eadward. Yet underlying the mordant amusement in his voice was something else. Curiosity, perhaps? Prurience? It had come to her attention that there were certain rumours concerning Eadward.

Did his crafty mind now guess something of the strange, unsettling feelings coursing through her? One lightning glance at his face told her that he did. Another glance told her that he dared her to take this further and he thought that she did not have the courage.

He was wrong. She did. She had the courage and the will to match anything.

She fluttered lashes she knew to be outrageously long and flashed him a smile. She could produce the kind of smile that would swell any man's balls to bursting point. She was very beautiful and everyone knew it. What they did not know was the attested fact that the reality of her fell far short of the appearance.

She had been made all too aware of it. But she did not intend that Eadward should find out. So she moved her hand, very gently, sliding it upward with deliberate tantalising slowness, across the exposed flesh of the male slave. Eadward could sweat. From now on, the terms would be set by her.

She returned her attention to the thrall.

She would never be at the mercy of anyone's will again. Eadward would see she was not afraid.

How could a mere thrall have such fine skin? It was heaven to touch. Rich. She let her fingers trace with a slow and deliberate sensuality the smoothness of the inner forearm, the veined hollow of the bent elbow, then spread out over the heavy swelling fullness of the upper arm. Fine masculine skin.

It had a fascination that transcended the lesson she was about to teach Eadward. A fascination that was as unexpected as it was unsettling. This was about showing Eadward she was in control of her life, not him.

Nothing must threaten that control.

She fixed her mind on Eadward, on what was at stake, on the losses she had suffered. On her determination never to suffer like that again.

She made herself go on with what she was doing. Her hand tested the tightness of male muscle, nay, caressed it in every naked and licentious detail.

She milked it for all it was worth. She let every nuance of sinful pleasure, every trace of the dark, dangerous, nerve-stretching exhilaration that coiled inside her show in her face, in the flagrant movement of her hand over another man's flesh.

She did not so much as glance Eadward's way. She kept her eyes lowered in a semblance of modesty that was nothing of the kind. Her whole concentration, every shred of feeling, every sense, was fixed on the unknown, golden skin, on the slave's flesh, and Eadward would know it.

She waited and let him sweat. She let herself sweat. She could feel the faint pricking of perspiration on her upper lip. She hoped he could see it, and then she no longer cared. Her only awareness was the slave's skin; there was nothing in the world but its warmth and its texture and the sweet, forbidden exhilaration building inside her.

Her eyes drank in every naked detail: the tiny scratch on the upper arm, the strand of hair that had fallen forward across the man's shoulder. It was reprehensibly long hair; it shone, with a light that seemed to have nothing to do with the sun. The stray strand clung to the lightly oiled skin, just in the hollow between upper arm and body.

Beyond the soft coiling tendril of hair lay the chain. Her hand had to slide underneath it, the hard unyielding metal scraped against her skin. The iron links, toughened, fire-forged, clinked. For one instant she imagined the cold, dead weight of that metal on her own flesh, stifling, inescapable.

She tore her mind away from the thought. She made herself push her hand farther, down and across to settle on the thick, naked torso. Warmth, the smoothness of the body oil. She caught its scent, rich, unidentifiable. Foreign. It smelled of a heat and languor that flourished somewhere far south of her land.

Her fingers slid with sweet ease across that lightly oiled surface, releasing its tantalising scent, feeling the hardness of the muscle beneath. Her hand tested the firm shape of the chest wall, her fingers moulded themselves round its surface, found their place, would no longer move.

She touched ribs rather too close to the skin's surface. She felt the slave breathe and something strange happened around the region of her heart. She was lost, out of the carefully conserved and so necessary control. Ensnared in the touch of another person, trapped in the sensual spell of her own devising.

Nothing else existed.

Nothing but the thrall under her hand.

She turned her head, judging it so that the thin, filmy material of her veil and the artfully curled blond hair that escaped under its edges, just brushed across the golden flesh, the hard, dark nipple. She let her breath fan out across his skin.

She felt the sudden jolt in his rib cage, heard the

gasp so quickly suppressed. The thrall could disguise nothing from her, not when she was so close, not when she touched him so.

But he did not want to give in to it, the untameable thrall. In truth, he could not. She could sense every silent effort of the struggle for control in that hardened body. It was quite ruthless and it succeeded. But he must breathe. No one could stop breathing. Though they might try to control its pace and its depth, they could not stop it.

Her slim hand stayed exactly where she had placed it, and he must breathe. The faint involuntary push of that wide rib cage against her fingers was too fast, too shallow. The feel of that, the knowledge of it, was impossibly intimate. All of her awareness was concentrated on that small living, unstoppable movement. The weight of her hand increased against its slight pressure.

Just touching someone like that could not be so intoxicating. But it was. She could not stop. She wanted more and she wanted him to want it.

She wanted to make him want it. He had to. Why that was so gut-wrenchingly important she would not allow herself to fathom.

Her hand pressed harder, heavy, insistent, against him, felt the instinctive resistance, felt the waiting, bated stillness of another human being, a man. The moment stretched out between them, belonged only to them, and at last she felt the small catch in his breath that escaped his will.

It undid her, feeling that reaction. The power and the sheer dizzying excitement of it built up inside her until she thought her shallow breath came as fast, nay faster than his and heat touched her face.

It was impossible to get enough.

She moved her hand higher. Higher, until she could feel the quick strong beat of his heart.

"My dear, if you handle the goods any more I shall be obliged to buy whether I wish to or not."

She did not know whether the cold jolt of dislocation was in her own flesh, or the thrall's. She blinked, like someone awaking out of fever dreams.

"Do you still think that this is entirely suitable?"

The double meaning in Eadward's words was deliberate and there was an edge to his carefully amused voice, as though having provoked the reaction he had sought he was now infuriated by it.

She snatched her hand away, fighting for control of her face and her voice.

"I am not sure."

He could make what he liked out of that. Rowena shook her head to clear it of the strange, heady sensations, which had so bedazzled her senses and played havoc with her judgement. It had all been pretence to put Eadward in his place. It was nothing more.

"You are not sure? Lady?"

She stiffened. She should be careful of the King's Reeve. He was not in her power yet. She tossed him a melting smile that begged his indulgence.

She took a step backward and turning her head, she inadvertently saw the face of the slave.

His eyes were grey. As grey as slate, without any of the redeeming softness of blue. The hardness of those eyes could kill.

She took another step back. Their expression when they looked at her…they were eyes that saw, that had seen, far too much. They saw and assessed everything: the cynicism of the trader, Eadward's pride and hidden anger; the exact measure of her own behaviour.

They were not afraid.

She suddenly realised what the powerful force was that beat so strongly it could burst through the barrier of flesh and blood.

It was anger.

The force of that anger cut straight through her, twisting her innards into knots. She took a breath that was almost a gasp. She reminded herself that the man, whatever burned inside him, was no more than a thrall. In chains. She wrenched her gaze away. Eadward filled her sight. Eadward, the sunlight glinting on the thickly twisted silver at his wrists and the jewelled hilt of the sharp-bladed *seax* slung at his hip looked what he was: a lord and a thane, fit companion for a king. What the world called a man.

But in spite of her will, her eyes turned back to the slave.

''I hope you are not trying to sell me a penal slave,'' said the thane's voice behind her. ''I do not want something that causes trouble.''

She had not thought…was all that dazzling power and symmetry merely the brute body of some criminal?

"Never," oozed the trader with complete confidence, "born to the life."

She glanced up at the thrall's face. The trader lied. She did not know how she knew because the slave's expression did not change. But she was certain.

"Eadward—" she began, but her words were cut off because the silk-decorated edge of a sleeve flashed in front of her eyes, striking straight to the slave's head. This time she did gasp, but the hand fastened not on the chain where she expected it to, but in the long hair. Its grip was savage. Eadward pulled, with a force that snapped the man's head sideways, twisting his back. So that she saw it, expertly exposed to the sunlight, the unmistakable marks of a flogging across the strong, naked shoulders.

She suddenly felt sick.

"Surprised?" inquired Eadward, and the triumph and the malice in his voice mocked her. Then in growing viciousness to the trader, "What did you think you were trying to sell me?"

The jewelled hand was still tangled in the hair, dragging on it.

The touchiness of Eadward's pride was legend, even for a thane. Rowena knew from experience that if she hazarded but one word of protest she would make things worse. Tenfold. She stood in silence, she hoped with no expression on her face, and watched.

The trader, distracted by the public nature of the altercation did not shut up.

"Lord, not here, please. If you would—"

"If I would what? Do you realise who I am? The King's own Reeve of Lindherst. I would kill this piece of scum of yours if I wished."

"Lord…"

Eadward's other hand shot to the long, single-bladed knife suspended in the gold-chased scabbard at his belt.

The merchant's mouth opened but no more sound came out. He did not seem able to move. Neither did she. The only thing that moved was the slave, so swiftly and so unexpectedly she did not believe what she saw. She did not know how he could have broken the warrior's grip or how he could have evaded the jewelled *seax*. But he did, while Eadward's hand still fumbled.

His slate-grey eyes held murder.

Eadward hesitated, knife gone slack in his hand. Rowena watched the high colour of indignation drain from his face and realised he was afraid. It lasted only an instant, before he remembered he was the King's Reeve, and armed, and the other man was in chains.

But one moment of fear was enough. People, traders, farmers, excited townsfolk, stared.

She risked one more glance at the thrall. He had not made a sound. He was not even looking at the King's own Reeve of Lindherst, standing there with the useless knife in one hand. He was looking at her and the fierce eyes held a strength that was inviolate. She shivered. The strength was untouchable, like the abandoned recklessness of the *fæg,* the death-doomed.

Or of those who had known despair.

He had made Eadward afraid, and there was no fear in him. The ghostly shape of an unspoken idea formed in her mind. An idea every bit as reckless as the slave's courage, every bit as abandoned, in all probability just as doomed.

"We are not interested in the kind of merchandise you have for sale. Come, Rowena." The hand of the King's Reeve, with threads of silver brown hair trapped in the rings on its fingers, fastened over her arm.

She took a step but the idea in her head would not let her follow him. The reckless-eyed man, the stranger in chains, was not afraid.

He was for sale.

He was a slave constrained to do others' bidding. Eadward's hand dragged on her arm. Eadward. She needed help to deal with Eadward. Not the ordinary kind of help. What she wanted to do, what she had to do, did not require ordinary skills. It required the reckless sort of courage that took no account of either the odds or the risks.

She stopped.

"Rowena."

The slave still watched her. Her head churned with wild possibilities, and with all the reasons why those possibilities would not work.

The slave trader yanked on the dragging chains in a fury of disappointment to bring his merchandise to heel. The chain snapped tight. The thick iron ring cut through the skin on the slave's neck. She actually saw the blood. Somewhere at her shoulder she heard a hiss of satisfaction from Eadward.

The slave did not so much as flinch. The death-*fæg* eyes held hers for a moment longer and then they looked away.

"Dead flesh," hissed Eadward. His laughter floated round her ears.

All calculation and all reason flew out of her head.

"Yes. We are interested. We will take it. I will buy it. Him."

Eadward's laughter choked off. "Rowena! You cannot be serious."

The fingers round her arm tightened with enough force to cause bruising. Rowena gritted her teeth. She did not take orders from anyone anymore. Not even a King's thane. She would never let anyone make decisions for her again.

"I am."

A small crowd had collected round them, a crowd of hostile eyes on the King's tax collector.

"Rowena…"

"I thought it might be amusing." She smiled. She watched Eadward. Eadward watched the crowd. It was tax collection time.

"Twelve mancuses," she said to the trader across Eadward's sudden silence.

The huge Frisian shoulders turned. *"Twelve?"*

Eight was, of course, the usual price but she wanted it finished, no haggling, before Eadward got over the shock.

"Twelve. I will send my steward. Eadward?"

"Twelve?" said Eadward, the shock of her extravagance compounding the shock at her defiance.

"Come, Eadward. You are dining at my house tonight. We will have enough time for discussion in private."

Eadward's glance at the crowd was venomous, but just slightly unsure. She took advantage of that uncertainty, moving forward, taking her companion with her, laying her hand over his and leaning slightly against him, so that the curve of her breast touched his arm.

She had never done such a thing with him before, never allowed the slightest hint of physical familiarity. Given any encouragement, Eadward was not a man who would be content with hints. He expected to bed her. In his mind it was only a matter of time. He was enjoying the chase, but he was becoming impatient. She was taking something of a risk.

But then she had already taken a risk that was insane.

There was a moment when she thought his ill humour might be stronger than his lust, and that King Ine's Reeve might really choose to display his power. But the physical temptation, the novelty, of touching her proved too much. And she had already provoked his lusts most wantonly by what she had done with the slave.

She felt the well-muscled arm clamp down on hers in a grip that still hurt a little and was probably meant to. But he would do what she wished. The smile on his winsome face held triumph and the ghost of its usual satisfaction.

She had permitted enough to compensate for fondling an overexpensive male slave of dubious origin. And then buying it.

The slave.

Her feet crunched on the gravel path. She would not look back over her shoulder.

But she did.

They unchained him. He scarce seemed to notice it. He watched her. She could read neither relief, nor apprehension, only a fiercely controlled attention that would have drawn the secrets out of a runestone. It spoke of a will that was unrelenting.

"Rowena, I was speaking to you."

"Of course. I am sorry," she said smoothly, turning away from all the disturbing power she had just purchased. It was then that she realised there was something in Eadward's eyes that was going to demand compensation for her boldness. She had not paid nearly enough. Not yet.

Behind her, she could feel the clear gaze of the slave, like a knife in her back.

She forced her face back into its smile.

What in heaven's name had she done?

CHAPTER TWO

"FETCH ME MY PURCHASE."

"If you mean the silk thread, Lady, it is on your table. If you mean the barrels of wine, or new scythe blades, or the suckling pigs they are—"

Rowena glared into the disapproving eyes of her steward. The tightness that had settled in the pit of her stomach got worse. "I mean the other thing I bought. The—"

"The man, Lady Rowena?" enquired Ludda.

"The slave."

It was not unusual to purchase a slave. Granted, there had not been one on her estates in living memory. Her father had not approved of... She closed her mind on what was too painful for her mind to bear. She was in charge now.

"Fetch it. Where is it?"

"The Lord Eadward—"

"Eadward?"

"Undertook to see the man housed."

She stiffened. Eadward was just one of the guests who would be feasting with her tonight here in that other expensive novelty she had recently purchased:

her town house in the now thriving port of Hamwic. She was entertaining to show it off. Her guests included some cousins-in-law and a kinswoman of the Ealdorman. She needed a favour of the Ealdorman. The Ealdorman outranked Eadward.

Eadward, King's Reeve, always assumed too much.

"Fetch him. It. The bondsman. Now."

But Ludda, hang him, took his time. Doubtless to show her he was put out. She paced the small confines of her chamber and the unwelcome knot in her belly tightened.

She glared at the sunlit courtyard outside the open window. It was still warm, but the shadows lengthened. It would soon be time for the meal. For her guests. The ones she had to impress.

At last.

She flew to the cushioned window seat, adjusted the long blue skirts of her fine woollen kirtle, fluffed out her filmy veil, straightened the embroidered edge of her sleeve. The latch clicked. She raised indifferent eyes, arching her carefully plucked brows. Ludda shoved something through the doorway.

The door slammed shut with a finality that said everything.

She was alone with the thing she had bought.

She had forgotten quite how tall he was, how large, what his eyes were like. She thought of what she had to do and the uncomfortable feeling inside began to seethe. One part excitement to two parts…fear.

The unknown man, the savage who was afraid of

nothing, not even Eadward's steel, stood in the shadows. He did not move. A stray beam of sunlight caught the edge of his hair, making it glow with gold. No, not gold, silver. The reflections in the light brown hair were silver; not even yellow sunlight could change that. In fact, the hair was not light brown at all, it was that rare and wonderful shade called "ash." It was fascinating and…she took a breath. She was not here to be fascinated.

The creature was a slave to be used. To achieve her revenge. Bounden duty of those who survived.

"Come here."

"Lady."

It was a deep voice and quite steady. He had an accent, foreign, obvious even in that single word. He moved. There was no delay, no reluctance, only a certain assurance that he should not have. Perhaps it came from the fact that he had not always been a slave, whatever the oafish Frisian had tried to say. Or perhaps just from an awareness of physical superiority.

Well, for all his strength and for all his will, he was going to do exactly what she wanted.

"Stand there, in the light. I wish to see what I have bought."

He might be free of the chains but they had tied his hands. She had not expected that. The tightly bound arms pulled his shoulders back and forced the thick muscles of his chest into sharp relief. The hot sun from the open window seemed to slide over the shining, naked skin. She looked at—

"Beren's bones! What have you done?"

"I fell over."

The deep voice became the more foreign and exotic as he went on.

Her gaze travelled from the bruise on the left side of his face to the bruises still forming on the right side of his ribs.

"You fell over? Twice?"

"Slaves fall over a lot. It is traditional."

The voice held no expression but the slate-grey gaze flicked over her with a knowledge and a contempt of her that had the power to make her insides crawl. Knowledge. That same knowledge was in her, deep down.

Eadward. Eadward, whose pride had been slighted. He would have had to avenge himself on the object of his displeasure. She should have known he would not just leave it. She should have realised. Slaves had no rights and no protection except that provided, or not, by their owners. She should have prevented this. Out of duty.

Prevented it? She had provoked it. Her fault.

The thrall's eyes simply stared at her, the way they had stared down Eadward in the marketplace.

It worked.

She found herself examining the fresh rushes on the floor and the conscience, once so tender, the easy pity she had been wont to lavish on other people, stirred in some forgotten corner of her mind. Weakness. The weak got trampled on. The weak were killed. And they brought death where they should have been able to protect. She would never walk that road again.

It was unfortunate he had got hurt. She had not intended it. But she was in too far to withdraw now. The only way was forward and the thrall was the key. She knew it in her bones.

One did not apologise to a slave but…perhaps it might give him another reason to do what she wanted. He had to do what she wanted.

She stood up so she could eyeball him without cricking her neck. More or less. She prided herself on her height as much as her slenderness. But he was still taller than her. She arranged her mouth into a sneer.

"What are you called?"

"Wulf."

"That is it? Just Wulf?"

"What else should there be?

"Lady," he added. But it was an afterthought. Impertinent wretch. And there was more, she knew it, by an instinct that had no basis in the expressionless mask of his face.

Mask. It was a mask and there was more behind it than she cared to think on. She should ask his proper name. She should pursue it.

She looked into the flint-grey eyes boring into hers and found she didn't want to know. It was far too dangerous. She didn't want to know anything about what lay behind those eyes and that exotic accent.

Besides, there was only one rule that applied to enchanted strangers. You did not ask their true name, because if you did, they left you and went back to whichever otherworld they had come from.

But she had not expected things to be quite this difficult, not when they had pushed him into the room with his hands tied and she could have him hanged if she wished, with no penalty except the disapproval of the church. She wondered if he quite grasped that. Perhaps she should help him along.

She let her gaze rake over him. The face first and then the body. She let him see her examine every detail, the bruises, the awkwardly bound arms, every inch of exposed flesh. Her gaze moved down to the coarse dark trousers, their fullness tightly cross gartered from knee to ankle to show off the shape of the leg. She finished with the cheap, clumsy shoes. She let every judgement show in her face. She had to show straightaway who was master.

She walked towards him. The knot of tension inside her tightened with every step that shortened the distance between them. She kept the sneer on her face. She stalked round him.

"So, thrall," she said, disdaining to use the no-name he had presented her with, however much it fit his predatory silver-grey eyes, "just what have I bought for twelve mancuses?"

"What you see." It was not just the unlikely shape he gave to the words, but the way his voice moved. In a single lilting muscular sweep. It was the strangest and most beautiful sound she had ever heard. If you kept listening to that, it would ensnare you out of your senses. Except, it held a sharp edge of contempt, a contempt that was insufficiently disguised. Doubtless she was supposed to discern it.

But he had an insolent tongue on him. She would curb it.

"What I see? And what do I see?" She stopped in front of him, too close, breath tight in her chest, the dark knot twisting inside her. She must show him mastery. Her way. She couldn't go on living as she was. There had to be a way out.

Raising one delicate finger, she placed it lightly on the middle of the slave's chest. She let it rest there for one moment and then drew it down, slowly, across the solidity of the ribs, the sensitive skin of the flat belly. Her touch was not harsh, but it was not a gesture of indulgent sensuality this time. It was a gesture of power and he should know it.

He did.

She felt the tightening of the muscles in his belly and heard the faint hiss of his breath.

"I own you," she said to that contempt and that suppressed anger, "all of you, and I want to know whether I have got a bargain."

She let her hand drop, fast, a deliberate shock against the slow drawl of her words. It slid across the lower abdomen, the beginnings of a broad thigh, to the bulge of his male sex.

Her fingers but caught the outline of that thick, heavy flesh, no more, and then her hand was gone. Because the shock and the unexpectedness, and the branding on him of her undisputed possession were what she wanted. But that momentary contact, the fleeting touch of her hand over that hidden, secret part of him was enough to strangle her breath.

She clamped her mouth shut on the gasp that rose in her throat and the black tension laced with fear, the consciousness of deliberately doing something wrong, forbidden, stabbed through her like the shaft of an arrow. Her gaze flew to his face. But she could not see it.

He moved.

One step backward, one half step and a slight turn of the body. That was all the reaction she got.

The tension inside her head splintered into flying shards of relief, self-justification, triumph, exhilaration and the dark threads of guilt. She had achieved her aim. There was naught that he could do. His strength meant nothing while his hands were bound and he was a slave, a piece of property. Hers.

She looked on the averted head, the face hidden by the rich fall of his hair. He did not move again. He would not dare. That was how life was.

She stood with the breath wrung out of her and looked at the way the sunlight clung to every tense muscular curve of him, at the delicate angle made by the naked shoulder and the bent head. She could just glimpse beyond the curtaining sweep of his hair his downcast eyes with their thick brown-gold lashes.

All hers. She took a shuddering, steadying breath. He would do as she wished. She had set out on the road to victory, to redemption, at last. She took the step that would close the gap between them.

He looked up.

Her heart slammed against her ribs.

It was not submission in the slate-grey eyes, but a challenge. A challenge that was primitive and fundamental, without restraint or the slightest consciousness of the unbridgeable gulf between their stations.

It was not bravado. It was real.

Fear shot through the deceptive fog of her triumph, making sweat touch her skin. But running through that fear was another response, one that knew no reason and was as primitive as anything that burned in the slave's eyes.

The heat of his gaze would not let her go and the moment stretched out until she thought the sinews of her body would break. There was nothing in the hot, silent room, nothing in the entire world except the man no more than a breath away from her and what lived in his eyes. The future, her purpose, all the bitter burden of the past dissolved from her consciousness.

Nothing but the challenge and the charged awareness that stretched between them. She couldn't let it go. She touched him.

Her hand just skimmed the very tip of his shoulder, as soft as a piece of thistledown. That was all. But it wasn't all. As soon as she touched him, she was lost. The connection that had burned along the thread of her will and his flared white-hot, consuming everything. She was drawn into its heat by a power she could not have stopped. Not even if it had meant her death.

Her body sought the touch of his, came to rest against him, was accepted wordlessly, was subsumed by his strength. His feet moved a little farther apart, fluid muscle braced instinctively to take her weight, just as though he had been expecting it. As though he had known what she would do.

His body took the compass of hers. Easily. No effort. You could be lost in that sort of strength. It seduced just by its very completeness. Her bones seemed to melt into it, her flesh cleaving to the long, clean lines and deep muscle, pressing against his back, one solid shoulder, the bound arm, the taut curve of his buttock, the ripened swell of his thigh. She could no longer see his face.

The closeness overwhelmed her. Just the feel of him, as though it was he who held her in thrall. All she knew, the very boundaries of her awareness, were set by his size and his maleness, by the hidden power so at variance with his captive state.

It was enough to drive her out of her mind, this desire for him. The conflicting emotions inside her, the fear and the need and the sheer primitive excitement of him, fused into a savage pain, a raw and desperate hunger that would never be slaked.

Except by him.

She wanted him to feel it, too. She wanted to know that the echo of her own terrifying hunger had its place inside him. She wanted to feel that strong thrall's body move and tighten and grow desperate with the feelings that tormented her. She wanted someone to want her that much. Him and only him.

If he wanted her, if he… The memory of her hand covering his manhood scored her skin, burned her mind. If he really wanted her what would it be like? If a man really wanted a woman with all the fierce single-mindedness she had seen in his eyes, the sort of desire that was real, not a bitter pretence?

Her eyes closed. She imagined that thick, heavy flesh she had touched hardened, desperate, driven with the same aching need that clawed through her. She wanted this man, this stranger, to want her so much that there was nothing that he would or could hold back.

No one had ever wanted her like that.

No one ever would, because she was ever a disappointment. That was the truth. The truth she would not face.

This man, more than any, would not want her. He was a thrall bought in the market, a thrall who despised her.

She had to stop. Now, while there was a thread of dignity left. She tried to pull her hand away and because she was so clumsy about it, so painfully wrung out, she sensed what she would otherwise have missed.

The slave's shoulders were so tense under her hand that the small, pathetic, defeated movement of her fingers made his skin shiver.

She had done that. The disdainful, overproud thrall was not inviolate to what she did at all. So her shaking hand reached back and touched him, in wonder, this time. Her fingers moved over the smooth flesh then… caressed it, and the bunched muscles moved with her touch. The longing dragged claws through her heart and she knew it was doomed. Because it would never be satisfied with less than what it truly desired: trust.

Her hand buried itself under the weight of the stranger's hair; her face buried itself in his neck. Even though she knew it was pointless. She couldn't stop herself. She felt the slight movement of his head, not away from her, but towards her.

The cruelty of that slight movement took her breath and the longing clawed its useless way through her heart. It made her know just how deeply she craved the man's warmth and all the comfort his formidable strength might bestow. If she could just rest in that for one moment, feel that unconscious strength take just some of the weight pressing on her heart, the way it had taken all of the weight of her body.

She shut her eyes. It was false, what she did, as false as anything that had happened to her in her life. *If* was for the weak and for dreamers. She had trusted the enticement of its promises like the child Eadward had likened her to. Never again.

She must take care. She must see things as they were. She took a steadying breath but that only made her inhale the scent of the slave's oiled skin, the beguiling scent released by his warmth—dark, full of foreign spices, and under it the scent of him. Man. Clean heat and the promise of such power as would ravish the senses, just as it had done in the market-place.

The market. You could not lose your mind over something you had picked up in a marketplace. She forced herself to remember that, the dirt and the degradation, the heavy chains, the scales ready and waiting to weigh out the money. Twelve mancuses and Eadward's ruthless face. There had been no weak-mindedness in Eadward. Eadward was a master at exerting power over others. Eadward had known exactly what to do. She had to be equal to that. Equal to anything.

Her mind cleared and she raised her head from its rest in the warm curve between the thrall's neck and shoulder. Her fingers were still tangled in the richness of the ash-brown hair. She twisted her hand round, gathering up one heavy swathe.

It coiled round her fingers, thick and rich and quite sinfully long. It was clean, like the rest of him and underneath, where it had lain against the warmth of his back, just lightly touched with the aromatic oil. The scent teased at her. She lifted the hair higher, fanning it out through her fingers, letting it go. Sunlight struck through the falling strands, warming it and making it glow like a net of light. She caught the wild shifting tangle deftly before it could cover his skin.

That skin, and hard muscles underneath, rigid with

a sense of power that was leashed, so savagely suppressed.

She took another breath and willed herself to the same strength and to clear thought. Even though her senses were still half in thrall to him and her other hand yet rested on his warm skin.

His skin. She saw the thin bruising wound where the iron fetter round his neck had cut through its surface, the patch of dried blood. Her fingers on his shoulder touched the edge of a purple-red mark, a raised, inflamed welt of scarring, hideous in its obviousness. The man had had to be kept in chains. He had been flogged because he was a criminal. That was what she was dealing with. That was what she had to bend to her will.

She straightened her back. She let her hand stroke with as much seductive lightness as before, across the largest scar. The pads of her fingers slid across twisted, distorted flesh, the scarring unrelievedly ugly, frighteningly deep. Perhaps it still pained because she felt a reaction in him that was quite different, jarring.

Thoughts writhed unbidden in her head: about how much such a thing would have hurt, might still hurt, about the horrifying extent of the damage and how long such suffering would have taken. She swallowed sickness, suppressed it. No place in this world for pity. She steeled her will. Her lips opened.

"You are a penal slave, are you not?" Her voice, biting and contemptuous, sounding quite in control, sliced through the heady, sun-warmed air of the room. "That is what I wanted."

CHAPTER THREE

HE MOVED. She thought she was prepared. But there was less than an instant between the toughening of the muscles under her hand and the movement. She jumped back. All she could do was fling the heavy mass of hair over his shoulder, smothering his face, stinging against his eyes.

To her surprise, it almost made him lose his balance. Because of his hands. She had not considered the effects of that. He could not save himself. She reached out by impulse, but he twisted away from her in a movement that did not quite seem possible and landed in a wrenching thud against the wall.

She controlled a gasp and sought in her frightened mind for the words that would finish him.

"Thrall…" But she could see his face now and the grey eyes were on hers, and whatever she had wanted to say was annihilated.

He straightened up, using the wall to lean against, until she was painfully aware not of the vulnerability of his bonds, but of his height and his size.

"What you wanted," said the foreign voice, "was something to whore on."

Her heart nearly stopped but the eyes never wavered from hers.

"You thought you would buy it for yourself. Perhaps it is not so surprising if all you have got is that silk-clad *nithing* you were with. Or is it the silk and the jewels that bore you? Did you think some half-naked savage might be more amusing? Some helpless thrall who could not say no?"

The look in his eyes was not to be borne.

"Well? Lady?"

It hurt. Though there was no reason why it should. He was a slave.

There was silence in the room and then, "I think you bought the wrong man."

Anger was the only salve left for her pride. She lashed out with it because she had no other defence against his eyes and his words.

"Really?" She nearly spat it. "Is that what you think? Well the fact of it is that I have bought you and I can do what I will with you. I could add to that fine collection of scars you have. I could take your life."

"Then do it."

The challenge between them had shifted ground. There was such reckless force in his eyes that she stepped backward. Those terrible eyes held no taint of fear for her very real power over him. Only a conviction that was absolute. The words *death-fæg* drummed through her head again. What he had could only be the strength of someone who had faced the worst imaginable and come through it.

She did not know whether in his circumstances she would have such courage.

She did not know.

This was more than she could take. What, for pity's sake, did she think she was going to do with a brute beast like this? She should get herself out of it. Now. She had made the biggest mistake of her life. She had been witless and self-indulgent and utterly wrong. There were no possibilities of rescue in this and there could be no honour.

How Eadward would laugh. She had just wasted twelve mancuses on a hell-fiend. She should sell him back for whatever sorry bargain she could get.

Eadward had told her so… No. She could not give in now. She could not possibly let Eadward's view of things be right. She raised her head. She was a thane's daughter. She was not worthless.

She met the slave's eyes with the same complete and unyielding determination she saw in him.

She would make this work, one way or another. She would not believe she was so utterly mistaken.

"I have a proposition for you," she said. Her gaze matched his. Her fine mouth achieved a sneer. "And it is not what you would flatter yourself into believing. Tell me, thrall, just what did you do to merit spending the rest of your life as someone's slave? No, do not even think of telling me you were born to it. You would be about as convincing as that oaf of a Frisian. Was it theft, perhaps?"

"No."

The disdain in that was well done. It almost sounded genuine.

"No? So what did you do?"

Silence. The only weapon of the powerless.

"Did you injure someone? You might as well say it. It is nothing to me."

More silence. Something worse, then?

"Abduction, perhaps?"

Not a flicker. Hang him. What use was he going to be?

"You must have done *something*."

"No."

"Brawling? Breaking the peace?"

Was he not capable of anything?

"A blood feud?" That, at least, would be useful.

"Forgive me, Lady. I seem to have disappointed you." The subtle shift in the fighting ground between them was not lost on her. The words were meant to bite but…a lightning flicker of amusement passed across the eyes that were so unsuitable for a slave. She caught it. She caught everything about him. If he had the gall to laugh at her she would kill him. She… It made his eyes look quite different, briefly warm and full of light, yet still with that underlying challenge that stirred the blood. Was that what he would look like if he ever—

"Just what are you thinking of?"

She started. She had bought him for a reason and she was here to assess his potential for criminality, not bed sport. What a disaster that had just been. She clamped down on the thought, on the raw stirrings still clamouring inside her, ready to flare into life again even though she did not wish it.

She hardened her expression. ''I am thinking of what you have done that you stand before me as a slave. What was it?'' There was only one thing worse she could think of and it made the coldness seep into her heated blood. ''Killing?''

She had hit it. Coldness grew as the eyes changed, completely. He shook his head so that sunlight danced across the entrancing folds of his hair. She blinked all that wild brightness out of her eyes. She would never believe a denial from him again.

''No.'' The finely wrought lips shaped the lie. She took a breath but he had not finished speaking. ''I would not call it killing. I would call it murder.''

The coldness deepened. It was not a lie at all. It was the truth. A truth, she suddenly realised, looking at his eyes, that held more shades of meaning for him, more edges of horror than she could begin to guess.

''Murder?'' He could not mean it. He could not have done it. Murder was a bootless crime, unatonable, honourless.

''Aye. It was no fair fight. I took the life from someone who was completely helpless.''

''What did you do?''

The horror was still at the back of his eyes, held there. She thought for one instant there was pain, and then she thought there was not. Everything was controlled, ruthlessly. He spared himself, he spared her, nothing.

"I broke his neck with my bare hands."

She swallowed and she willed herself to be anywhere but here in this room with a man who had beguiled her senses, so finely it had almost broken through the defences of her innermost self. A man who admitted to murder.

Yet it was what she wanted. A ruthless, honourless beast.

"The proposition is theft. The reward is that which you lack—freedom."

It was impossible to disguise the reaction to that. The eyes blazed with all the brightness of a firedrake across the night sky. With the same speed. And then it was gone. But he was caught.

"And silver," she said, just to clinch it. No mistakes. "I knew you would see things my way in the end. I—"

"No."

The shock was so great she thought she had misheard him, that he would say something else, call that single syllable back. But he was no longer even looking at her. She was left with her mouth open, staring at a bruised profile outlined in sunlight.

"*No?* What have I done? Offended your honour?"

"What a surprise that must be to you. I will not steal to enrich your coffers."

"*Enrich my*...did I say this was for gain? Did I? This is about honour. My honour. My dead father's honour. My—'' She stopped. She had never meant to say all that. She was shouting. She did not know who might have heard her through the open window. She was a fool. But she had to make that contemptuous voice stop. She had to strike the intolerable disdain out of those eyes.

She took a calming breath and realised with horror that her throat was tight. She did not want to cry. She had not cried since the day they had carried her father's body back and she had looked on his mutilated face.

She knew all about honour. Just as her husband had known all about the lack of it. Husband and father dead and…the other death.

''You know nothing,'' she said to the contemptuous eyes, ''nothing. Just remember that. You are my slave and I have offered you more than you are worth. Obviously. It was a mistake. I really think you should be back in the marketplace, where you belong, don't you?''

Let some other fool take him. She had done with it. She—

''No.''

''What? Can you not say anything else?''

''Yes.''

''*What?*''

''Yes. To the bargain. I have decided I will take it.'' A pause. ''Lady,'' he added as an afterthought.

She choked. It was bizarre. It was impossible. It must be the money. It must be…she did not understand a thing. She was still shaking from the unwanted memories he had forced out of her.

"You must be the most exasperating, ungrateful, mind-numbing fool I have had the misfortune to meet in my life—"

"I was not aware that you had bought me for my brains," and then, while she was still gasping with rage, "What happened to your father?"

But she was not to be caught off balance this time. She had her tears under control, buried, where they should be. "He is dead," she said, "just like my husband." So many deaths and— She would not think of the last death, the one that had been her fault, the one that was no death at all. She would have done anything to— She cut the thoughts off. They would break her. She was in control, had to be.

"Death will be what awaits you if you get caught in theft. Because of what you are. A slave. Do you understand that?"

"And I thought you were going to change my life."

"I will, in good time. Just as you wish. So do not even consider betraying me. You will not speak of...of your duties to anyone." Her words rushed, because she had to reestablish control. Show him she had his measure.

"As far as the rest of the world is concerned you are just some thrall I decided to buy. There will not be any special treatment because of what I want you to do. I will not tolerate any familiarity and I do not expect any resentment over it."

"Resentment? Lady, you relieve my mind."

If that meant what she thought it meant she would personally hamstring him—

"Lady, I think we are about to receive a visitor."

"A visitor?"

"The King's Reeve of Lindherst. As soon as he can escape the attentions of your other guests."

He had half turned towards the window and that was what let her see it.

"For heaven's sake, what is that?"

"The King's Reeve getting agitated?"

"No. There. On your hands. It is—"

"Blood, I expect."

He did not even look round which told her exactly what he thought of her. The sickness came back. She had not realised…she had not realised because she had not bothered to think about it. She had not noticed how tight the rope round his wrists was. She had just made use of an unexpected advantage. She had…she no longer wished to think about what she had done while he was in that state.

But there had been no blood then. Surely she would have seen it.

When he had lurched away from her and she had thrown the hair in his eyes. She remembered his shoulders and his back hitting the wall and if the bonds had been that tight…

"Why did you not say something?"

He turned his head and the answer lay in the blankness of his eyes.

''Turn round.''

Her voice was as cold as January ice, and angry, but she could not help that. She was so furious with herself over this whole appalling business. She was so furious with a witless thrall for making her feel ashamed.

''Turn. I will cut the rope.''

She unsheathed the *seax* that hung at her girdle where other ladies hung household trinkets. It was finer than Eadward's. It had runes of power etched in gilded silver down the blade, ancient, arcane. *Tir,* victory, repeated three times and *Os,* rune of the mind.

The blade had been her father's and before that his father's. For how far back no one knew. Victory. Victory had not been her father's in the end. He had not been able to turn aside fate.

Perhaps she would, with the slave. Perhaps she would redeem…everything. She had the strangest feeling as she approached him, as though the possibilities she had given up were in fact still there, shimmering under the surface of the sunlit air. If she took just one more step towards the thrall the whole world might move into a different shape.

She took it.

It was an insanely risky thing to do. Somewhere in her mind the word *murderer* turned. She touched him and this time the terrifying power of him, the inner anger, pierced through her skin.

But she could not stop. The runes on the knife seemed to glow under her gaze in the slanting sunlight.

The one set near the hilt burned her eyes. *Os.* She realised what it was. It was a rune that loosed fetters. Of the body or the mind.

"I will set you free. Such a thing will not happen to you again. The runes will seal it."

She did not know why she said such a thing. It sounded like a promise. Wyrd. Fate.

His skin was bruised and cut round the rope. His flesh was already swollen so that the rope had sunk into it. Her hand tightened on the knife. What had been done was wrong. That was the only conscious thought in her head.

She cut the rope. The blade was stone-sharp, battle-sharp. The thought of making a mistake, of touching the swollen flesh with that killing edge burned at the back of her mind.

But the rune blade never wavered and he helped her. She did not know how he could do it but the corded muscles of his arms tightened, forcing space where there was none, iron-hard against the rope's bite.

He never made a sound but she knew his breath, felt the fierce unshakeable control and wondered at its power and where it found its strength.

The rune blade severed the last threads of rope. The skin beneath was crushed and broken and there was blood but the knife's bale had not touched him.

She had set him free of his bonds, but there was scarce time for that thought because he moved, and she was reeling with her back jammed against the wall and no breath. The fingers of her empty hand thrummed.

The shape of her slave's body was feral. It was one sinuous unbroken line of power from the flexed feet, the bent knees, the crouching hips, the flaring shoulders to the arching curve of the neck and the flung-back head. One lightning glimpse of his face told her that the murderous rage she had sensed in him had slipped the leash.

The eyes belonged to a place where there was no light at all.

That should have been the thing that terrified her most, the lack of light in those fierce eyes. But it was the one thing about him that stopped her from screaming.

It was like watching a beast caught in a trap. She hated trapping.

"No one should have done that to you."

It was impossible to tell from his eyes whether he heard her. But the rune blade, shining trough the sunlit air like an extension of his hand, lowered. The bright fall of his hair shifted in the light as his head bent.

He was examining the knife.

Then he looked at her. The wildness in his eyes had been replaced by a fierce concentration that examined her with the same thoroughness he had given to the blade. She had never been examined like that before in her life. Her skin crawled with it. But she couldn't move. Not so much as one muscle.

He took a step towards her. She remembered that a

trapped beast was as likely to turn and rend its rescuer as it was to accept aid. Her breath made a small rasping noise in her throat.

He kept walking. He stopped when he was so close that he filled her sight, to the exclusion of all else. She could not even see the knife blade. Only him. The granite-hard face, the thick rise and fall of his bare chest as he breathed. He rested one hand against the wall beside her head. Blood on his hands.

She could not move. Not even her head. He leaned closer. She did not think it was possible for him to be closer, but he was. When he breathed, the hard wall of his chest touched her breast. She could feel his thigh against hers.

''Do you have any idea, Lady, what you have done?''

The whisper of his breath touched her face. When she breathed, her breasts pressed against him. But she must breathe. No one could stop breathing.

''Do you know,'' he said again, ''what you do?''

His flesh pressed against hers and the scent of him was all around her. From his shining skin. From himself. Born of his power. She opened her mouth. But that let the scent and the whisper of breath from the finely wrought lips inside her lungs.

''Do you not know?'' said the dark exotic voice for the third time, like the repetition of some terrifying witchment. She felt the weight of his body, nay only sensed its fullness, because it was still held back, lightly. If it was not, it would crush her. He could crush her, before she had the slightest chance to cry out.

It had been madness on her part to loose his bonds. She had held the trapped beast in thrall. She had provoked its savagery and then she had unchained it, and now it would turn its savageness on her.

Any thoughts otherwise had been nonsense. Dreams.

Well, if that was the case, so be it.

She tilted her head backward so that she could see his eyes. They were ice-clear. The anger inside that was so powerful it had seeped through his skin was hidden. Neither could she see anything of the maiming pain that he would feel through his lacerated, blood-soaked wrists. Everything, all that, was utterly denied. That was probably what allowed him to kill people, as he chose.

He was nothing but a murderer. Yet she had held him. She had held all that fierce savageness, all that damaged strength in her arms.

She had felt the secrets of his breath. She could feel it now. The rise and fall of his chest was too fast. The fierce eyes were darkly shadowed. She had felt his strength and yet she knew that the ribs of that powerfully built torso lay too close to the surface of the smoothly oiled skin. She knew because she had touched them. The weight of him, held by a hair-thin control from crushing her, was yet not all it should be. The terrifying strength was stretched so tightly because he was exhausted.

He had not actually hurt her. She knew beyond fear or reason that the hurt was inside himself.

Her breath swelled against the tautness of alien muscle.

"I know what I do," she said in answer to that threefold question, "and I would change naught."

The sane part of her brain told her that despite all she had sensed of him, he could still kill her. He could probably kill any man living.

The grey eyes widened. They held hers, and then the hand beside her head moved. The sane part of her brain remembered what he had done to someone else with those hands.

Her body flinched. Primitive instinct. Unstoppable. But there was no knife, no flexed fingers, just work-roughened warmth, palm open, like a token of peace. The warmth touched her face. Just briefly.

Perhaps not peace. She could still see his eyes. Truce.

Her pent breath exhaled against his hand. Her head dizzied with the relief of still being alive.

"You are a riddle without solving, Idess."

Her breath came out in a rush this time and as misplaced as such a gesture was, her mouth tilted itself into a smile. So that the edge of her lips brushed against the pad of his thumb where he still touched her. He could not say "Lady," not without thinking, not without forcing himself, and yet he had called her Idess, a woman of uncommon power and ability. Also a creature of myth.

''Do you know what an Idess does?'' she asked on the edge of the intoxication of relief and that reckless, misplaced smile.

''Makes firm the fetters.''

''Aye. Yet some pick apart the chains. Those are probably the crazed ones. Like me.'' The rogue smile vanished like smoke, because although she was whole and scatheless, she had lost the thrall: danger, criminality and...possibilities. She could not hinder him from leaving, even though by doing so, he would imperil his very life. They would stone him to death for a runaway if they caught him.

She did not believe for one moment that that thought would be enough to stop him.

''I have unchained you,'' she said. ''Do you think we shall both rue it?''

She watched him. She watched the grey eyes so close to hers. But he only shook his head so that the wild fall of hair rustled.

''Nay. It is too late to unchain me now when you have already made fast the fetters.''

''What do you mean?''

''Are you deaf? I gave you my word.''

''You—'' She bit it off, once again too late. The unsaid words, that thralls were not exactly oath-worthy like other men, made the ice-eyes glitter, just as though they had been said.

He released her so abruptly she nearly sank down into the rushes. She had had no idea her legs were so weak and unsteady. Something was pressed into her hand. She flattened herself against the wall to stop herself from falling. The sunlit room seemed suddenly cold without the thrall's touch.

She was holding the rune blade. It was hers again. She briefly considered sinking it up to the hilt between a pair of scarred shoulders. But she couldn't. And he knew it.

She put a shaking hand to her face. There was a tiny wet trail along her cheekbone. His blood. He was staying. She felt the blood like a sealing of a pact.

He was watching through the window, standing in the shadows at the side so that he was not visible from without.

"Eadward," he said. Just that one word, not *King's Reeve,* not *Lord.*

Eadward.

She made herself stand up, take two steps forward. She could still see the source of the blood at the thrall's damaged wrists. "I will send someone to you." He didn't look round. "But...I must go."

He turned his head then, and she got the gleam of his eyes.

"Aye. You cannot keep a Reeve waiting while you dally with a thrall, can you? But tell me one thing, Idess, before you go. Who am I supposed to rob?"

"Him," she said.

"Him?"

"Yes. The King's own Reeve of Lindherst."

CHAPTER FOUR

RUSHES FLEW from his ill-fitting shoes, cascaded in an endless rustling fall. His feet paced the woman's bower like a chained wolf, impossible to stop.

The dark rage of hell that had smoldered in the slave trader's chains had caught flame when she had had him bound. It was the last thing he could bear. It brought too many memories. And in the moment she had released the bonds, that flame had burned through all the hard-won control he had.

She had seen that with terror. But it had not made her flee before the black creature he was. The woman had an Idess heart. And now he was stuck with her.

Wulf's fist hit the table with a force that sent red-hot pain through his damaged wrist.

She was not an Idess; she was a *hægtesse,* a hell-spawn. Nothing else could account for her power over him.

The instant the Lady Rowena had set his hands free he should have crushed her, beaten her brains out against the wall she was clinging to and left her body outside for his namesakes to fatten on.

But at the mere thought of his hands on the Lady's warm, fragile skin he could feel his balls curl.

He hit the table again but what raked through his mind was the will to crush the breath out of her in quite another way, with his body, skin to skin, his lips fused against hers and his tongue as far inside that fire-spitting mouth as his manhood inside her soft woman's body.

He knew the touch of her body already, far too intimately. He could sense it now. He could feel how all that pent-up passion would ignite for him, how that smooth, delicate flesh would soften under his, melding round him and enclosing him in its heat. He would have her desperate with the need and the pleasure of it until she had no breath left but to whisper his name, that single despised syllable would be all she had left in her devious little mind to say.

But the only sound was the gasp that tore from his own throat and it was his body that was breathless and shaken. Only from his own imaginings.

He leaned his head against the window frame and let the southern breeze of Wessex lift the hair from round his face and his shoulders.

He was a fool. He had given the word of what had once been a thane, a nobleman, an owner of a large slice of an even larger kingdom, to a spoiled stupid brat of a woman.

He was exactly the kind of fool his brother Athel-brand was, and Athelbrand, slave of lusts, had brought the wrath of an entire kingdom down on his head, on all their heads.

The memories clawed through his mind, unstoppable. The acrid smell of woodsmoke choked his throat. The gut-wrenching screams of the man, nay the child in a man's body, the boy he had murdered, shattered the silence of the room. The foul taste of his own blood polluted his mouth. The sound of the boy's pleading voice would never leave his ears. It had begged mercy from those who had taken his life and yet left him to linger in torment.

There was no mercy on earth and the memory of that death was something he would never be free of, even though there had been nothing else he could have done. Even though there had been no other choice that, in pity, he could have made.

He took a huge retching lungful of air, the soft, warm air of the alien south. He hated it with intensity. It had no soul. Not like the air of his land.

He had to get back there. He had to find Brand and he had to find the man who had ruined his brother's life. He needed revenge. He could not have got this far, fought and manoeuvred his way back from the bleak flatlands of Frisia, back to the Kingdoms of Britain, to be stopped now.

It was Brand who needed him. The hell-spawn woman needed no one. Least of all some low crawling slave to right her wrongs for her.

But she did. He wished he had not seen the moment of truth, when the wretched woman had mentioned her dead father, and the arrogance in the blue eyes had threatened to dissolve into helpless pain.

He knew too much about pain. That was a vulnerability, like a scar taken in battle. It left a hidden weakness that had to be guarded against and compensated for lest it drag you down a second time.

He had never been able to stop meddling in other people's lives. But he could not do it again. Not this time. He was not truly bound. An oathless, honourless thrall could not be bound by a word as a thane would be. The thane no longer existed. He was as dead as the murdered man.

Wulf turned towards the door, even as his mind screamed out at him that walking through it was no longer possible.

The door was open. Before his eyes had time to make sense of the shadow outlined against the light, his body made its own preparation, knees flexed, weight balanced, hands deceptively loose at his sides. He choked.

It was a small maid of no more than five or six winters. She would hardly come past his knees. She took a step forward. Enormous blue eyes gazed up at him in reproach.

"You were supposed to come to the kitchen," she said. Her voice was sweet and had something almost familiar about it.

What on middle earth did she think she was doing?

He made his body relax and tried to speak without alarming her.

"I was supposed to come to the kitchen?"

"The butter's boiled."

Butter.

He had enough to contend with, without stray maidens who had domestic problems. He considered how to get rid of her. She began frowning.

"To make your hands better," she said.

I will send someone to you. But…not even the *hægtesse* could have arranged this.

"*You?*" he said, at the end of his patience.

It made her jump and to his alarm her lower lip began to tremble. Had he snarled hard enough to terrify her?

"I have to," she wailed and burst into screeching tears.

He had no idea what to do. Why in heaven's name had he raised his voice? He took a cautious step towards her. She did not flee. She just sobbed.

He was not one to be sentimental over children. But she was pathetic. He was aware of a helpless desire to pat her russet-brown head. Only his hands were such a bloodied mess he could not touch her. The hands that until now had been so ordinary, suddenly seemed too large and strong and she was as thin as a twig.

He knelt down beside her. He was stuck here anyway, for better of for worse, for deception and theft and incomprehensible problems with cookery.

"All right," he said over the terrifying noise. "I will go to the kitchen. We can both look at the butter."

The howling stopped. She looked up, huge blue eyes swimming with incipient tears and he suddenly realised whose daughter she was.

"WHERE IS THE LADY GODIFU?"

"In the kitchens, I think, Lady, with the new slave."

"The slave? What? Why?" demanded Rowena. That savage brute she had bought was with her daughter? Alarm nearly choked her. Not Gifta, not small, terrified Gifta.

Gifta was so fragile. She was... Rowena could feel the familiar claws of helplessness and guilt that she could not take away her daughter's cares.

Gifta was not fair game in the duel of wills that existed between her mother and some desperate criminal.

"Lady, I think they—"

But she did not stop to listen. She charged across the courtyard and burst through the kitchen door.

She did not believe her eyes.

The brute, now clad in a coarse grey tunic of un-dyed wool that did not fit him, was sitting at the far end of the worktable. His arms were stretched straight out in front of him, the sleeves of the tunic rolled back to the elbow.

Standing on the bench next to him was a small girl with long red-brown hair spooning great dollops of some evil-looking goo onto his lacerated wrists.

"Keep still," commanded Gifta the terrified, "or

you will make it…fall off,'' she added as the mixture slowly slid towards the wooden tabletop.

"It is not, perhaps, enough?'' asked the savage criminal with a humility he had never shown to his mistress.

"One more.''

"Gifta! What are you doing?'' But she knew, and the knowledge clenched her heart. Gifta had decided to add the slave to her collection of lame animals which had to be healed. No. Please not. If that was so, she would never let him go.

"Gifta,'' she said, alarm adding sharpness to her tone, "it is time you were in bed. I have come away from the feast specially to say good-night.''

Gifta dropped the spoon. Drops of goo splattered.

"I just have to put the bandage on. Then I have made him all better.''

There was a look in her daughter's nervous eyes that said everything she dreaded most. The guilt and the helplessness were soul-cutting. She could not force her daughter away from the object of her pity now. It would do a damage she was not prepared to inflict.

"Very well,'' she said, trying to make her voice sound reassuring and unconcerned, as though this was of no importance at all. Then to the nurse, who was hovering uselessly in the background, "Help her.''

She would have much to discuss with the nurse on the morrow.

She waited. It was an almost unbearably awkward process because Gifta insisted on doing most of it herself and no one was game to stop her. Rowena could not bear to look at the criminal's face. She suffered agonies, expecting at any moment that fiery self-willed impatience to burst through. But it did not. He did not speak, except something to Gifta, so very softly that Rowena could not hear it. That made her furious. How dare he?

"That will do. Bed."

She captured Gifta's hand, still sticky with whatever foul potion she had been concocting, and led her as far as the door.

"Mother."

"What?"

"You must not tie him up again. It will hurt him."

She stiffened. It was impossible to have the rightness of your actions questioned by a maiden of six winters and be found wanting.

Besides, they had not been her actions. She had not ordered it. It had been Eadward.

But the memory of the indifference that had left someone bleeding while she played games she blushed to think on was not so easy to shrug off. She reminded herself that the man was her slave. She was being as pathetic as Gifta. She—

"I do not tie Brocc."

Brocc. The half-tamed badger recovering in the upper paddock at Healdsteda from a broken foot. A badger, for pity's sake. There was some difference between a sick badger and a man who had been enslaved

for unspeakable violence and who stalked round looking like King Ine about to declare war on Mercia.

"It is not a thing for you to worry about...oh, all
right, no I will not. Yes, I promise. Nurse, take her. I
will be there in a moment."

"Yes, Lady."

The nurse and her impossible daughter vanished and
she was left with the untidily bandaged murderer.

She sat down on the other side of the kitchen table.

Where did she begin? How did she protect someone
as innocent and damaged as Gifta from this? How did
she keep her daughter away from a dangerous and
forceful man the child was naïve enough to regard in
the same light as a badger in need of nursing?

How could life possibly get more complicated?

She took a breath and stared at the table.

"My daughter," she began, forcing the words
through gritted teeth, "is soft-hearted about people's
injuries. Also those to animals." That should put him
in his place, right down there with a lame badger.
"We make allowances for her age and her innocence
but that is all. It means nothing."

"Lady."

You could tell nothing from a single word like that.
He began unwinding the cloths round his wrists, awkwardly. Lumps of dark goo fell out.

For heaven's sake.

"What is that?"

"Woad. Boiled in butter."

"Woad?" she said in alarm, glancing at her own

hand and looking for blue stains. "But is that not for—"

"Burns." She heard him laugh. "I have one."

The last of the cloth came off and she saw it.

"What? How did you—"

"We forgot about cooling the butter before applying it. There is an irony in there somewhere."

"Oh, no. You did not—"

"Upset the child by letting her know what she had done? No. You need not worry."

His voice taunted her but when she looked up the eyes that met hers were very steady. She looked at the infernal, painful mess of his wrists. It seemed an odd kind of forbearance to be found in a murderer. But if Gifta's peace was at stake, she was not going to question it.

"Thank you," she ground out, so low that it was almost inaudible. The look of disbelief she got froze her tongue. She felt the same mixture of guilt and fury towards the thrall that Gifta had forced out of her by babbling about badgers. She could not stand it. The man was the scum of the earth.

He had been kind to her child.

"You might have called me a riddle without solving," she burst out. "But you are worse."

"I?"

Her heart beat too fast but she had to have this out with him. "You prowl round like a…a wolf out of the forest, filled with a fierce passion to tear something into pieces, and then you stop yourself. I do not un-derstand why.''

''No, I do not imagine you would.'' Just his voice, just the directness of the wolf-eyes, was enough to make her burn inside with the memory of her reckless behaviour in the marketplace, of the way she had handled him.

She glared. ''I have always found desperate passions a liability.''

The burning inside touched a fine line along her cheekbones. She tried to will it away with a cold mind-strength like his.

''Perhaps, Lady, you have not had my opportunities to learn self-control.''

''You mean from being a thrall,'' she spat.

''No.''

''*No?*''

''That merely tested what was already there.''

''You are trying to tell me your nature is as cold as ice?''

''Aye.''

The pitiless eyes and the perfectly commanded body bore witness to the bleakness of that one syllable. But every instinct screamed out in her head that it was not true. She had felt it, seen it. She had held him in her arms and the power of the rune blade had let her see into his soul.

She looked at the flint eyes. How could anyone be so wrong about themselves? What could possibly make them commit such an error of judgement?

"Nay. If it was not thraldom, it was something else made you breathe ice."

The tilt of those firm lips held more irony than amusement. "Then it must have been necessity. I belong to a kindred ruled only by its impulses. Someone had to deal with all those things they could not."

"And that someone had to be you?"

"I was the most suited. I am the only one in the family who thinks."

One of her misplaced smiles bubbled to the surface. She could not stop it. He had an effect on her like the strongest Frankish wine, even though he was so dangerous. Perhaps because he was.

"And this kindred of yours—" But she had baited the wolf too far. The coldness in his eyes could freeze all it lighted on.

"They are not your concern. Lady."

She remembered what he was, what his family would be. A race of murderers.

"How right you are. Just as my daughter is no concern of yours. I will not have a criminal so much as approach her. You will remember that in the future, thrall." She took a huge breath. "You are here for one reason only and you will do exactly as I say, is that clear?"

She stood up without bothering to wait for a reply she was unlikely to get. But the message was there. Let him heed it. She called someone over to clear up the mess and rebandage his hands.

"You can wait for me in my chamber."

She went back to Eadward.

HE WAS GOING to fall asleep. There was no help for it. He tried to fight it off, but it was impossible. Wulf leaned his head back against the wall of the Lady Rowena's bower. The dull cloying bands of the exhaustion that came from too little food and too little sleep for too long would have their revenge on his body. Not even the ache of the bruising on his face and his side and the pain in his wrists could keep him awake.

In the last moment before oblivion he allowed himself to think of Brand and tried to formulate the apology in his mind, as if it could travel several hundred miles north to Iona, or wherever else in the world his exiled brother had taken his high-born leman. If she had not left him.

His eyes closed and there was nothing else in his mind but winged thoughts.

It was a sort of mind-game he played in the blackest moments, pretending that he and his reckless brother could still communicate without words, the way they had fancied they could when they were children.

But that was stupid. Besides, if he had been half as close to Brand as he had thought, his brother might have confided in him. There might have been some warning of disaster. There might have been some way he could have prevented it, could have rescued Brand from the mess. The way he always had.

The way he was not doing now. Because he had been caught by the wiles of a *hægtesse* and…a child. Wulf could still feel the sticky little fingers twining round the hideous mess of his hand, at least, round a couple of his fingers and half a thumb which was about all she could manage. All in order to lead a complete stranger in the direction of the kitchens and all the comforts of boiling butter.

It seemed impossible that something that innocent could live. You would expect it to be crushed at any moment in a world that had no value for such things. But then there had been enough to crush that small spirit already. The child had no father. He remembered the wounded eyes, and then in the exhausted confusion of his mind, they were no longer the child's eyes but the tear-filled eyes of the woman, beautiful beyond belief. They were the last thought as consciousness slipped from his mind.

He heard her come back. The sound of the door and her light footsteps were unmistakable. It was dark except for the small glow of the bronze oil lamp he had lit on her table. Her steps sounded unsteady.

Half awake, half locked in the deadness of exhaustion, Wulf forced his aching eyes to open just a little. He had propped himself up against the wall on the cushioned window seat. She came towards him, a slight shape, indistinct, wrapped in her cloak and her floating veil.

He should speak before she got any nearer. He must not let her think she had a total advantage. Again. But he could not get his throat to work. It was still stuck in dreams.

But she stopped before she reached him and after studying him for a moment, turned away towards the inner room. Gone, like some elf in the mists of the night. His eyes began to drift shut, but then she turned back, directing her unsteady feet towards him. She swayed. He stiffened. Was she not well, or…ale-glad? He caught the sweetness of mead on her breath as she leaned over him. Her normally deft fingers fumbled at the brooch that held her cloak. He took breath to say something but then it was lost, smothered under clinging folds of fine wool, still warm from her body.

She had cast her cloak over him. The undeft fingers brushed it away from his face, began a painstaking arrangement of its billowing folds across his shoulders.

He did not believe it.

She tucked it in with careful consideration round his feet. He should stop her, but this new vision of his owner was too fascinating. He had an insane desire to laugh. His *hægtesse* as lady of mercy? It was impossible.

Her narrow foot caught in a loose fold of material and she nearly fell on him. She giggled like a naughty girl and then sighed and the mead on her breath just about knocked him senseless. Too sweet.

Like her behaviour.

He framed a withering remark, wondering how she might react when she was drunk. It died under the soft touch of her lips. They landed on his face, missing the bruise by a hair's breadth and then they trailed down across his skin to light on his mouth for an instant that was hardly measurable in time.

The reaction through his body was like fire, molten, stronger than the strongest pain he had ever felt. But her lips were gone, before he could even move a muscle and she danced backward, nearly tripping over the table.

It was just as well she moved or he would have sealed his own death by flinging her to the floor and taking her right there and then. But she was gone, out of his reach as she always was.

She righted herself, laughing, and then she said quite clearly, "I am so tired it hurts."

He sat up, but she had already vanished into the inner room.

He watched the door close, leaving him suddenly helpless with fury, not just with her for her arrogance, but with himself for the reaction of his body. She should not be able to do that to him.

One day, he would kill her.

THE NEXT TIME he woke, it was completely. Every sense stretched. They came in through the outer door. Had the stupid woman been too drunk to lock it? He should have checked. He should have known. He pushed the anger and the exhaustion to the back of his mind, forcing himself to stillness, watching through slitted eyes.

There were two. They spoke softly. One went straight for something on the table. The other, armed, went straight for him. Not with caution, but with the confidence of one who knows his victim has no chance.

That was his mistake.

He left it until the last possible moment and then he moved, taking the man unawares, smothering him in the clinging folds of the cloak. The *seax* missed, but not by as much as he expected. It tore through his tunic. But his movement was so unexpected the knife went flying and he drove his opponent backward into the other, sending both crashing back against the table in a rending of splinters that would have wakened the dead. But not, apparently, the Lady. He was terrified she would come through the door from her bedroom into the middle of this.

He had better make it quick.

He did.

He hit something and dislocated a knee. A fist slammed into him but it only connected with his body and it meant that the other fool had been confident enough not to have drawn his knife, and now he did not have time. He kicked. There was a shriek. Still nothing from the inner room.

"The table. The casket."

But Wulf had the *seax* by this time and he was quite ready to use it.

"I cannot…"

"Leave it."

They fled for the door, the one who could still run dragging the one who was lame. There was a denser darkness against the night sky in the doorway. A man's figure. It vanished as the other two launched themselves through.

The fighting urge to pursue, to finish what had been started was overwhelming. But thought was stronger and the urge that wakened was stronger still.

There had been no movement from the inner room. None of the intruders had expected any. Wulf slammed the heavy oaken door back in place one-handed, rammed the bolt home and surged across the room. The force in his body burst the lock on the woman's bedchamber door.

It was not dark. She had left a branch of extravagant wax candles burning beside the bed. He was there in two strides, ripping the bed curtains apart. She lay quite still.

CHAPTER FIVE

WULF FLUNG HIMSELF down beside the bed and touched her face. Warm, quite warm and tranquil and he could feel her breath against his hand. Relief hit him with a force that unleashed shock. He sat on the floor and buried his head on the bolster beside her face. Her long corn-gold hair was soft under his skin.

He did not want to think about the strength of what he felt.

He made his mind focus where it should be: on what had happened and why.

It would have been useful if the Lady had thought to mention that his duties might include the prevention of theft, as well as carrying it out, if he possessed the slightest clue to what was going on.

He concentrated on getting breath back into his burning lungs. The very tips of his fingers still touched vulnerable flesh. What in heaven's name had her arrogance and her deviousness led her into?

And him.

Breath could only be achieved in racking gasps and the pain in his wrists clawed at self-control. But self-control was what he was used to. He forced his breathing back into a bearable rhythm. He raised his head. There was fresh blood soaking through the cloth on his right wrist but not that much. He pulled the edge of his sleeve down and clamped his hand over the mess. The knife had scarce touched him and the rest was just bruising. He could ignore it.

She had neither woken nor moved and yet she seemed so calm and peaceful. He did not know how much mead she had drunk but it must have been a considerable amount. He let his head fall again beside hers. He could still smell the honey sweetness on her breath, though not as strongly. It was cloying and…there was something else, something that had been disguised before by the drink.

Poppy.

I am so tired, it hurts and the touch of bewilderment in her voice that he had put down to the drink.

His heart lurched. How much had they given her, whoever it was who had wanted her to sleep soundly while they had invaded her room? Not too much, please heaven.

Her breathing still seemed so natural but what they had given her could kill it.

He wiped his hand free of the blood and pushed down the covers over her shoulders. Her pale skin and white shift gleamed in the candlelight, smooth as fresh milk. He slid his hand lightly across her flesh, heated and relaxed by sleep. His fingers touched the smooth material of her shift, glided over it. Silk. Who else but she would have a night rail made of silk? The hardened skin of his hand, so foreign to all that softness, skimmed the swell of her breast, touching her as gently as he could, finding the steady beating of her heart.

She was well. Just sleeping. There was nothing to fear.

He was aware again of the gut-wrenching relief and with it a burning anger that someone could have made such reckless use of her. She suddenly looked so fragile. She was, in spite of all her spirit and her spitting words. For him that made her a more difficult opponent. For someone else, it had meant an opportunity.

He thought of the King's Reeve attempting to kick his ribs in while he had been bound. He thought of the unidentified shape he had glimpsed through the open doorway. It had been no more substantial than a night shadow. But every screaming instinct told him it had been real. Told him, proofless, who it had been.

Eadward Reeve. The Lady's dear friend.

He let his hand rest against his owner's sleep-warmed skin, feeling the beating of her heart, the almost imperceptible rise and fall of her breast. She was so beautiful like that, all smooth voluptuousness, no spitting edges. Her body was one warm curving line and her face was quite relaxed, small and lost among the pillows. So different from its usual stormy arrogance.

If he had as few scruples as she had, as Eadward the Reeve had, he could...he could not even think

about it. If he did he would do it. He got up abruptly.
Pulling the clothes roughly round her shoulders.

He strode back into the other room. It was a sham-
bles. He left it so. All he wanted was the casket.
Locked. At least she had had that much sense. He
smashed it open. Not gold or silver or coins, but pa-
pers. He fished one out, careful not to get blood on it.

x vats of honey
xxx ambers of clear ale
ii full-grown cows

He nearly laughed out loud. A list of estate dues?
Someone would risk drugging and robbery for an estate list?

He fished out the next sheet.

xx cheeses
xii geese

And so it went on.

Ridiculous. Not of interest to anyone.

Unless, perhaps you were King Ine's true and faith-
ful tax collector. Lay the wind in that quarter?

He dropped the box as though it was of no consequence among the rubble, found more cloth to tie
round his wrist to stop the blood as best he could, one-
handed, and went back into the bedchamber.

He would feel better if she woke but he doubted she
would before morning and then probably late. He did
not want to try and force her awake unless her
breathing became too shallow.

She was well. Truly. He watched her dreaming face.

He should go back and get what sleep he could under the useful cloak.

He could not leave her.

If something happened. If she became worse…he had given his word to this bargain.

He always kept bargains. Besides, she had not paid him yet and he had to keep her alive that long.

He maneuvred himself across to the other side of the bed and then stopped, one hand resting on the fineness of silk embroidered curtains, the other on the richness of the bedclothes. Everything inside him revolted at it, and the black anger that never left him, day or night, rose up like bile. Everything he touched turned in his mind to what he had lost. All that he had valued not for its worth but because of what it represented, an island of civilisation wrested out of a barbaric world.

It was gone, his island, like the person who had created it. Only the slave-creature was left. The unkillable. The living undead. The unavenged. That creature no longer belonged in the kind of world the Lady Rowena inhabited, could not be forced to step back into it.

He drew back, and yet the woman's face, so pale, so frighteningly defenceless in its drugged sleep, held him.

He could not leave it.

He lay down. It was harder than sleeping on bare boards, on damp earth, on stinking fetid straw.

He turned. His hand touched her. Just her outflung

arm, nothing more. Nothing to fire even the most lust-crazed youth. And yet it did him. All the wildness locked inside him, all the leashed rage, all the fierceness of despair, seemed ignited in one burning flame of desire for the arrogant witch, the fragile slender reed beside him, robbed of all defence by forced sleep.

He bit his lip until there was blood, his fists clenched and his body burned. The tightness in his loins ached with the force of his unspilled seed.

All that held him back was what he had been. What he no longer was and would never be again. That was the irony of it. Cold, clear thought, somewhere far above the savage body of the murderer and the beaten thrall, could see that.

You could not be stopped by something that no longer existed. By something that had failed and had no purpose.

But he was.

Even the black creature he had become would bind itself against what it seemed the King's Reeve had planned to take.

He stayed facing her, her long fair hair trailing towards him, gleaming in the shadows, the outline of her body, sensed as much as seen. He reached out towards it, placing his less damaged hand on the warmth of her side, lightly, without fuss. She did not stir, did not notice, had no awareness that he was there. But he would know if her breath became troubled. He would know if she woke.

He closed his eyes. Hours later, he began to drift.

His thoughts were no longer clear and cold, but muddled as wraiths floating through the luxurious dark of the rich woman's bed. There was nothing left in his body except the sour aftermath of conquered pain.

She would want to flay him when she woke in the morning and found her thrall taking his ease in her bed.

She would be mortified.

She would have to stew in it.

She would wonder. And she would not like it.

THERE WAS SOMETHING in the bed.

How odd.

Rowena could not remember it being there last night. On reflection, she could not remember anything about last night.

She was ale-sick. She had the worst hangover in the world.

Except…she could not even remember drinking that much.

The thing in her bed breathed. It must be alive. Rowena put out a cautious hand, not too quickly because of her headache. Her fingers tangled in cloth, found a shoulder, a torso, a compact hip-bone, the lean, spare, unmistakable shape of a man.

Cuthred. Except that her lawful husband, just lately, had been getting fat. Too many years of good harvests and…Cuthred was dead.

A wave of nausea clenched her belly. She would not think of Cuthred dying. She would not. She squeezed her eyes shut and concentrated on the immediate problem of the man in her bed. Her hand appeared to be tangled in the hem of his tunic. Why was he wearing his clothes in bed?

Some people were very odd.

Why was she in bed with someone who was odd?

She tried to think but there was only a vast pain-filled space where her brain should be. She turned her head towards him. It was not easy. She managed about half-way and caught the faint suggestion of spice.

The slave.

She distantly remembered buying it.

She did not remember getting into bed with it.

She had a vague feeling that she ought to be alarmed. Or something. She would think about it when the fog cleared out of her head. In the mean time, all she craved was the blessed oblivion of sleep. If he would just keep still she could…was he ticklish or what? His tunic was very scratchy. Perhaps that was his problem. She did not like such a tunic. She tried pushing the folds out of the way. It was ripped. Had she done that? She did not think so. But it was very convenient. She found skin. She put her head on it.

She slept.

"WHAT THE DEVIL do you think you are doing in my bed?" shrieked Rowena. The waking, this time, was complete. Panic at the alien male figure she was somehow entangled with crashed into her consciousness.

"Get away from me," she screamed. "Do not dare touch me. You—"

"Good morning—" offered a rather raspy voice with an entrancing foreign accent. A heavy head moved in a ripple of silvered darkness.

She put down the bolster she had just been about to beat the intruder with.

"—Lady," said the voice.

He always forgot. Miserable thrall. It was deliberate. What in the name of all the saints was he doing in her bed?

"Get out," she screamed.

The recently purchased slave sat up. He had all his clothes on. He was trying not to laugh.

She flung the bolster in a fury not unmixed with terror.

It hit.

He fell off the end of the bed.

Served him right. She buried her head between her upraised knees and tried pulling handfuls of her hair out by the roots. It did something for the headache. But not for the shock of waking up in bed with something you had just bought and had no recollection of inviting. At least he was gone now.

She groaned and bit the bed covers.

Ale-sick did not begin to describe it. Her head pounded and her eyes felt as though they were going to fall out. Her stomach…she would not think of her stomach. She came up for air, great lungfuls of it. No sign of the slave. Perhaps he had very properly fled in fear before her wrath. She peered cautiously over the side of the bed.

He was sitting in a heap on the floor, his gleaming head buried in the bolster. His unnecessarily large hands were clenched into fists and his shoulders shook. He looked a mess, even from what she could see of him.

Had he hurt himself? Had she petrified him with the consequences of her rage?

Slaves who forced their miserable bodies on other people were taken away and gelded.

She would make up her mind about that later.

If only she could remember what had happened. But she could not. The only thing left in her head was fog. And pain.

She stared at a sheet of dishevelled pale brown hair that did nothing to disguise the breadth of the shoulders underneath. Surely she would not have disported herself with a thrall? But the alternative, that he had crawled into her bed while she was asleep and ale-sick and defenceless and had…had rutted himself on her was insupportable.

She would kill him. She…she suddenly remembered kissing him.

He had a mouth like hot black silk.

Heaven help her. She had invited him. She must have.

She could not remember.

She could not stand not knowing.

She was going to have to ask him. Discreetly. The very thought made her flesh crawl.

There was no other way.

She laid her head back to ease the pain. Choosing a tone that she hoped reflected lofty disinterest, she began, ''Thrall, I hardly expected to wake and find you beside me.'' Would he take it to mean he had outstayed his invitation or that he had had no invitation at all? ''Just what did you think you were doing?''

''My duties, Lady, as I understood them.''

His duties? His *duties?* She closed her mind on the memory of groping the contents of his trousers only yesterday.

But he would not dare. He would not dare to think that he was entitled to disport himself with her at will.

His voice sounded rather muffled and unsteady. Guilt? Dreadful realisation that he had erred? Mind-numbing terror?

''Thrall, I believe some further instruction on the precise nature of your duties may be required.''

''Aye, Lady. It was all rather more than I expected.''

''What?'' She sat up and immediately wished that she had not.

''I really do not think you explained things very well. It was something of a…surprise. But I think I acquitted myself extremely well under the circumstances.''

The conceited whoreson. Did he actually think to boast of his prowess? She swallowed. She did not know what his prowess was. She eyed him and came to the conclusion it was likely to be considerable. And he had…exercised it on her? She really would kill him. Then she would probably kill herself.

At least it would stop the hangover. She groaned.

The gleaming, tousled head moved instantly at the sound. The slave looked up.

"Are you all right?" His expression did hold concern but behind it…behind it she could see the traces of laughter. Light glowed in his eyes, dampness clung to the thick lashes. His mouth, that mouth she had kissed, was curved.

She remembered the shaking shoulders. He had been laughing at her.

"You whoreson," she snarled and looked for something else to throw. "How dare you? Did you learn your behaviour on the threshing floor that you—"

He stood up.

"Lady, I learned my behaviour here. If it does not please you, perhaps you should teach me better."

Her jaw dropped. He was her slave, hang it. She could do what she liked with him. As for him, he had no right to so much as approach her, let alone talk to her like that or…whatever else he had done.

If he had done it.

"I should teach you the lash," she said, "it seems to be the only thing you understand. Or have them make a eunuch out of you."

She would have him crawling for mercy, begging her to spare his balls. She would—

He threw back his head and laughed.

"Is that what you were checking for yesterday when you said you wanted your money's worth? I can assure you it is all there and I have had no complaints yet."

"You…you…"

"Of course, whether I might wish to *make* any is another matter after—"

"*What?*"

Whatever blood was left in her veins drained away. He must know. That sharp mind and that virile body knew. That she did not measure up to what her beauty promised, to what everyone else thought. He knew she was a failure and she could have no pride left before him.

He was watching her with that suddenly intense scrutiny that saw through walls. He knew. He had had her. Either that or he had been talking to Cuthred's ghost.

"You are naught but a peasant," she spat. "Do you realise what I could do to you, you…"

The terrifying eyes hardened.

"Aye. I think you have told me already. You need not worry, Lady. I would not so waste myself."

That dizzied her out of her head. She buried her face in her hands so that he would not see, would not guess the sickening flood of her relief.

He did not know, and he must not see her weakness. Not him of all men. But she felt so ill. She tried to lift her head but it would not move. She heard the hiss of the rushes as his feet closed the gap between them.

"Do not dare to approach me."

Her voice would have frozen a blacksmith's furnace. But not, apparently, her thrall. She felt his hand touch her bare shoulder. She wanted to shrug it away but it would not move.

"You were ill," said the foreign voice, "that is all and we had unexpected visitors. I did not wish to leave you."

"I do not—"

"It is all right. There is nothing you need to worry about now, but I have much to tell you."

There was actually pity in his voice and his hand was so warm against her chilled flesh. It felt so very comforting. She had not found anyone's touch a comfort since—

"I also think you have much to tell me, Lady. About—"

"No!" she yelled in desperation, and thoughts of her father and Cuthred and illness and deaths and sorrow and lovelessness all jumbled in her aching head. All the thoughts he made her think. All the things she wanted to forget, because they would only hamper her in what she had to do. She snatched herself away from that disturbing touch and her gaze was caught not by the strong masculine hand, but by the messy, blood splattered bandages at his wrist and the coarse sleeve of his cheap tunic.

"Do not presume beyond your place," she said, "slave," and looked straight up into the stone eyes. He would look away. He would remember what he was. But his memory was as imperfect as his behaviour. He just looked at her as though she was three inches high and that was two inches too much.

"If you do not wish to speak, perhaps you would like to come and see what happened to the next room. If you can…manage so much. Would you like me to help you out of your bed?"

Rowena glared.

"That will not be necessary."

"No?"

"No."

She sat up. The bedclothes slid down and she was suddenly aware of how close he was and the fact that she was only wearing her night rail. And that they had just been discussing whether or not he had bedded her and how thoroughly.

"Get out of my way."

She slid rapidly out of the warmth of the covers. She reminded herself he was only a possession. She grabbed for her cloak. She could not find it. She had done something with it last night. What? Her hands flailed about seeking something, anything, to hide herself against the thrall's gaze. She snatched a woven rug off the bed and stood up.

She had meant to stride across the room. But the floor tilted alarmingly. To his credit, he did manage to catch her before she hit it.

She thought, after what she had said, that he might just have let her drop. But her weight was lying against him and her head was muffled in scratchy wool. She buried her hands in it because it was actually rather frightening, the way the room span and her head throbbed, and the weakness in her legs. She did not know what was wrong with her. It could not be just too much mead.

She tried to raise her head and touched skin where more tunic should be. Her hand was fastened on the fraying edge of a huge rent in the heavy material. Her stomach clenched.

"Thrall, how did you manage to tear something quite that thick and...serviceable?" She swallowed the word *coarse*.

"Someone's knife."

"Someone's *knife?*"

"I told you we had visitors."

She saw the snaking line of the cut across his side, all black dried blood and reddened flesh. She let out an oath.

"I did not...are you..."

"It is nothing."

"Nothing?"

It was not nothing. It looked awful. Her hands tightened their grip round the solid warmth of his body and she was suddenly frightened not just for herself but for him. It was an unexpected feeling, vaguely akin to the way she wanted to shield Gifta. Except you did not want to protect large and strong men. They protected you. Sometimes. She shut the door on memory, turning in the shelter of her slave's arms and looked at the wreck of the outer chamber.

"Beren's bones."

CHAPTER SIX

ONE SHE-GOAT

Rowena shuffled vellum and surveyed the disaster. She was sitting, wrapped in the rug, on the window seat. The slave stood beside her, large, solid and reassuringly indestructible, despite the bruises and the knife cut. She would have to do something about his wounds. Something decent this time, not Gifta and a panful of woad and boiling butter.

iii wheat sheaves

She glanced across at the solid legs of her purchase. She would be lucky if there was anything left of him by the end of this.

He seemed to be possessed of incredible patience. He just stood beside her and let her swear and groan and tear her hair and issue threats against kings' reeves.

And he was brave. She had to admit that. She had not been deceived in her choice.

One cow or a small whether

"I have said all that I can and I think, Lady, that you owe me an explanation," said the patient one.

She looked up at the unslavelike face. The incautious movement sent a bolt of lightning through her head.

"Owe?" She had forgotten just how arrogant he was. "I do not owe anything to a thrall. I—" she tempered her voice. Because of the headache. She tried to think. She would have to tell the slave something.

He shifted position slightly beside her and the ripped tunic gaped. She could see the painful line made by someone's *seax* marring the lissom turn of his side and the dried blood on his skin.

She had to tell him. Well, some of it, anyway. This was what she had bought him for.

She screwed up the page in her hand. At least a miserable worm like him would not have had the wit to be able to make out the letters written in precious ink.

She glanced at the room again and the casual destruction.

"Did you have to break my table?"

He appeared to consider it.

"Yes."

"You are going to be more trouble than Eadward." There. At least she had said the dreaded name. "The King's own Reeve of Lindherst is a thief."

"Ah."

No surprise. Not a flicker. Well, he probably thought she meant of things like gold and silver.

"Not a common thief. He collects the taxes, but he somehow manages to take more than is due and not all of it finds its way to King Ine. I realise you can hardly expect a Reeve to be totally honest, but it is more than a little cream with Eadward. It is scandalous and it gets worse every year.''

She straightened her spine and raised her drugged head.

''I shall prove his crimes to the Ealdorman, to the King, to the entire world and I will see him known for what he is—a thief and…perhaps a murderer. I will have him punished.''

''A…murderer?''

Like you. She glared at the coolly inquiring face. For pity's sake, why had she said so much about Eadward and her father's death? They were only suspicions anyway. Black and unthinkable. It was the hangover. It was her anger at the invasion of her bower and at the way she had been used and left helpless.

She did not discuss her father's death with anyone.

''You do not need to know.''

''No? I am hired to steal something as yet undefined from someone who turns out to be a thief himself, a very common thief I would have thought, who is prepared to use assault, drugging and possibly murder to get what he wants. I am supposed to prevent all this but not to know what he is after or why? I think I need to know why someone is prepared to risk all that to steal a piece of parchment.''

''It is vellum.''

She thought she came quite close to being belted

over the back of the head with the remains of the casket which the slave was holding for her.

Instead he put the pieces down very carefully on
what remained of the table. She was aware of a slight
shudder of relief.

"It may seem strange to you," she said as kindly
as she could, "that anyone should risk theft over
parchment—"

"Vellum."

"Yes, vellum," she continued, not kindly at all,
"but for those of us who can actually read, such sheets
of *vellum* can serve as a record of what has been done
and of what should have been done. This," she explained, waving the crumpled sheet under his ignorant
nose, "is a list of the king's *feorm*, the taxes due on
an estate of ten hides.

"It is for Acleah, my morning gift on my marriage
to the Lord Cuthred," she added, unfurling the sheet
to give him a slight taste of just how rich she was. He
would be dumbstruck. In fact, he was looking suitably
impressed. His shapely eyebrows had risen almost to
his hairline. And this was not even her major estate at
Healdsteda that she had inherited from her father—

"You got ten hides of land for your morning gift?
It must have been a very impressive wedding night,"
observed her slave, "perhaps I really did miss my
chance. Look out, you have dropped your vellum. Allow me."

"You ignorant peasant, I do not need you to…"

"Do you think you are going to be sick?"

"No! Yes. Mayhap."

She could not move. She was stuck, bent double, trying to retrieve the wretched piece of parchment. Vellum. She could not raise her head without swimming out of consciousness.

"Just try turning a little towards the window and move much more slowly."

Someone had opened it. The fresh morning air skimmed over her suddenly heated skin like heaven's blessing. If she breathed very slowly and did not move again, she would be all right. She let her head fall back onto the cushion. It felt quite rough against the side of her face. It must be the embroidery. She moved her head in irritation. It moved with her and all of a sudden it was the most comfortable thing in the world. She closed her eyes against the light.

When she woke, it was to a feeling of vague bliss. If one were transported to paradise, it could not feel better. It was like floating in the air but being safely anchored to the ground at the same time. Safe. That was the word. She had forgotten what it felt like. Blissful. Lazy. Warm. With a hand stroking her hair. She liked that. She smiled.

The hand stopped.

"Ah. The Lady of the ten-hide estate is back with us."

She looked up. Grey eyes. Watching her. Not soft at all. Not like the hand that had been stroking her hair.

Had it?

Or had that just been part of her dream?

She moved. Not fast this time, but with a certain amount of force. It got her nowhere. Her hands were tangled up in the slave's arms and her head would not raise itself from the scratchy wool of his tunic.

"Let me go."

"If you wish."

But he did not release her immediately, as he should. The large hands held her with complete assurance, no clumsiness, no deference. She could feel the rough warmth of his palm on the bare skin of her arm, underneath the cloak, high up, nearly at her shoulder. The muscular heaviness of his forearm touched her breast and the thin material of her silk shift seemed no barrier at all. She was leaning into his arms, her body knew the outline of his, felt its lean, spare shape, the unexplored power in it.

The grey eyes were so very bright.

Her heart thudded in a way that had nothing to do with the lingering effects of opium.

"Yes," she said. "I do wish it."

He moved and she pulled away but her movements were slow and uncoordinated. Her fingers got briefly muddled in the rent in his tunic, tangling against the smooth skin of his side, the rough, soft feel of the body hair on the center of his chest. She dragged herself away, lurched forward so that his arm skimmed lightly across the curve of her breast. It was an unintentional touch but she could feel her skin tighten in reaction, drawing her nipple into a peak of excruciating sensitivity, sending a jolt of feeling inside her that shocked.

She bit her lip, hard, to stop the betraying gasp that rose in her throat. The jolt of feeling sliced straight through her, out of control, bringing the sharp heat of thwarted desire between her legs.

She looked away, towards the cool air from the window. Her hand clutched the cushion with a force that should have broken her nails.

There was silence.

She kept her face towards the slice of the courtyard visible through the gap in the shutters.

She felt his hand cover her clenched fist on the cushion. She was ready to scream at him then, to lash out if he dared to try and take advantage of her frightening, volatile state. But the touch was not like before. It was not assured, but quite tentative, like something offered, not taken.

She tried to speak but nothing but a strange sound came out of her mouth.

The hand closed over hers. She wanted to push it away. But to do that she would have had to let go of it.

"You should come and rest, Lady. There is no need to speak more today."

She nodded very carefully. It was what he should say and then he should go. So that she could retire to the sanctuary of her bedchamber and think about her problems tomorrow. But now that she had received the due politeness that she deserved, now that her slave's touch seemed to hold the proper degree of deference, she found that she would speak. Just to show she was not some weak-kneed woman who could not hold her own in a world made for men.

Her free hand tightened on the list of taxes for a well-run and profitable estate of ten hides.

"This," she said, "was the beginning of my father's evidence against Eadward."

"Your father?"

Rowena took a breath of air from the open window, a breath that steadied all the grief and all the weakness out of her and left only the determination.

"Yes. My father wished to put a stop to what Eadward was doing. Eadward's greed had taken him beyond the bounds of what could be tolerated. I mean it was not just a question of harrying reluctant churls and cottars and firing the odd village—"

"He burned a village?"

"Yes," she said, distracted from what she had been going to say. "It does happen sometimes if they do not pay and they never want to pay. It was not as if it was on our land—"

"Sometimes they cannot pay."

"Oh they can unless it is two bad harvests in a row, or cattle disease or something. I have never had any problem on my lands—"

"Which village did he burn?"

"Some village on the King's land, so I suppose it's Eadward's anyway to do with what he likes." Why was he distracting her when her head ached and she was trying to tell him of Eadward's greater crimes? "Ditchford, I think—"

"You *think?* You do not even know?"

She glared upwards and found the slave's eyes boring into her as though she had burned the wretched village personally. Her much-abused stomach clenched.

"What I *think* is that Eadward murdered my father."

There was a sudden silence during which the slate-grey eyes became quite different.

"I am sorry."

She became aware that she was still holding his hand only when she felt it move around hers, surprisingly gentle in spite of its rough skin. Whoreson. He would make her cry if he looked at her like that. Why could he not just stay obstinate and insulting, the way he truly was?

She snatched her hand out of his. She did not want the pity of an insect like him. She fixed her gaze on the courtyard outside the open window.

"I was trying to tell you," she said, "that Eadward had turned his attentions to important landowners."

"Like you?"

That was better. The irony and insulting tone of voice back to full strength.

"Yes," she said, to make him realise where she stood in the scheme of things. "From what I finally managed to get out of Ludda—"

"Ludda?"

"The steward. My father told him." The words stung. Her father's chosen confidant had been his steward. After all, he had not had a son to talk to, only a daughter.

She blinked drug-aching eyes and told herself firmly that her father had only wanted to protect her.

"My father had decided to confront Eadward, to give him a chance to explain, reform. Eadward was…is a friend, a fellow thane. But before my father could do so he was ambushed on his way home from Hamwic. He took the shortcut where the road passes through the edge of the forest. He was killed."

She heard the thrall move. She did not look round. Just sat with her back straight and her face turned away from him. She did not want him to touch her, not then, not even the gentle non-challenging touch of his rough hand. Especially not that.

He must have known. He must have sensed it. Because he let her alone.

"I see," said the foreign voice behind her. Just that. Just two inane words that meant nothing. Except…they meant everything. They told her that he knew. He knew just what it was like to be hurt by such loss. Perhaps because of who he was.

What he was.

"Eadward, *everyone* said it was Bulla Fire-Blind. He is an outlaw, with a gang of wolf's heads at his back. He hides in the forest. He waylays travellers and robs them and very often, he kills. He was caught. They put one of his eyes out with a flaming brand but then he escaped. And now that is what he does to people if they resist him. Burns their eyes out and then kills them.''

The slave did not say anything this time. But the quality of his silence was like wound-balm. She did not know how it could be but she wanted it to go on forever, that silence, not even touching. But then she heard his voice.

''Eadward?''

Just that one word, but it captured all her fears and her doubts and all that she could not bring herself to believe.

''I do not know. It happened before my father had a chance to speak to him. Eadward had no reason then to suspect what my father was about. I know Eadward is greedy and a thief, but to arrange the murder, secretly, of another thane. I cannot make myself believe it but…'' *Just like I would not have believed he could have drugged my drink to let his henchmen search my room with impunity.*

If she had not had the forethought to get herself a slave… She looked at the stone face and the tough body she had purchased.

''I want to find out,'' she said. ''I will find out. That is what I bought you for. Eadward is afraid that I have more evidence than I actually have. Evidence of his fraud should be easy enough to get. The rest…'' She caught her breath. ''What you have to do is steal Eadward's copies of the other lists of estate dues and the lists of what he actually sent to the king.''

"Is that all? Would he keep such records?"

"Aye. Eadward is like a flame-snake guarding treasure in a burial mound. He has to gloat over what he does. That is his obsession. That and amassing riches. I would say that he takes those lists out every so often and reads them and knows what he has done and…that is his pleasure."

Her hands twisted in the embroidered cushion.

"I will lull Eadward's fears. I will make him think I know nothing, that I am too stupid to suspect. But when the time comes, I will take you to the royal estate at Lindherst. And you will steal the parchment rolls for me."

Rowena's gaze fastened on her purchase. She had to know whether Wulf, the slave, had the stomach for this. Because however strong he was, however much he wanted his freedom, the penalty if he was caught was death. Not many men could face their death in cold blood, even if they could in the heat of battle.

He was watching her. She saw straight into the grey eyes and they were not as she expected. They were wide and dark and they seemed to look at things that were not there.

"We are going back to Healdsteda. It is the estate I inherited from my father. It is the nearest to the royal estate at Lindherst." *It is also the only place where I have ever felt any peace.*

"I know where the lists are likely to be, I can show you how to recognise what you are looking for. It will not matter that you cannot read. In fact, that will be a defence for you against a thane like Eadward.''

Would he be able to do it? He was a villain by trade, by very definition, and he had to do as she wished to gain his freedom. Yet she needed to assure herself he would stick to the bargain. She tried to catch his gaze. His eyes were actually turned on her but she did not think he even saw her. His eyes looked straight through. She had to ask.

"Will you do it?"

"Me? I have said so. Besides, I like the thought of the King's Reeve as a greedy flame-snake. I have always had a fancy to fight a dragon. Like Beowulf in the story."

Rowena opened and shut her mouth. This was not some childish fancy. He did not even seem to be listening to her.

"Beowulf was incinerated for his trouble," she snapped.

"Aye. Beowulf took a hero's death. But there is no need to worry. I tend to choose otherwise."

If the situation had not slid somehow beyond her control once again, if her head had not been pounding to the exclusion of all reason, she would have thought that was a choice he bitterly regretted.

Ridiculous.

"You will do as I say," she said to put him back on the straight and narrow. "You will—"

"What I will do is stay till Lamas Tide. No longer. That is it.''

He deserved thrashing for such a presumptuous tone.

But…he was hers until *Hellwaran*, First Fruits. Yet it was not long. It would come so soon. She swallowed a peculiar and doubtless drug-induced pang of regret.

It would be long enough.

After that, he could go where he wished. He was hell-foot already. As far as she was concerned, he could end up where he belonged.

CHAPTER SEVEN

THE KING'S REEVE arose early. He wanted to be in time to wish the Lady Rowena God speed on her journey to her estate at Healdsteda.

He yawned. Tomorrow he would be back at his post overseeing the royal hall at Lindherst. The two estates were such a convenient distance for visiting.

Eadward allowed the yawn to stretch into a smile.

He donned dark grey trousers, a fine linen shirt and then the tunic with the silk decorated sleeves he had worn yesterday. His hands fastened the buckle of his sword belt, richly decorated with boar shapes as befitted his manhood, inlaid with gold as befitted his rank. He adjusted a carved, leather-lined scabbard mouthed with gold, touched the protruding gold embossed hilt wrought about with snake charms. The thickly twisted arm ring at his wrist flashed in the dawn light.

Silver. It struck a discordant note.

It should be gold. After this harvest, it would be. He would see to it, as he had had to see to everything. Life had not dealt fairly with him to make him the eighth and little-prized son of an ambitionless man, a thane of moderate rank who could do nothing but breed on his long-suffering wife like a jack rabbit.

Eadward had had more intelligence. He had fought and flattered his way into the rank of King's Reeve. The only reward from his loving father had been to cut him out of the share of the family inheritance which should have been his. Because Eadward had had the ambition to make something of himself, his fatuous father had believed that he needed no help. One burden less.

He gazed at his reflection in a sheet of highly polished bronze. The reflection was good. It would soon be better. Wealth would make it so. Wealth could satisfy all the cravings of the soul.

Eadward smiled and stepped outside into the grey morning light.

CUTHRED'S CASTOFF looked well on horseback. He had to admit that. Strumpet. She had played the ice queen with her husband and now she tried it with him. That particular pose was beginning to wear thin. Even now, just with the sight of her, he could feel his man's flesh harden. It should have been slaked on her. Last night.

She saw him. His smile became utterly beguiling. He took care to add a hint of concern. Because she was still pale from her recent and mysterious illness. But the small burst of pleasure he got from that was not nearly enough to compensate for his frustration. His plans had gone awry.

If it had not been for the thrall... He, it, was still there, standing oaflike and silent across the other side of her courtyard. Unshaven, unkempt. Still alive. Eadward's hand tightened on the gold-embossed hilt of his sword. If his men had had any ability at all they would have stabbed the creature through the heart, not merely added to the scars on his worthless hide.

The thrall had not yet paid in full.

At least someone had known how to treat such a brute. He thought of the disfiguring, fascinating stripes across the fellow's back. If he had been there to see that punishment administered...frustration ground through him.

What a waste of effort his plans had been. Or so it seemed. He could scarce believe from the witch's bewildered and pathetic behaviour that she could truly be harbouring any evidence against him. She was far too stupid.

"Lady!"

Rowena's gaze turned away from the contemplation of a tangled fall of gilt brown hair and an unhandily mended tunic. She shivered in the dawn coolness.

"Eadward."

She forced her mind away from unsettling eyes and an unshaven face hewn out of granite. The flash of gold and silver, and a hint of garnet dazzled her eyes. Eadward looked brilliant. He was smiling. The way he always used to smile at her.

Her horse shied and he reached up to steady it. One capable hand caught her bridle, the other settled on her silver chased stirrup, brushing lightly against her ankle above the soft leather shoe.

"I have heard nothing yet from the Port Reeve about the robbery," he began.

Eadward had seen to that for her. He had taken up the attempted theft before she had even thought what to do.

"When I think what might have happened to you…"

Rowena shuddered, not just from the cool air. "Aye. It seems I was lucky." She darted one lightning glance at the dishevelled figure standing beside the cart. Eadward saw it. The hand around her ankle tightened.

"You know, Rowena, that I am speaking only out of concern for you when I say you were not wise in purchasing that…*thrall*. I fear you will have a sorry bargain for twelve mancuses." Eadward's fine thane's voice must carry clearly across the yard in the stillness of the air.

"You should be careful of men like him, Rowena. I worry for you." The hand smoothed its way across her ankle, so discreetly, hidden underneath her skirts. None could see. Except…except the thrall standing straight across from her. She could feel his gaze even through the distance that separated them, sense its heat and power. So strong. He looked like a cutthroat compared to Eadward, like something that should be running with Bulla Fire-Blind.

"Low criminals," said the thane's voice, "and outlaws, wolf's heads. There is no vice to which they would not stoop. You do not know, you have never dealt with such brutish scum. As the King's Reeve, I see such things all the time. I would spare you. You should let him go, Rowena. You know nothing about his past. It is obvious he is a criminal from the marks on his flesh.''

The horse sidled because of the way she moved in the saddle. Eadward steadied it effortlessly, his touch warm on her leg.

''Leave him to me, Rowena. I will take care of it for you. You know I have always wished to help you.'' Eadward's smile would have melted ice on the North Sea. ''Think on it. We both know what outlaws can do.''

She stifled the gasp of hurt. But Eadward must have heard it. His eyes darkened in concern. His words roused all the grief, all the fears that were too close to the surface, too vulnerable.

The horse plunged, for no reason this time, startling both of them because they were so lost in their separate thoughts. Eadward jumped back, swearing. A movement, tiny, scurrying, caught her eye.

''Mouse!''

Gifta's piping voice. There was a flash of russet hair. The horse reared.

''No!''

She fought with the reins, with her feet, with all of her weight and every ounce of strength that she had. The horse pulled left, nearly unseating her, nearly losing its footing, but it pulled away. Not far enough. The hoofs slashed through the air. Something else moved in a brief blur of grey.

"It is all right. I have her."

It was the thrall. He had Gifta. Russet brown hair cascaded over his arms, small white hands clutched at his disgusting tunic. He had her child. The world went briefly black, as though she would swoon, and then she was aware of masculine hands on her reins, steadying the horse with well-trained skill.

"Eadward…" It would be all right. He had the horse under control. The slave had her child. Gifta…Gifta must not be upset. No one must frighten her further—some idiot screamed. Gifta's nurse launched herself, screeching, across the courtyard and tried to drag the child out of the slave's arms.

Nothing could have been calculated to terrify Gifta more. The child screamed in return, clinging to her refuge like a limpet.

"Idiot," snapped Rowena, "leave her alone. You will only frighten her."

Rowena leapt from the saddle, past Eadward's irritating, restraining hand. He was saying something. She did not care what. She just wanted Gifta. She—

"Seize him," yelled Eadward's voice, bellowing across the confusion with all the authority of a King's Reeve. "Seize the thrall. Free the child."

His men surged forward.

"But—" She could not move. Eadward's hands closed over her shoulders.

"Rowena, leave this to me."

One of his men had managed to secure Gifta. The rest held the slave. Somewhere round their feet a small furry creature made an unhindered dash for the freedom of the stables.

"Mouse," said Gifta. Rowena thought Eadward might go off in a fit. His body, rammed against hers, vibrated with it.

"*That* was what this was about? Of all the stupid—"

"Gifta!" she said, her voice cutting across his with all the abruptness of her fright. "Come here. Give her to me."

Eadward's man looked not at her, but at Eadward. For one second, one second that held an endless age of time, no one moved. She felt the fury in Eadward's body. She saw it in his eyes and quite equally he must have seen the fear in hers.

But he did not speak. He just watched her.

"Eadward…"

"Of course. Hand over the child." His eyes seemed to come out of a trance. His voice was laced with reproach for his man's hesitation. He smiled. But she could no longer bear that smile. She launched herself across the courtyard and Gifta swung into her arms.

She clung to her daughter's small body. Somewhere over her head, Eadward was talking, about how she should not have had to suffer such alarms and distress. About how the cause of such a disturbance should be punished.

"Cause?" she said, forcing her gaze away from Gifta's head. "There was no cause. It was just an accident. Just—"

Eadward's men still had the thrall, holding him, like a beast trapped in a snare.

He hated being trapped. The thought came to her with certainty. There was no need to do it. Why—

"Eadward, what do you think you are doing?"

"My dear, I will not allow you to be distressed for any cause. People should know that. Some people need teaching."

"But—" It was too late. *She* was too late. Eadward's shoulder tensed and then released with the smooth ease of years of weapons training, thane's training. There was not even time for breath before his hand struck. Nicely judged. Every last ounce of weight behind the blow. Perfection in force and balance.

But it did not strike as she expected. The warrior's hand did not smash into her slave's face. It cut slantwise, the edge of the outstretched hand chopping with the precision of a blade across the body, centred exactly over the knife cut in the slave's side.

Blood burst in a bright wave, the smooth-fierce body she had caressed doubled up, ripping against the hands that held it defenceless. Eadward's eyes glittered, though his breath came hard. Eadward knew. Eadward knew what to do, where to hit.

Blood had come away on his hand. Rowena's arms tightened round the child, burying the small face against her tunic. She expected Gifta's screams. There was one lodged sickeningly in her own throat. But the child seemed too frightened, or too stunned, to cry.

"Why did he do that?" The words were no more than a whisper against the skin of her neck. The child's breath the only warmth in a world gone cold.

Eadward's eyes, glazed, absorbed, utterly intent, slid from the contorted body of her slave to her stiffened face.

"For you," he said, as though it were she herself who had spoken. The smile was back on his face.

She told herself it was not particularly extraordinary. It did not do to cross a thane, especially not if one was only a thrall. That kind of insolence was punished. Instantly. However anyone wanted.

"But it was just an accident."

She felt Gifta's little hands tighten on the embroidered front of her tunic. The child's eyes held shock and the shadow of nightmares. The shadow of the look they had held when some culpable idiot had let her see the mutilated body of her grandfather, the hopelessness they had held at the bedside of her dead father.

"Mother...he should not do that. Mother!"

She saw what the child's sharp eyes had seen. Eadward's right hand flexed for the next blow. She understood that the slave had seen it.

Blood welled through the side of his tunic where Eadward's blow had burst the wound. Three people held on to him. He should be desperate, screaming, but he was not. He had not so much as glanced at her.

He watched Eadward. His face held exactly the same expression it had held in the marketplace. His eyes were blood-angry. She saw his feet arrange themselves and his knees bend slightly in that seemingly effortlessly balanced stance that took years of relentless practice to achieve. She recognised it because her father had been the best warrior for forty miles and he had been afraid of nothing.

But he could not win. There would be death.

She told herself it would not come to that. She told herself the punishment was nothing extraordinary. She told herself that this was one of the less palatable aspects of life she had toughened herself into ignoring.

There was one split instant of time between the thought in Eadward's mind and the readying of his trained, warrior's body.

She put Gifta down. Her hands gave the child a small push to send her scooting in the direction of the nurse. Her body moved with the same concentrated efficiency as a warrior's.

She landed on Eadward's tensed shoulder.

"Eadward," she cooed it, heart thundering with the speed of hailstones, her tone conveying complete ignorance that this might not yet be over. She slid her hand over muscle sickeningly tight.

"Rowena, what—" he was so intent on what he was doing he had not even heard her approach. She let her body touch his, lingeringly. She smiled into heat-glazed eyes.

"Eadward." She breathed it. "No one could exceed

your care of me. No one.'' She had placed her body between him and his target. She had no weapons. None but those that women had. Words and looks. And the hidden thoughts of the mind.

"I want to thank you." She smiled with a look that melted. Eadward's jaw slackened. His eyes still dazed with a heat that terrified. She made her hand keep touching him. She drew her body back, just slightly, just tantalisingly out of his reach. But still in front of him, still between him and the slave.

"Gifta's tired and this has been distressing for her." She glanced across at the nurse trying to stifle her hysterics and clutching with feverish hands at her charge. Gifta was surprisingly silent, watching them with eyes as deep as the lake in the forest at home.

"I should get her home as soon as I can. It is a long journey for her, for all of us. I will just get her settled with the nurse, then we will be away. You will come over from Lindherst to visit me at Healdsteda before the week's out, will you not?" She squeezed the tight, deadly, shoulder. She slid her hand down the arm tense with hideous power.

"You did give me your word on that." She found Eadward's hand. There was an edge of blood on it. Eadward blinked.

"You know I rely on you." The hot mist in the dark brown eyes cleared at last. No, perhaps it just changed into something else.

"Of course. You will be seeing me at Healdsteda. You may be sure of that.''

She bowed her head. It was over. At least, this part of it was. She allowed herself to step away, keeping it slow, although every muscle in her body screamed to flee. She placed herself so that to follow her Eadward had to turn his back on the slave, move round with her if he did not want her hand to slide out of his.

He moved with her.

Rowena turned her own back on the thrall. But not before she had looked into the fierce, unbreakable clarity of his eyes. They robbed her breath.

She had not imagined that what she did would be taken at face value not just by Eadward, but by the thrall. Her face flushed with a sudden unstoppable heat. Eadward would no doubt believe it was because of her closeness to him and her boldness in taking his hand. But not the thrall. He believed quite otherwise of her.

She had just saved his neck, hang him. She had…not everyone would think Eadward wrong in what he had done, even if there had been no secret score to settle over the robbery.

As for her, she was blameless in this, nay more than that, *praiseworthy*. No one, except her lawful and duplicitous husband, had ever dared to doubt her motives. No one. Not since the day she had been born. Her mother might only be a fond memory from when she was Gifta's age. But her father had loved her all her life.

Her father had prized her above everything. She

knew that. Yet doubts, past and present, unacknowl-
edgeable, writhed inside her.

Thoughts that would not stay leashed since she had
purchased the impossible thrall.

She should have let Eadward dismember him.

She closed her eyes briefly against the sight of seeping blood. The very thought made her sick.

But even so. He had to learn, her thrall, to keep his
place. Especially in her life.

He would learn. She would see to it.

And once she got home, once they got to Healdsteda, everything would be right.

THINGS WERE WRONG at Healdsteda. It was obvious.
But Wulf could not, at first, place the source of that
feeling.

The estate must be reasonably large, judging by the
number of buildings. Not that you could call any estate
in the South truly large, not like the vast lands of the
North.

It looked prosperous and the deepening gold of the
corn in the fields gave promise of a good harvest.

People ran out in swarms to greet them. The Lady
was obviously pleased to be there, but…the only one
who was entirely natural throughout the whole chaotic
scene of their arrival was the child. She bounced round
her mother, squeaking about something or other, her
fright over errant mice seemingly forgotten.

"I want to show him the new puppies."

"Later," said the *hægtesse* in the voice designed to depress the pretensions of the importunate.

He squatted down to pick up some of the purchases from the Hamwic market which were being carried inside. Something thudded into him at speed, smacking squarely against the knife wound. The ground hit him.

"I want to show him now," demanded Gifta, small hands scrabbling after his sleeve.

"No," said the *hægtesse,* "leave him…" For once they were in complete agreement. He had a brief glimpse of the decorated hem of the Lady's gown in front of his eyes. He considered raising his face out of the dirt but it was suddenly too much effort. He could feel the faint warmth of blood under the new bandages.

He thought she might have touched him, and then for brief black seconds there was nothing.

In the end, it was the steward who started to pick him up out of the dust, glaring at his Lady with a depth of disapproval Wulf could only silently admire.

"If ever there have been some foolish starts today…and yesterday—"

"Thank you, Ludda. Perhaps you could take him into the hall."

Wulf decided the steward's glare was nothing compared to the Lady's. He remembered the hidden anger when the Lady had talked of her father's confidant. Perhaps Lady and steward did not get on. It would hardly be surprising.

He made some effort to get to his feet so that the man, Ludda, did not have to try and lift his weight. Ludda kept hold of him which, on the whole, was probably just as well. But as the world resolved itself into something approaching its normal shape he realised what he did not want to see.

The Lady was worried out of her wits about the child. The steward was worried about the Lady. In a circle gathered round them were the worried faces of the inhabitants of Healdsteda, staring at them with a kind of helpless mixture of need and uncertainty.

The only problem at this estate was in its heart.

It was exactly the sort of problem, in another life, he had been able to deal with. The sort of human puzzle he had been trained to solve since birth, whether it related to a band of warriors heading for battle, or the complex group of people needed to create the necessities of life out of a northern wilderness.

The Lady Rowena strode towards her hall with her daughter clinging to her hand. Ludda started dragging him after them. He was aware of dozens of eyes watching. No one said a word. They were like people trapped under a curse, waiting for something to set them free.

It was not going to be him. He could not make himself do that again.

WULF WAS SITTING on the wall bench inside Rowena's hall with a litter of small hounds and the child crawling round his feet. One of the pups swarmed its way

across the bench next to him. He reached out for it
absently before it fell back over the edge, running his
hand across short dense fur. The small beast stretched
out, relaxing its body against his hand, the way all
animals did for some reason when he touched them.

He let his head fall back but the waves of pain and
sickness beat through him. He closed his eyes and
tried to concentrate on something else, like recon-
structing his copy of Boethius' *Consolation of Philosophy* entirely from memory. There were some very
salutary thoughts in it, particularly about the fickleness
of fortune. He kept one arm clamped across the knife
cut.

They ought to at least think of moving the child
away before the blood began to soak again through
the stained wreck of his tunic. He tried to say so but
the words would not get past the dry constriction of
his throat.

Something touched him. Slender fingers adorned
with gold. The fine white hand which had so recently
been feeling its way across Reeve Eadward's body in
much the same way that it had felt his pushed a swathe
of heavy hair out of his eyes, brushed the unbruised
side of his face. How she must be enjoying this.

''Hurry up,'' she snarled at someone unseen, ''and
where's Gifta's nurse? Let her take…'' She had realised. At last. He moved the lump of lead that had once
been his head out of her reach.

''Clumsy oaf.''

If he had not been so near to the edge of unstoppable fury himself, he would have laughed. She sounded furious. She sounded…frightened.

He managed to prize one leaden eyelid open. She wasn't talking to him.

She was exchanging glares again with Ludda who was clutching a beaker. He had expected her to snatch her hand away when he moved his head. She had not. The hand had moved with him, had moulded itself round the shape of his cheekbone. The fingers had found their way into the roots of his hair. Her grip was unsteady.

"No," she snapped, "give the cup to me."

She leaned across him. The hand on his head stayed put even though it made the movement awkward for her. He slid out of her way before he got an elbow in his ribs.

"For heaven's sake keep still," she hissed like an irritated viper. Her hand brushed vaguely at hair that was no longer in the way. The softness of that gesture was no match for her voice. She would not give up that small connection to him. It was almost as though it was an offer of reassurance. That was ridiculous. People did not offer to give him reassurance, they took it. It was what he was, had been, there for. Sorting other people out.

"At last. Here. You had better drink this." The ridiculous hand slid farther into his hair, curving round the nape of his neck. She was going to lift his head. She obviously didn't realise how much lead was in it.

She slid an arm under his shoulder but she could

scarce move him unaided. He did not seriously expect her to try, which was why he did not move, at first. But she did try, with the same persistence she had shown before.

Her body leaned over his, touched it. He felt her warmth, the soft curves of her. He could smell her scent like summer flowers. The irritating veil she wore teased across his skin, the way it had once before. Awareness of her, that same awareness, burned through him like a fire bolt. For one instant he thought it burned her because her breath caught and her eyes widened.

And then he saw that what lived in her eyes was fear.

He sat up, straight through the pain, breaking her grip on him because it was the only thing to be done. She was staring at him. She had a cup in her free hand. It was made of Rhenish glass, its shape richly ornamented in a design like animal claws. It would be worth a small fortune. She pressed it forward, still with the frightened look in her eyes.

"You have to drink this."

He took the cup out of her fingers so she would not have to touch him again. Light hit the dark green glass, making it glow like summer leaves, the smooth coolness of it fitted with the ease of familiarity into his palm. He closed his mind against memory.

He nearly choked at the first swallow. He had been expecting the sourness of her indifferently brewed ale, but it was not. It was wine, strong, heady and most definitely not from the dubious vineyards of England. It was Frankish, rich and luxurious and of a quality hard to come by. The taste was as familiar as the glass.

He could not drink that.

He lurched to his feet. Hounds scattered across the floor.

"What is it?"

He had a brief glimpse of the Lady's pale face and then his eyes focussed on the hall. It was a cavern of sunlit walls and shadowed heights, the pillars were carved, gilded, painted in colours: red, dense blue and a rich green the colour of forests. The walls were hung with tapestries in colours deeply subtle and more varied. A thin plume of smoke in the centre of the room, released from the fire that must never go out, summer or winter, wafted its lazy blue trail upwards into the soaring denseness of the thatch, towards the gap that allowed a glimpse of the infinity of the sky.

If someone ripped the heart out of your body and then held it up before your eyes, forever out of your reach, this was what it would feel like.

He did not know he had even taken a step until he heard the rustling of agitated feet behind him. But he was aware of sunlight pouring over him from the open window, where before he had been in shadow. The Lady Rowena was clutching at his arm.

"It is all right," said her voice, "I know there must be so much strangeness for you...."

It was all as familiar as the taste of the fine wine. Yet not so. As his sight cleared, he could see the differences. The proportions of the hall were all wrong. It was smaller, not so long. The tapestries had strange scenes, Wessex scenes, doubtless, soft-edged and crowded. The sense of the sky and the forest just an illusion of the mind.

"I do not like it when you look like that."

Like what? A madman probably. That was what he was. A madman with too many memories, trapped in a stranger's hall.

"Then let me go," he said, because the pain was no longer in his ribs or his arms or his face, but somewhere deep inside.

The fingers on his arm fluttered in agitation. She was so close, closer than she must want to be. The filmy whiteness of her veil drifted across his vision.

"Go?"

He remembered his promise, what he had bound himself to. He could feel the grasping hands of all the other ties that lay around him now, in this terrible luxurious place, waiting their chance.

"Outside then. I only know I cannot stand this hall."

"Indeed?" He felt the sudden stiffening of the body close to his. Her voice bit. The fingers laced round his upper arm bit. She obviously did not take kindly to any criticism of her appalling death-trap of a hall.

He went anyway, the air outside was a blessing against his burning body, the vicious ache of tiredness in his eyes.

She sent her steward after him with instructions to

take him to the priest. She did not come out and this time the people of Healdsteda avoided looking at him.

He was aware of only one pair of eyes that followed his progress. The child watched him from the corner of the building, a hound cub clutched in her arms.

CHAPTER EIGHT

NOTHING COULD TOUCH HER.

Rowena sipped scandalously expensive imported wine out of her glass beaker and let her head fall back onto the nearest cushion. It was one of a set embroidered with a banqueting scene from the life of Saint Judith. A woman after her own heart. Judith had known what she was about when she had beguiled Holofernes and then chopped his head off. A woman of resource.

There was more than one man round here who could do with having his head chopped off.

Healdsteda. Her home. It was unspeakable bliss. At least it was now that the fey and bloodied thrall was gone. She glanced round the hall softened by the evening light. It was beautiful, high beamed, hung with tapestries, the heavy table in front of her still littered from her meal with the plentiful fruits of the earth.

The thrall had looked at her hall as though the very air of it had choked him.

The thrall. At least she had not had to see him again. He had spent the remainder of the day with the priest.

She poured more wine.

Father Bertric knew medicine. Much better than Gifta with her concoctions of woad and boiling butter. She had sent new clothes for him. Good ones, not the coarse rubbish he had been wearing. Castoffs from Cuthred's things. Dark blue cloth. Fine and a delight to wear.

A guilt offering? She had no desire to believe that.

The thrall was trouble. Eadward had been right about that much.

Eadward of the heavy hand. Harsh, mood-proud, hot-tempered…charming. Thief and abuser of those less fortunate. And murderer? She did not know.

There was only one more thing she could try before robbery.

She swallowed the last of the wine.

She got up. It was impossible to rest, even now she was home. Healdsteda was too full of unquiet ghosts. The loud voice of her father, his strong footsteps ringing through the hall. The way the house had come alive when he was there. It had been so all her life. It had continued after her marriage during the frequent visits she and Cuthred had made here. Cuthred, her father's friend, her husband. It had been such a perfect life. Perfect. She would have it no other way. Admit no other memories.

Rowena's fist struck the silk-embroidered cushion.

Why could she not rest? Be at peace? Lay the unquiet ghosts?

It was the thrall's fault. She had never felt so restless, so utterly confounded, as she had since the moment she had bought him. She thought of her hand resting in his hair. She thought of the terrifying way that had made her feel.

Air. She was choking. She went outside. The cool breeze of evening played with her hair and her filmy veil, bathed her wine-heated face in freshness. The wind had a bite to it that had not been there before, surely? Had the autumn wind turned northerly already? If so, it was early this year.

She should have brought her cloak. But she did not want to go back into the memory-filled hall. She shivered, walking on, her mind miles away, full of conflicting thoughts.

The soft sound of laughter brought her to herself, sly laughter, female laughter, almost a…giggle. She looked round and found she was beside the priest's hut.

Father Bertric?

The laughter came again, borne by the cool breeze. It came from the priest's herb garden. She had no desire to go in. She had already had words with Father Bertric over the question of the slave's manumission. She could not satisfactorily explain to a priest why she was not prepared to set a fellow human being free. He had actually dared to try and prick her no longer existent conscience.

It was infuriating.

Yet she valued Father Bertric's opinion.

That was even more infuriating.

The laughter came again. She stalked through the small wicker gate.

The first thing she saw was the back of Father Bertric's bare skull. The second thing was her slave's bare torso, an expanse of translucent gold in the ruddy evening light.

The third thing was Father Bertric's niece, a strapping wench of fifteen winters, blessed with thick flaxen hair and an enormous bosom. The bosom trembled beneath an ineptly woven expanse of bright green cloth. It was the wench who was giggling. Her gaze rested on the thrall's golden flesh like one of Gifta's overexcited hound puppies watching a slab of meat.

Rowena came to an abrupt halt. What in heaven's name did her purchase think it was doing disporting itself half-naked in a borage patch for the entertainment of some slavering trull? He seemed to have made a remarkable recovery.

"Good evening," she observed.

They jumped. All three of them. Even the half-naked thrall.

They had obviously been enjoying themselves too much to hear her approach.

"Good even, Lady," they chorused. Well, two of them chorused. The third seemed to run out of breath before the last word. Mayhap due to a sudden chill of the lungs brought on by exposing himself to the damp night air.

"Why are you not wearing the tunic I sent you?"

Rowena demanded, ignoring the fidgeting priest and the slavering maiden.

There was a flash of something in the fierce grey eyes that took her by surprise.

"Because it…" the eyes glanced from her to the priest and something was bitten back. "I was afraid it would not fit," offered the thrall, falling back on practicality.

"Oh." She could scarce argue with that. Yet it had been Cuthred's largest and loosest tunic. Had she so miscalculated the difference in size between her late husband and the slave? Her irritated gaze swept across acres of exposed flesh marred only by the clean line of a bandage expertly applied by Father Bertric. At least that much was done. That much was off her conscience. The thought of Eadward's hand still had the power to make her shudder.

She made a close assessment. There was a lot of him, to be sure. But then there had been quite a lot of Cuthred. Perhaps it had just been arranged in different places.

She remembered how heavy he had felt in her arms. She swallowed. With the slave everything was so…so exactly placed, so symmetrical that you could not have done without one ounce of that gilded flesh. In fact if anything he could possibly do with more of it to cover such an expansive frame of bone and muscle. How could a creation of such potent force possibly be too thin? Did he not eat…

She became aware, all at once that the rather prom-

inent blue eyes of the strapping wench were raking
over the thrall's body with a similar degree of attention, ogling every angle of light and shadow. Except,
Rowena was not ogling, of course. Unless…perhaps
the wine had overheated her blood. She felt quite…
She transferred her gaze to the slave's face and en-
countered an undisguised irritation that surpassed her
own.

She had forgotten quite how arrogant he was when
he was not half-dead.

"I still think you could have—"

"I had no desire," cut in her slave, taking as little
care to keep the irritation out of his voice as out of
his face, "to rip the shoulders out of anything quite
so…fine." This final word appeared to be a last-ditch
effort to cover what he really wanted to say with some
token attempt at respect.

"He's nearly bursting out of his seams as it is,
Lady," put in the maiden, helpfully.

Rowena's fascinated gaze followed the direction of
the wench's overbold eyes, farther down, to where the
fine dark wool trousers strained over the compressed
muscles of her bondsman's thighs where he knelt in
the dirt. She was aware of a sudden rush of warmth
in spite of the chill wind. She tried not to imagine
what would happen if something did burst. Freya's
handmaid, here, would probably swoon from an ex-
cess of frustrated lust. Rowena wondered whether she
might, as well. Idiocy. She would never drink wine
again.

"What on earth are you doing kneeling in a borage patch anyway?" she snapped, in a desperate effort to regain control of what was becoming an utterly ridiculous situation.

"Weeding."

A suppressed giggle escaped Freya's handmaid. The priest glared at her. Rowena glared at her. The slave glared. He got to his feet. The effort that took was very well disguised. But not from her. He was not recovered at all. Not yet. Not by a long way.

What had Father Bertric been thinking of? She had sent him to the priest for rest and attention to his hurts. And perhaps a sermon or two on the follies of pride.

Or on the vanities of men who wore their hair too long, she thought, as the cool breeze wafted errant locks from the source of her earlier downfall in her direction. A stray strand caught her cheek. Her skin tingled with memory.

She swatted the bright strands aside. They felt like cold gossamer on her hand. She jumped, and as the slave moved from the ruddy glow of the sunlight into shadow Rowena saw that there was no colour in his face at all. Father Bertric grabbed his elbow.

"I did warn you, my son, how things would be with you for the next couple of days unless you rest. I told you I expected no payment for tending your hurts. Let me—"

"Let me—" suggested the strapping wench.

"No," countered the priest and Rowena as one.

"My niece came over from Alfred's farm to help

me with the housekeeping,'' explained Father Bertric cautiously letting go of the elbow, ''a most willing girl—''

''So I see. Is it not rather late? Perhaps your niece should be making her way back to Alfred's farm before it gets too dark.'' Rowena smiled at the flaxen-haired maiden. The trollop, her avid eyes still on Wulf's naked shoulders, bobbed a reluctant curtsy and seized her basket and departed most unwillingly into the sunset.

That the thrall-turned-gardener accompanied Rowena back towards the hall of disasters without protest was surely a further sign of his discomfort. Or perhaps it was just that the north wind had frozen his throat. It had certainly frozen her now that the sun had descended below the roofs of the buildings. Rowena wrapped her arms around her body and wished more fervently for her cloak.

The slave walked on, oblivious alike of the cold and the way the sun's afterglow and the deep blue shadows alternated across his bare skin. He must know what he looked like and what it did to people, surely. He had reduced Freya's handmaid to a writhing torment of female lust.

''What an idiotic wench that was.''

''Who? Oh, Father Bertric's niece? She is full young.''

She was. Precisely eight winters younger than Rowena.

The massive shoulders beside her shrugged, light over shadow.

"Are you not in the least cold? This wind is freezing. It should chill you to death." She looked for gooseflesh.

He laughed unexpectedly. It made the tight muscles of his abdomen ripple.

"It is the north wind. It has not reached a quarter of its power yet. Besides, what could it do to me? We are old friends." The strong, rather harsh face lifted into the wind, so that the cold moving air touched his skin, snagged at his trailing hair, lifted it from his neck just as she had done with her hands.

She shuddered, as much from the awareness of that memory as from the sight of the pleasure in his face. She was afraid of that kind of pleasure. She was foreign to it. Her husband had told her so, and now she shunned it. But since she had seen this man, since she had touched him, sinfully touched him, she wanted it. She wanted to know what it was like. Wondered, achingly, how it would feel to give yourself up to that elemental pleasure, to know what it meant.

The thrall knew the secret magic. She could see it in him, feel it through his touch. But he did not seem to know that he drove her mad with that knowledge, drove her mad from the sight and the feel of him.

The knowledge he had was simply part of him, like his beauty. He seemed to be truly unaware of how he looked, or of how he affected people.

Perhaps it was because he was only a thrall. She

had to remember that. He had been overawed by the splendour of her hall, after all.

But he did not hold himself like a thrall, or move like one and, hang him, sometimes he did not know how to think like one.

Rowena suddenly wanted to learn about him, wanted him to tell her what his life was, had been, before this. Even though it should not matter to her, or impinge in any way upon her thoughts.

"Thrall—"

But he was already speaking, the cool grey eyes fixed on her, all trace of softer thoughts gone.

"Lady, I will not wear such clothes as you sent me today. You should know that."

Peasant. He was looking at her as though she had committed some crime.

"They were good clothes. Better than you deserved—"

"Aye. Better than I deserve."

She had done him a favour. She had… "They were my husband's clothes," she snapped so that he should know just how big a favour.

"Aye. Well they might have suited him but not me."

"What?"

"Cloth like that? Embroidery? Lady, I am what I am. Dressing it up makes not only a fool out of me but out of you."

A fool! A… Rowena swallowed what she had been about to say. She had not thought about that, except…maybe she had. Arrogant swine. Why was she always in the wrong when she was with him?

"You will wear what I give you to wear and you will do what I say. For all your fine protestations, I think you do forget what you are to me." *Just as I forget.*

"No. I think not. I believe I know exactly what I am to you."

Suddenly all she could see in the fading light was the whiteness of the bandages round his chest and at his wrists.

She swallowed bile and forced herself to spit out the words that had been pressing against the walls of her chest all day.

"Thrall, you have to know that I did not intend what Eadward did to you this morning to happen."

Silence. No reproach because he could not. But the quality of the silence did it for him. Or perhaps it was just the conscience she had thought was buried but which seemed to take on a new life whenever her slave was around.

"I know what it looked like when I…when I went to him and…and I know what I said, but believe me, that was the quickest and most effective way to stop Eadward."

"Lady."

He did not believe her. She had said something in good faith, something unwelcome to her that she did not need to say and the scum of the marketplace did not believe her?

It was so impossible that she choked.

"Feeling unwell, Lady?"

"No! No, I am not and if I were it would be no concern of my slave's. Do not presume, thrall, to overstep the bounds of your station."

"Ah. I will remember that in future."

She thought of how he had saved her from Eadward's thieves, the kindness, the unutterable comfort of his arms when she had been ill from Eadward's drugs.

Why did she have to think of that now?

She took a breath and said with as much truth and disinterest as she could manage, "You do not know Eadward as I do. But I can assure you what I did was the only thing I could do. Besides, it worked."

Let him challenge that.

He did not. There was a pause, during which she felt as though she was being assessed down to her shoe leather, but all he said was, "I see."

You could tell nothing from that. Not whether he believed her or whether he did not.

They were back at the hall, standing in the glow of the torches. It was nothing to her what he thought. She should make an end to this.

"I suppose you are sleeping in the hall?" If he could get over his distaste of it. Well, it was either that or the threshing floor, or—

"No."

"Oh. Then where?"

"Wherever you are sleeping."

"What did you just say?" Rowena's gaze fixed on the powerful, sensual, half-naked man she had bought as though it had been nailed there.

"You are going to sleep where I... How do you dare to say that?" Her voice nearly rose off the scale. She fought to get it under control. She fought not to look at the light sliding over his muscles. "Do you think I am like that witless farm girl slavering over your attributes like Freya's acolyte in a fertility dance?"

"Like..." her powerful sensual purchase choked on laughter. "Freya's acolyte? Father Bertric's niece? Was she slavering? Over my...my attributes? Never tell me I missed my chance again? And with a fine healthy wench like—"

"Healthy is one word for it and as for chances," said Rowena, their last discussion on this subject stinging her mind, "do not flatter yourself that you would be worth a morning gift of ten hides."

"No," he said sadly, "you have the better of me there. They might pay ten hides of land for your favours but I am only worth twelve mancuses."

Her face burned, despite the coldness of the wind.

"Yes," she snapped in fury, "and something worth only twelve mancuses belongs on the threshing floor."

"Do you fancy a night in the barn then?" he asked, as though this was some bold but nonetheless interesting proposition.

She seethed. Was he doing this on purpose or what? He was wearing his patient look which told her noth-

ing. He was blocking the way to her chamber and he
did not move.

"Well, you certainly look like an ox that should be
spending the night in a stall. Get out of my way."

"Lady," he said humbly.

That was better. She barged forward into the shadows and ran smack into his chest. The only compensation for that was that she made him wince. But he
had hold of her arm and she could not move.

"I am sorry," he said, "you paid for me. You get
my services. Oh, not that kind," he said to her indrawn
breath and her beating heart. "You would have to pay
me a lot more than twelve mancuses to get me to do
that."

Whoreson, she thought, with such force that it
should have been heard in the cold air between them.

But it was not cold. She could feel the warmth of
his skin through her dress and feel the soft whisper of
his breath against her throat. And the strength of his
hand around her arm. She did not want to feel that,
any of it. His eyes caught her gaze, held it, and there
was none of the barbed mockery left.

"After what happened yesterday and after what
happened this morning, you are not sleeping anywhere
farther away than I can hear you call me. If you need
me." His breath fluttered the thin film of her veil,
shivered over her skin, was lost in her hair. His eyes
gleamed in reflected torchlight. His skin, his bare
warm skin, gleamed hot red and cold black in the
flickering light. Smooth across his shoulders, lightly

dusted with fiery gold hair across his chest. So powerful and yet so human and vulnerable against the coarse white cloth of the bandages.

He had not been cowed when Eadward had hit him, though Eadward could have killed him. Just that look in his eyes when he had raised his head. He had not given in and she did not think he ever would.

She had met a will she would find hard to bend to her own uses. It was not a welcome thought.

"You would have to wait a long time for me to call you, thrall. Now let me go."

He slept on the floor of the outer room, across the door to her bedchamber. She gave him the set of St. Judith cushions.

CHAPTER NINE

THERE WAS AN ART to using an axe to chop wood, just as there was an art to using a battle-axe to hack through someone's chain mail. Wulf had been taught the wrong one.

The heavy blade landed with a dull thud that sent ringing shock waves through the disaster of his wrist and the damage to his side. He resisted the impulse to swear and adjusted his stance and the angle of his arm.

He had slept late but the *hægtessse* had still not risen from her silk canopied bed. He should not have thought of her. His mind filled with her and her devious thoughts. He was a fool for believing any word that woman said and she had not told him near half the story yet, the devious Lady Rowena. Not the half of it.

Wulf raised his head and a small breath of wind from the north stole through the yard, cooling his hot skin, drying the small bead of sweat that had formed at the base of his throat. He hefted the blade. It was thick, ill-made, in need of sharpening. It was next to useless but…just once. There was no one to see.

He closed his eyes. He imagined Bone-hacker, the long handled battle-axe he had won from a Danish mercenary. It was in his hand, steel-bright, finely wrought, the socket inlaid with silver, the haft bound in its copper sheath, the blade curved downwards and inwards to allow for an overhead blow. He saw the face of the King's Reeve. At the last moment that face faded before another, born of memory, a face with colourless eyes.

He opened his eyes and struck with perfect balance and with every ounce of force he possessed, nothing held back, the way you struck in battle. The huge oak log split in half with a crack like Thunor's thunderbolt. Wulf leapt back out of a hail of splinters. Something hit him high up on the arm. He felt the wetness of blood. He did not give a damn. His breath exulted with freedom in the painful mess of his chest. He flung Bone-hacker, the battle-axe, over his head, swinging his whole body in the familiar rhythm. The axe landed buried up to the neck in a stack of beech.

"I would hate to meet you on a battlefield."

Wulf spun round. The man was tall, well dressed. A churl of some substance. He had the kind of eyes that missed nothing.

"I thought Dunn chopped the wood."

Wulf assumed an expression the Lady Rowena would have likened to that of an ox in its stall. "Dunn is sick."

"Ah." The irony in the word was masterly. Wulf was suddenly aware of the irritating bandages. "You met my daughter yesterday with her uncle the priest. Pretty girl. Blonde.''

''Oh. Was she? I mean, yes,'' corrected Wulf politely. The fellow would doubtless be proud of the wench. All Wulf could remember of Father Bertric's niece was the giggle.

The shrewd eyes crinkled. ''Your first answer was better.''

Rowena's cool, low voice making derisive remarks about slavering and fertility rites rang in his ears. A well set-up farmer's daughter was not to be compromised by a slave. He should have seen this coming. Wulf turned to free the axe. The man would go now that he had the assurance he wanted.

''My name is Alfred,'' said the voice behind him. ''I live near Ditchford.''

''Ditchford? The village that was burnt?''

''So you know? My wife died in the fire.''

''I...I am sorry.''

There was no change in Churl Alfred's face. But Wulf had become an expert at suppressing before other people any inconvenient emotion. It was an art he recognised in others.

''I do not see things turning out much different with the dues they want this autumn.''

There was no need for a churl to even speak to him. Wulf's eyes watched the strong, shrewd face. He was not one to kick opportunity in the teeth.

''Things may change. I am interested...the Lady Rowena would be interested in what you have said.''

"Her? You are new I suppose. Otherwise you would know what good friends the King's Reeve and the Lady's husband were."

The Lady's husband about whom he did not need to know. *Thank you,* she had said as Eadward had appeased his vicious tastes on him. He felt the anger that had no death surge inside him. He felt the pain of Eadward's blow, the soul-killing fury of being held down, trapped. It brought other memories, worse, unacceptable. His mind blanked them out.

The Lady Rowena and Eadward. It was not possible. She had said... His mind remembered the kind of look she had given the King's Reeve, the way her hand had caressed his arm, much the same way she had caressed him. With the same result. He had done exactly what she wanted. The thought was like ashes.

"If you want my advice, lad, you will keep your head down. Just like the rest of us."

The bitterness in that last comment was understood on a level beyond reason. It was understood by the person who had once owned not just land, but peace, that untouchable quality that some Latin-tutored priest would have called civilisation. That peace was gone, as completely as the burnt village, as completely as the thane who had owned a personal heaven. He tried to tell himself he did not meddle.

"Wait," ordered the nonexistent thane. Wulf swallowed back the command. "If you would allow it," he amended to Alfred's bowed shoulders, "I would speak further of this with you. But not here."

"Quite sure about that, are you, thrall? Then you had better come to the farm." There was the faintest sign of crinkling in the weather-beaten skin around the world-weary eyes. "Next time my daughter is out."

"WAKE UP."

Not moving was deliberate because the anger inside him, the deep memories that should never be stirred, were blacker than the shade of the trees above his head, blacker than the nightmare that clung tighter than the remains of sleep. The darkness was total. Never since he had woken in chains had control of that lightless force been so difficult.

"Wake up." The voice, disembodied, scarce penetrated the blindness of mind and body.

Something stabbed at him through the bruising. He moved on the grass at the edge of the forest, every muscle a dense aching mass of pain. The pain took the edge off speed but gave the strength of fury. The movement—

He stopped it. How he stopped he did not know. But he did.

"I want you to come and see Brocc." Eyes the blue of cornflowers, sun-bright, brimming over with light and a trust that was horribly complete.

He fell over onto his elbows.

"You have to see him," piped the Lady Godgifu, Rowena's child. "He was not well but I made him better. Like you."

The reality of the present came back, the present of

Healdsteda. He looked up into the dazzling light in the child's eyes. She smiled. Heaven knew what she saw in the black remains of his soul to bring out such a smile.

"You will come?" Her delight was as strong as steel and as fragile as a spider's thread.

He had no idea what she was talking about. Why would she ask her mother's purchase to go with her? He did not want any involvement with the tiny maid. Did she not have other children to plague? The nurse? Anyone?

"Brocc is my badger. He hurt his foot."

A badger? "It depends," said Wulf. His voice croaked. The only recognisable thought out of the strands of chaos was fear that the blackness would show through and extinguish the light in the child's eyes. "Does he have stripes and whiskers?"

"Of course he does." The smile dissolved into giggles. "You are silly," crowed Rowena's daughter. "Come on."

THE PATH to the badger's pen was not one to be taken in your best clothes. Rowena's annoyance grew. She had overslept. A thing she never did and now she was making herself later than ever. But it was impossible to leave without saying goodbye to Gifta. The child would panic.

But why could the stupid nurse not keep her charge where she was supposed to be? At her singing lesson with Father Bertric. Not roaming about the woods and paddocks.

Rowena stopped and hauled a piece of briar out of her kirtle. If it ripped, someone was going to die.

She managed to disentangle the material intact at the cost of a scratched finger. Someone was going to die anyway. She sucked the finger.

Brocc lame-foot lived just over the rise. She ploughed onwards and paused at the edge of the clearing.

The badger dozed in its pen, almost hidden under its shelter of plaited hazel twigs. There was no sign of…she turned round.

"There it is. Catch it. Hee hee."

Rowena wondered whether she was always to be lured to the haunts of her slave by the sound of female giggles.

The Lady Godgifu, her face bright red, her hair straggling out of its braids and grass stains on her skirts, leapt from one unshod foot to the other yelling instructions at something crawling through a patch of flowering willow herb.

"Left," screamed her daughter, then more helpfully, "no, right. Under there."

Rowena watched as the new tunic she had sent the thrall, her father's plain and carefully woven tunic, snaked with astonishing speed through juicy green stems and rose-coloured flowers. She winced as it narrowly missed a stray briar.

"There!"

The right sleeve lunged perilously close to the
brambles.

"I got it," crowed Gifta, like King Ine blithely ap-
propriating the deeds of the more successful of his
hearth companions. She sounded so happy and
yet…such happiness in Gifta turned almost inevitably
these days into overexcitement and then…

A swirl of tangled ash-brown hair emerged from the
vegetation, a pair of pale blue shoulders in a tunic
achingly familiar, a tunic she had only given up at the
cost of painful memory. It fitted. She looked from her
slave's unreasonably broad shoulders to his face. It
was turned half-away from her, so that she saw the
unblemished side of it. There was a piece of rosebay
willow herb caught in his hair.

His face wore the same expression of idiotic triumph as her daughter's. It smirked. It…the stupid grin
made his cold grey eyes glow and his face look so
young, as young as hers. The unfettered happiness in
it caused a pang somewhere round her heart, a painful
reminder of how uncomplicated life had once been.
But the feeling was mixed with something else, something breathlessly sharper. Something that had to do
with the beguiling way the sunlight touched fair skin.

She glared. She was not here to be beguiled by
some snake in the grass, or possibly the wild herb
patch. Life was not uncomplicated. She was on her
way to see an Ealdorman of doubtful loyalties about
a matter of betrayal.

An Ealdorman outranked a King's thane. An Eal-

dorman held justice in the palm of his hand. An Ealdorman was the only one who could prevent her, and
her crawling slave, from theft.

And now she was late. She…her prostrate slave balanced himself on one elbow, her father's sleeve set
squarely in a patch of damp earth. The other grubby
hand was upraised in the gesture of the victor of a
battlefield holding up his enemy's severed head. In his
earth-streaked fingers was the most disgusting insect
Rowena had ever seen.

"Ooo," squeaked Gifta, transported, "look at all its
legs."

The slave looked, with a skin-crawling thoroughness.

"No meat on them," he pronounced in his wild and
fantastical accent, "but look at the body on it." The
obscene crawling object was brandished in the air. "A
feast!" Man and child broke into incomprehensible
laughter.

Rowena stepped forward into the sunlight.

"To be roasted on a spit?" she enquired. "Or
boiled, perhaps?"

Two pairs of eyes were turned to her with a satisfying mixture of surprise and guilt. She arranged her
fine skirts becomingly and stared from overexcited
child to suddenly wary thrall.

Her slave sat up, squashing an unwary willow herb.

"Crushed," he said, "in honey."

Small bright traces of amusement lingered in the
eyes directed at her. Rowena straightened her back.

She was not here to exchange jests with something that wished only to roll about in the mire. Yet some unruly part of her almost wished to respond. She focussed on mud and insects. She moved her decorated skirts away from an offensive bramble.

"Family recipe?" she asked, raising her freshly tweezered brows. It invoked something slightly dangerous in the glowing eyes which enabled her to concentrate quite well on her rightful annoyance. Her brows climbed higher and she directed her gaze down the pleasing lines of a nose she knew to be flawless.

But it was Gifta who spoke, breaking the almost palpable line of tension between her and the dishevelled and kneeling slave.

"It is for Wrenna, of course," she declared and began giggling.

Of course. The wren with the broken wing set by the falconer who should be training merlins and goshawks.

"Gifta! Look out for the—"

"What did you think—" began Gifta's overexited squeak.

"—puddle," finished Rowena as the leaping feet took unerring aim.

"Eek," ventured Gifta. They both surveyed mud splashes. It was the moment when Rowena realised what Gifta was wearing.

"Why," she demanded, "are you wearing your best dress to hunt insects?" A fulminating glance at the thrall.

Gifta's shoulders hunched.

"I was going to come with you. So I wore my nice dress like yours so that the Ealdorman would do what I wanted, too."

"What?"

There was a choking noise from somewhere beside her feet. She turned round and glared with a look that would have reduced her best Frankish wine to vinegar. It was wasted. The thrall had collapsed into the undergrowth where he belonged. Flower heads quivered on their long green stems. She was reminded of the way his massive shoulders had shaken after she had hurled him out of her bed. If he dared to laugh at such an ill-timed, ill-founded, ill-famed statement from a misguided six-year-old...where had Gifta heard or thought such a thing?

"The dress is not so very dirty."

Rowena turned her head half a second too late.

"Do not!" she yelled with all the pent-up irritation in her heart.

The small grubby hands stopped in the process of smearing the damage over silk ribbons which had been carried at uncontemplatable danger and expense from Byzantium all the way to Hamwic, only to be ruined in insect-infested mud.

"I did not mean to."

To her credit, Gifta did not cry. But she was not a child to be shouted at and Rowena always did her level best not to. She would not have done it now if the wretched thrall had not created such a mess and then had the gall to think it, to think *her*, funny.

Somewhere behind Rowena there was a rustling noise from the slave in the willow herb. She ignored him and concentrated on her daughter.

"Never mind. Nurse will get it cleaned. Now run along back to your room and get changed," said Rowena in the firm voice designed to depress the passions of guilt and overexcitement alike, "and then it is time for your music lessons with Father Bertric."

"But I want to come with you."

"No," said Rowena, with the same firmness. Gifta was not to be involved in anything to do with her plans. Or to do with the thrall. "I will be back by tonight. Yes, that is a promise. Now run along. And no more insect hunts. Leave that to the falconer."

"Yes, Mother," said Gifta but Rowena could see her sidling round to the left, towards the patch of willow herb where the slave was. Quick as lightning, Gifta had picked up an earthenware jar. Something black and wriggling went down the neck of the jar and the stopper slammed into place. Gifta sped down the path, but not before Rowena had seen the look of understanding that passed between child and insect-hunting slave.

The coldness of fear clutched at Rowena's heart. It was succeeded by a wave of fury.

She waited until her fragile daughter was out of earshot and then she turned to face her purchase.

"Let me get one thing straight, thrall, my daughter

is no concern of yours. In future you will not approach her. There is not the remotest cause for you to so much as speak to her.''

''I did not—''

''Most of all, you will not encourage her against my wishes in such silliness as I have just seen.''

''But—''

''You seem to need reminding of just how things really stand. You are my slave. I have bought you and you must do as I wish. In case you have forgotten, I bought you for one purpose only, for your usefulness in my dealings with the King's Reeve. You have no other purpose here and no right to think you can involve yourself in any way with my family. Do you understand that?''

She expected some sullenness, knowing her slave. But she also expected submission because he had no other choice. In one heartbeat she realised she had only been granted the time to say this much because she had surprised him. Nay shocked him. So much that only now did the grey eyes begin to show signs of a fury that was a perfect match for her own. Nay, worse. It was bottomless. He stood up.

She took a breath, but her throat was too tight to allow it. She tried again, forced herself to breathe. She looked at the monster blocking out the sunlight. Dangerous. Such wilfulness in a thrall could not be permitted. She had to conquer it.

''Do I make myself clear to you?''

''Lady, I think you begin to. The fault was mine that I did not see clearly before.''

It was the perfect answer. He even lowered his head and the thick brown lashes veiled his eyes so swiftly that any lingering trace of that terrifying black rage was hidden.

Her relief was instant, swamping. Some part of her brain told her that this was too easy, but the relief was too welcome, too necessary. She took it. Because even someone as mood-proud as her thrall was obliged to see reality in the end. All was well.

She stepped forward with confidence, her gaze raking over the dishevelled and now chastened wreck that had just been crawling through the undergrowth.

''And for heaven's sake get yourself cleaned up. I do not expect clothes that…that I choose to give you to be ruined quite so quickly. You look a disgrace.''

From this angle she could see only mud and bruises and…the shifting play of the morning sun across his hair and the solid closeness of his body. He was so close. He no longer smelled of the sinful and exotic scents of the East, but of fresh air, and damp earth, and clean and potent masculinity. Like Siegmund returning from battle in the primal forest. Like Frey coming back to middle-earth to ensure the autumn harvest.

He made her skin tingle, just by standing so close to him. So that she could forget herself in that irresistible pull of attraction to his maleness, even in spite of her anger with him, or because of it. She did not know. And then what? If she did?

She would not think about that. She would not think at all. Not even for a very small moment. Because it would be disaster.

Her gaze dazzled against small shifting lights as the cold north breeze lifted the long swirl of his hair. The trailing purple flower head clung in its depths like some harvest token of Frey. Her senses filled with the heat of the sunlight around them, the rich scent of earth and ripening life and of…him.

Her hand reached out to pluck the rose-flower and was caught with shocking swiftness in a band of steel. It was not steel. It was his hand. As hard and remorseless as the traps that caught the forest game. She gasped. But he had let her go as swiftly and easily as he had caught her.

''A proper distance between us, Lady. Is that not what you wish?''

''Yes. Of course it is.'' Her voice snarled because she was so terrified that he might be able to see through to things as they really were.

''Then if my purpose lies in your dealings with the King's Reeve, should I not be accompanying you on your visit to the Ealdorman? That is, assuming what you wish the Ealdorman to do concerns the King's Reeve?'' Her second best silk-decorated tunic was examined with a thoroughness that made her spine tingle. She pulled the neck of it together and adjusted her veil.

"Yes, it does."

"I hope he appreciates the effort."

Oh yes, he will appreciate it, she thought. There is not a man living who does not appreciate my looks. And that is all they appreciate, because that is all there is. She shoved aside the feeling of emptiness inside called up just by the sight of clear grey eyes.

"We will have to see, will we not? At least I shall. You are staying here," and before the unthinkable happened and the slave countermanded her orders, she added, "I'm leaving Gifta here with her nurse. Eadward will not be at the Ealdorman's. If he visits anywhere, it will be here. I invited him, remember?"

"Aye, I remember." The air seemed to shimmer between them with more heat than the high sun could ever have poured forth. He did not believe her about Eadward. Not entirely. She could see it in the clarity of his eyes. It made her furious. At least it would have, if it had not hurt quite so much.

She stood in the meadow in the inappropriate glory of her second-best dress staring at a stranger who did not believe her. She had readied herself as best she could for the last attempt she could make before she pitched the stranger into the life-threatening risk of theft.

It had seemed so easy in the marketplace and now, deep inside, she did not want to make him do it. She knew he would. She knew he had the courage. He had proved that with his body, in the most elemental way possible when he had protected her from Eadward's cutthroats. From Eadward.

There was something about that which demanded fair return.

Yet she still needed him. She thought he might be angry enough to refuse what she desperately wanted. Someone to make sure Gifta was safe.

Of course the child would be. Not even Eadward would think to harm a child but…that awful moment when Eadward's man had had hold of Gifta, the eternity of coldness before he had let her go, still tortured her mind.

Perhaps the stranger saw that in the face she had schooled to remain impassive. He saw far too much. But the decision was made. She did not want to admit the possibility that the decision had been his and not hers.

''Take Ludda with you,'' he said, ''and remember your promise to be back before nightfall. I will be back at the house before you have left.''

He turned away. It was a dismissal. He had dismissed her as though she was the lackey, not him.

She watched him vanish into the cool mystery of the wood. The last flash of sunlight through the turning leaves caught the purple flower in his hair and then nothing, not even the rustle of the trees at his passing. Gone like something as terrifyingly other-worldly as a wood-wose.

She watched the forest's blackness. Nothing to say

he had even been there and she had not just dreamed him. She turned her back on the forest and walked down the hill.

To try the one thing that remained before theft.

CHAPTER TEN

THE EALDORMAN was an idiot. Rowena's heels dug into her horse's sides, urging it on to greater speed through the dark.

Only a wantwit would put the claims of his beloved third cousin Eadward above those of a King, especially a King as clever and determined as Ine. In the few moments she had snatched alone with King Ine's highest representative, he had been blind to every hint of hers. Nay, he had thrown out a few of his own. Along the lines of not bothering her pretty head about things that should not concern it.

Simpleton.

She would not have been so late on the road if she had not risked one more try with him. It had been useless. He had been more concerned with his foreign guest, some hulking brute who was supposed to be a secret ambassador from King Ine's ally, Osred of Northumbria. The ambassador had looked more like an outlaw. But then a wolf's head as an ambassador would have been appropriate for a young and vicious king like Osred.

Everyone knew Northumbrians were a tribe that was

lethal, however much they boasted of their superior learning. Northumbria was the most deadly paradox of the Islands of Britain, thick with schools and monasteries full of books from Rome. Ruled by a lawless despot.

At least she was now aware of where her slave had come from. The match between the accent of her thrall and the accent of King Osred's ambassador had been perfect.

Her thrall belonged to the race of Cain: a race of murderers.

She could not complain. He had actually told her so.

She glanced over her shoulder into the forest's gloom. She had heard it. She knew she had. Someone, something, was following them, and now it was moving closer. Now that she had taken the risk of cutting across to take the track between the high road to Hamwic and Healdsteda. To shorten her journey. Because she had to get home as soon as possible to Gifta.

She had promised.

There was no reason why Gifta should not be properly asleep and oblivious. But if the child woke to the dark and found the only person she had left in the world was not there... The consequences of that bit like pincers in her mind.

She had no reason to worry. But she did.

She spurred the horse onwards. The small escort she had taken with her closed up instantly, as though some part of her internal terrors lived in them.

There was something basic and primitive about the fear of the dark, about not knowing what fell creature every night-black shadow might hide: man or beast or worse.

The wooded track off the Hamwic road: it had only one meaning for her, a meaning laced with horror. She heard it again, hoofbeats behind them, separate and fast. It could not be. It must be imagination. Her own terrors.

But this time it was the men around her who quickened pace. As though they heard it, too. But they could not fear as she did. This was her nightmare, personal and specific, so insistent she could see it in front of her night-blind eyes: charred and blackened flesh round twin sunken pits in what had once been a face, strips of skin scarcely attached, bloodied and raw, hanging off the bones.

A tree branch whipped in front of her. She had not seen it with her nightmare-filled eyes. She ducked. Almost too late. The branch caught her shoulder with a thud that almost unseated her. She pulled the horse up sharply. There was a milling of men around her and then something else. The sound she had dreaded. But it came from in front. Other hoofbeats borne on the writhing wind. Horsemen. She saw them: a seething mass of movement, dark, blanking out the fitful light of the moon.

A scream lodged somewhere deep in her throat.

Part of the terrifying blackness detached itself, a huge, lightless shape, moving with the speed and the

litheness of a wolf. It made straight for her. The
banked scream took flight. The horse plunged at the
sound. She shortened rein, fighting to regain control,
but a hand seized the leather straps, engulfing her own
hands as though they were not there.

The light-eating shape spoke, its voice a single in-
distinguishable word of command, like the power-
word in a spell. The horse stopped.

The blackness turned to her.

It was not black at all. Her eyes caught the faint
flash of moon-silvered brightness through it, as though
from something hidden underneath. She looked up.
Her gaze fastened not on the hideous monstrosity of
Bulla Fire-Blind, but on the ice-grey, moon-silver, hot-
burning eyes of her slave.

She felt as though her heart had stopped. Her hand,
without the slightest command from her nightmare-
sodden brain pulled itself round under his, fastening
on it with the grasp of iron claws.

''You—'' It was the only word that her breath could
get out.

''Aye. Just as well. What the devil did you think
you were doing riding through the forest after dark?''
The force of anger in his words stunned. The dark
planes of the shadowed face gave nothing. The brightness of his eyes, the shifting silver gleams in the darkness of his cloak, dazzled the aching tension of her
eyes. Her breath came in patches.

Yet the grip of his hand matched hers. It might have
hurt if her brain had been able to register it. But even

if he had broken all of her fingers, at that moment it would not have been enough. She held on to him.

"Going home." She choked on it. "By the quickest route." *By the path my father died on.* "I—"

"Going home? Cuthbert's bones, woman, you would try the patience of an archangel. Why…" The oath, sworn by the foreign, northern saint, jarred through her mind. Northumbrians. A race of murderers. She tried to get her hand out of the death grip of his. "…did you not just—why do you keep looking over your shoulder?"

"Nothing. Just…I thought someone was following us I—"

"Stay with Ludda." Her hand was free. Her own again, without any effort on her part. She had not even noticed Ludda coming towards them. The Northumbrian spoke to him. Vanished.

"Lady?" She looked up from contemplation of her hand.

"Ludda! I thought I left you at home," she said, fright sharpening her voice. "I do not know why you thought you had to come chasing after me with a rescue party when—what on earth are you doing wearing a byrnie?"

"Seemed like a good idea," said Ludda mutinously. The tone of her voice, the one which had always been enough to disconcert her steward, had no effect on the mail-clad figure. His answer could have done as well for either of her snarled questions. "Shall we go?"

"But what about the thrall?" She put all the em-

phasis she could into that last word. Because the creature threw himself about as though he was in charge
and not Ludda.

"He will be all right. Knows what he is doing—"

"A *thrall*—"

"You are needed at home."

"Gifta?" The word flew out of her mouth before
thought could be formed. Her heart clenched with a
wholly different kind of terror.

"Now do not look like that. No harm done. Only
you know what she is like—"

"What? Just tell me."

"Cat got the bird."

It took a moment for the sense of something so
cryptic and inconsequential to sink in. Gifta's stray
bird. The injured wren the falconer was keeping for
her. Insects, disgusting ones with thin legs and meaty
bodies to be eaten crushed in honey. Gifta hopping
about in a state of overexcitement and the thrall en-
couraging her.

"No one's fault but she does take on. The falconer's
fair fit to cut his throat but Wulf had a word with him.
Wulf calmed the child down, too."

Wulf? She had almost forgotten what his name was.
"The *thrall?*" she yelled for the third time.

The barbarian from the North where they murdered
people for sport? The last thing she had done had been
to warn him away from her child. He had been supposed to stay in the house, but leave Gifta to her nurse.
"Why—"

"Child would not have anyone else."

THE NORTHERN BARBARIAN followed her to her daughter's room. He had caught up with them before they had reached the gates of Healdsteda. He had spoken to Ludda. Showed him something. She had seen him do it. The two of them had spoken in the low conspiratorial tones peculiar to men when they wished to exclude females from their world. She had not asked what it was. She had not spoken. The only reason he was still behind her was that she would not demean herself to order him away.

Could no one but her see what a savage he was? What a dangerous brazen opportunist? Did no one but her see what damage he could do? Rowena clenched her teeth. If the savage thought to advance himself here by exploiting the vulnerable fancies of her child he did not realise what or who he was dealing with. She was not afraid of anything or anyone when it came to protecting her child.

Her child. The thrall was irrelevant. The instant Gifta set eyes on her mother, he would know it, more clearly than any words of hers could tell him.

She paused on the threshold of her daughter's chamber. Warmth touched her chilled face and hands. Light from the glowing fire in the hearth and the polished brass oil lamps flickered over bright wall hangings thick enough to keep out any draught.

The heavy curtains round the bed were drawn back. Gifta was not asleep. All Rowena could see were huge blue eyes swollen with weeping. But the only one still making wailing noises was the nurse.

Rowena sent her away.

"Gifta…" Everything she had was in her voice and she did not care if the slave could hear it. All her love, all the care she had for her daughter. She moved with swift steps across to the bed, her arms held out. For a heartbeat it seemed as though all would happen as she saw it in her mind. Gifta's small thin hands extended in a mirror image of her own gesture.

Behind them the nurse shut the door with unnecessary force. The wind blew out the lamp beside the bed.

Gifta gave a terrified moan.

Rowena flew across the intervening space. "Gifta, it is all right now, I am here—" but it was too late. The tears started, for the fear of the half dark, for exhaustion and the dead bird. Something hit her arm. It was Gifta's hand.

"Go away," wailed a shaking voice. "You were not here. You said you would be here before dark. You promised."

"Gifta! I said I would be back tonight. I am. I—"

"No." The tearstained eyes fastened on something behind her shoulder. "Go away," said Gifta, pronouncing every word very clearly. "I do not want you. I want Wulf."

In the moment of shock, the small body slipped from her gasp, sliding down the bed like an eel. A blur of trailing white linen launched itself at blackness.

"Gifta…"

If someone had stabbed her through the heart, it would have hurt less. Rowena was not sure that she even breathed.

Her daughter slung herself round a murderer's neck.

"Let her go!" It was the sort of cry the dead and despairing might make as the executioner's axe fell. She lunged, with the primitive maternal force of a she-wolf. Her hands fastened round thickened, tensed muscle of the slave's arm holding her child. She pulled.

"No!" It was Gifta. The child screeched in the voice that held all her deepest terrors. Rowena saw, felt, what had caused that cry. A sudden wetness under her hand. Her ears caught the faintest of indrawn breaths from the slave. Her hand fell off. She had not done that. She could not have done it.

Gifta and the sight of blood. Something wounded.

"Let her go." It was scarce a whisper this time, because the taste of defeat in her mouth choked the words in bitter helplessness.

He did try. She could actually see it through the annihilation of her heart. There was none of the triumph she expected, not even disguised by the clever dissembler that he was. He really did not want the child to do what she had just done. The truth of that was something that even the consuming strength of her fear and pain and resentment could not mistake.

He tried to detach Gifta. But there was nothing to be done without more screams. Her daughter worked on instinct and the vulnerabilities of a nervous child.

She was quite oblivious to the adult undercurrents swirling round her.

She clung.

After a moment that had no breath of life in it, Rowena saw the slave's arms come round to support the small burden. They moved with the heavy, awkward reluctance of something forced. She could no longer look.

But something touched her. So lightly that it could hardly be felt, yet it made her whole body convulse, like someone in fits. The touch strengthened, just for an instant, with the force of the handgrip they had shared in the forest's dark. Every muscle in her body tensed as the hand, the unknown murderer's hand, slid down her arm, found her fingers, drew her hand into his and then placed it, just softly, on warmth covered by fine linen.

She thought her own heart would be broken into two pieces it hurt so much. There was an instant when Gifta's tiny body stiffened and she thought that the child would reject her. The instant passed. The little back under her palm seemed to melt its warmth into her skin. She could feel laboured breath. Then a sigh heavy enough to move a small strand of lamp-burnished hair off pale blue wool, a black cloak. Then quietness. Silence in the warm, flickering half light of the room.

She felt dizzy, sickened. The tensions of the day, the alarms of the ride home, all the nightmares in her head that would not stay properly buried, whirled round in her exhausted mind. They mixed into the greater aching hurt for her damaged child so that she could not support it. She could not support anything. Not even the weight of her body. The closeness of the room stifled breath, made the dizziness in her head worse.

She thought she fell on the bed. She felt the warm rugs, the straw mattress, something else, still warmer, living. She was hopelessly intertwined with it.

A heavy arm across her body, trapping her, long legs tangled with hers, the warm weight of a thigh, all bone and muscle. But not threatening. Relaxed, into an exhaustion as profound as her own. Still. Intimate. Her head rested on the goose-down pillow. Like his. And Gifta between them.

She touched Gifta's russet head. And then she looked at the familiar face of the slave. The unknown face of the stranger from some godforsaken land in the North. She could see the roughness of brown stubble and the fascinating length of his eyelashes. His eyes were closed, his lips faintly parted. His mouth looked so much more generous like that. Not compressed into a harsh uncompromising line. She could almost feel the familiar warm sweetness of his breath. But it was only in her dizzied mind, tantalisingly beyond the edge of sensation.

If she moved her head, she would feel it.

She did not want to feel it.

Gifta, curled up into a small ball between them, moved closer against her. Rowena's gaze dropped to the small head. So fragile. So easily hurt. So in need of protection.

She took a breath of strength. She fixed her gaze on the quiet face so close to hers.

"Do not fool yourself by believing that my daughter's childish fancies are going to change anything between you and me."

His eyes opened, bright, piercing.

"Nay, Lady. What a timely reminder that was. I actually believe I needed it."

"You have gone against everything I said to you concerning my child. You are not to involve yourself in her feelings. It seems you need more than words to tell you so, you insolent, encroaching thrall. You need—" He had insupportable eyes. Insupportable.

"I need what?"

"Flogging," she snapped, an instant before she remembered.

"Indeed?"

Her mind filled with the sight of purple, mangled flesh, the ugliness of the scars across her thrall's shoulders. "I…you…" but her voice became utterly suspended. She watched as something lightless and deeply hidden, something of terrifying power, was fought in the brightness her slave's eyes. Her whole body tensed like a bow string. Her eyes shut.

When she opened them again, there was nothing in the grey gaze except thought. Whatever she had seen, whatever emotion it was, had been conquered.

"It was you the child wanted," said the slave. "She was eating her heart out for you."

The words were what she wanted, what she craved,

to hear. They were said without malice. They felt like a slap across the face. Shame burned her.

"She was afraid something had happened to you and you would not come back," said the stranger who had just come chasing after her in the dark.

The words hung, expecting an answer. She had already told him about her father's death and he had worked it out, some of it anyway, the clever one, the one who could outface her and outthink her. The one who had just acted with more honour than she.

She said nothing into the warm, softly breathing silence and waited for what he would say next. She would say nothing more. She could not. They lay in silence. Touching each other, their bodies enmeshed, intersecting at so many points. Farther apart than the sundering seas.

He was not even looking at her. She had not the slightest clue to his thoughts. His gaze was fixed on the bed canopy.

"I suppose when you finally did come back the child felt quite safe enough to be angry with you."

Rowena blinked. Speech, movement, even breathing, quite probably, were impossible. Her body's only awareness lay in the small warmth of her child and beyond it the greater warmth of her slave.

"Have you not ever felt like that?" When he was not angry he had a voice like dark honey, smooth, full of the rich sinuous understated strength of the north. She remembered the honey darkness of his kiss. The soft startled breath she had stolen from him in the dark the first night she had had him, the thrilling heat of unexplored promise that had lain behind it. Her body, quite separate from her mind, surrendered a part of its tension to entrapment.

"It is how I would feel." How he would...*what the devil did you think you were doing*...and the way his eyes had burned. The fury she had sensed. Such fury when he found her on the forest track.

It could not be. Her slave did not care about her just as she did not—could not—possibly care about him. Any relationship they had was enforced. On her part by her need of his dubious skills and on his part by the simple brutality of choicelesness. Yet her heart swelled.

"I remember," said all that rough-smooth beguilement, "when I was just a bit of a lad..."

Just a...but her mind was not dizzy enough to accept that. She looked at the stark lines of a profile hacked out of rock. Impossible.

"The time my brother went missing."

A brother. The criminal thrall had a brother. Somewhere in godforsaken Northumbria. She held her breath.

"Everyone was running around screeching he had drowned because they found the boat drifting after he had been fishing. When he eventually turned up as full of himself as usual and started laughing, I gave him a black eye."

"You—" she looked at the rock profile. It was the

one with the fading bruises on it. "You are such a barbarian. You know that, do you not?"

"Aye."

One of the smiles she should not give in to twitched at her lips.

"And is your brother like you? Does he look like you?" Surely the world had not been inflicted with two such barbarians.

"I suppose so," said the thrall as though it was something he had not given thought to. It seemed that would be it, but then he added. "Mostly. At least he did. But…my brother always looked like gold. Gold stays perfect."

She did not know what to make of such a muddled reply from someone who spoke far too straightly. All she could think, lying in his arms in the half dark, was that perfect gold must be dross compared to the quality of something made out of moonlight and shadows. The intensity of that belief made shivers start inside her. The man in her arms, scars included, was the most beautiful thing she had ever seen.

Regardless of what he was.

She watched the clear sheen on his hair and felt the quietness of his breathing. Her thrall should not have secrets from her. She would get them out of him, or it would kill her.

But she did not know how. He was utterly beyond her experience. Except he was not. No man refused her.

"I see," she began, her voice as honey-smoothed

as his, "and just where is this golden, much-tried brother?"

"Iona." But he did not sound sure.

"Iona?" How far north could one get? "Is that not some monastery set up by the Irish in Argyll? Is he a monk?"

The quiet breathing intensified into a wordless sigh, the cool edge of which she could feel on the sensitive skin of her face, just.

"Lady, you could describe my brother as many things, but a monk is not one of them. More is the pity."

The skin-tingling sigh held an entire world of things she did not know. A quite separate world from hers. A world that seemed to encompass an unspeakable sadness and the complete darkness of loss. But yet there was light, like the small flashes of moonlight she had seen in the blackness of the forest track. She could feel his warmth. Not just the heavy, seductive warmth of the body covering hers but from the inside, from the quiet, understated words meant to soothe her, from the clear thought of his spirit.

. It did not seem possible, holding him and listening to his voice, that he could have murdered. There had to be a reason for what he had done. Something she did not know.

How could she possibly get him to tell her? She could not ask directly. He would not answer and she would lose the soothing words and the warmth of his touch. She knew that much. The brother was the key.

Iona. If he was no monk, why would he go there, except for sanctuary? For misdeeds again. For murder.

Or just as easily, as an innocent victim.

Northumbria, locked in the power of a feckless youth ruled by a vicious court, a court that thought nothing of dealing out death and dispossession. A court full of wolf's heads and murderers.

She took a breath. She knew how to get knowledge out of men.

"So," she ventured in her best, well-practised, man-provoking tone, "does he have an eye for a comely wench, this brother of yours. Does it run in the family, perhaps?" She let her dark gold lashes, a very good feature of hers, flutter across her eyes, timing perfect, fail-proof. She knew the instant she said it that she had gone too far. She did not understand why she had so miscalculated. But the controlled ease, the seductive warmth of her thrall vanished like smoke into a winter sky. She looked into eyes opaque as flint.

"Lady, your reminders are always so timely. No, that particular failing does not run in the family. More pertinent to our point, was it a failing of the Ealdorman?"

"The Ealdorman?"

"Aye." The flint-sharp gaze raked over every inch of her warmed supine body as it lay so close, nay entangled, with his. Her dress, her second-best tunic, her embroidered kirtle, were rumpled. The neckline, deliberately loosened earlier and which she had forgotten to retie, showed flesh. The finely draped skirts showed leg.

She had not got what she wanted out of the Eal-dorman and she had not got what she wanted out of her thrall. The indignity, the indecent intimacy of her position with her slave hit her.

She had wanted to know more about him for his sake as much as her own. He despised her for it. Well, he would get nothing from her, not her failure with the Ealdorman, not even the little she had found out about the origins of her thrall.

"Go," she spat, clutching Gifta's sleeping form closer against her and away from him, "get away from me. Get out. Now."

She moved. But he had already slid away from her, with the sinuous ease of some tempting and deceitful serpent. Gifta made some faint sleepy noise of protest in her arms and she softened her hold and laid her hand gently on the rumpled hair, terrified that the child would wake and make some impossible demand for the thrall.

Gifta. Gifta and the thrall. She had to have it out with him for her daughter's sake. Never mind how she felt. There was the helpless child to consider. Caught in the middle of some dangerous adult game she could not comprehend.

And Rowena still had need of the slave.

"Wait," she snapped, just as he got to the door. He stopped, with his hand on the latch, but he did not turn round.

''Go to my bower and wait for me there,'' she commanded. There was not the slightest movement and the thought came to her that he would not obey. But then Gifta made another sleepily protesting noise. Distracted, she bent her head to soothe the child. When she looked up, he was gone.

Eventually, she left Gifta in the nurse's care. She was reluctant to leave, reluctant to go back to her own chamber. Reluctant, most of all, to see the thrall.

Perhaps he would not be there. Perhaps his rebellious heart would have taken him elsewhere, perhaps she would not have to face him again tonight, face what was inside herself.

She went to look.

CHAPTER ELEVEN

HE HAD OPENED the window of her chamber. The night wind rushed through it, making the candles gutter and the oil lamps flare in protest. His face was turned to the wind, as though it was something he could see. There were countless stars.

"Thrall…"

He closed the shutters. The night sky was obliterated by slatted wood. There was only her and himself in the sudden closeness of the room. He must have felt it. He cast off the black cloak and it pooled, lightless, across her cushioned bench. But it had not been lightless.

"Were you wearing a byrnie?"

"Was I what?"

"Wearing chain mail? When you came to look for me before?"

She knew she was starting in the wrong place, but she could not speak of Gifta yet, and she had to know about what had happened on the road.

She simply got the look that blocked everything. "Is that likely?"

"Perhaps," she shot back. "Ludda was. You

seemed very thick with my steward. What did you speak of?''

The next look she recognised from the depths of experience. It was the look men reserved for women who stepped outside their allotted sphere of hearth and home. He would not tell her. He would rather speak to the steward, just like her father had, and she would be left alone to find her own way through the morass.

Her hands clenched into fists at her sides so that the heavy gold rings on her fingers bit into her flesh. He would not think she was worth—

''One of Eadward's men was following you. He took a shot at me when I chased him off—''

''Someone *shot* at you?''

''Aye, but he missed, if you can contain your disappointment. He would not have done it except I gave him…something of a fright. He had no intention to harm you. He just wanted to know where you were going. You should have taken Ludda with you. I told—suggested that you do so. I do not know why you refused to take him.''

''Ludda? What use would he—''

''More than you give him credit for. Ludda is—''

''My steward and my concern. Not yours.''

''Ludda is a man who prizes loyalty, a man who was not there when his lord was killed. You are all he has left. He would give his life for you.''

She flinched. It was so unexpected, so…true. Perhaps. But yet how would he know? He was a stranger here. He knew nothing about Healdsteda, nothing about Ludda. Certainly nothing about her. He could rot in hell. He deserved it.

"Was that what caused the hurt to your arm? An arrow?"

"The…"

He had forgotten the blood. Perhaps he was simply too used to hurts. He was certainly the kind of man you could cheerfully stick a sword through. But, what a terrible life it must be. She watched the grey eyes refocus and then she got that rare and extraordinary boon from his granite face, a smile.

"No," he said, "it was wilfulness."

"Wilfulness? *You* admit to wilfulness?"

"Aye."

"How?"

"I was chopping wood. It was just a splinter."

"You were chopping wood?" What did he want to do, cripple himself permanently from his injuries? "Dunn chops the wood. I did not ask you to do it."

"Dunn was ill." The smile vanished and the grey eyes suddenly took on the same look they had had when he had spoken about Ludda. Her spine stiffened.

"Dunn is always hale and if he was not, he should have told me, not got you to do his work for him."

"I offered."

"It was not your decision to make. It was mine. Dunn knows he should have spoken to my steward or to me. It was not your concern."

"No. Not mine. I would have thought that it was the concern of the Lady of Healdsteda to know that

Dunn has five surviving children and that his wife is near her time again. They all eat. He is also supporting his feckless brother who is in dispute with you over boon work for the harvest—''

She gasped. ''Dunn's brother is in the wrong. They are all a shiftless…well, perhaps not Dunn, but that does not mean—'' She stopped, as though he had spoken. He had not said another word. He did not need to. The most awful thing was that there was no longer the anger that had been there in his eyes over Ludda. There was pity. For her. Indisputably.

Her throat closed up.

''If you are trying to say that Dunn is afraid of me, that *anyone* at Healdsteda thinks I am so unjust that…'' She stopped, because her voice was coming out as the most disgusting rasp. She took a breath. She gathered up all the threads of strength that had been left to her out of her appalling, frightening, privileged life. She pitched her voice properly, as a thane's daughter should.

''I have had to fight for my place, to hold on to what is rightfully mine and to secure Gifta's true inheritance, against her male kin. I do not care what the law says, it is always harder for a woman to protect her rights than a man. And even men get killed.''

She took another steadying breath. ''I realise that it must seem so easy to you. To be owner of all this wealth. Oh, do not think I do not see how you despise me for it, you think I am a weak spoilt woman with all the riches in the world. Well I have had to fight for this, for people to know that I have the strength to hold on to what is mine.

"It may seem solid, all this wealth, my life, my daughter's, but you can have no idea how tenuous it is. There is no way that you would be able to understand…"

But he did. Incredibly. Impossibly. He had quite probably never owned anything more in his life than a spare pair of shoes but he understood. She could see it in the eyes that sometimes, could hide nothing.

She could see that he knew in every last soul-destroying nuance what loss was about. The pain of that was in his eyes, so deep, so bitterly deep. She could feel it like her own pain. His eyes held the all the bleakness they had held when he had first looked on her hall. But not the otherworldliness. Not the sense of looking at something else, some other place she could not begin to imagine. They looked at her, straight at her with all that wealth of feeling in them.

"What happened to your daughter?"

"I—"

She sat down on the cushioned bench. She was looking at his eyes and she could not say another word. She did not know whether it was because she was afraid of the horrifying memories the explanation would draw forth. Or because she was afraid of what was in his eyes. That sort of compassion would take apart any painful edifice you had built to protect your weaknesses. It could dismember a stone fort, piece by piece. It had that much power.

"You might as well say it. Whatever I might do, whatever I might think, it cannot hurt you. I am only here until Lamas and then I am gone. And Healdsteda and everything in it, and your daughter, will still be yours, safe and untouchable. But only if I know what has to be done to make that so."

It was true. The grey eyes, the like of which she had never seen, the stubborn, generous mouth, the fierce clarity of bone and muscle, were no more than a temporary arrangement. They had no significance in her life, in anyone's life here. Just a passing usefulness. All that understanding, all that frightening perception could not matter.

He would be gone after First Fruits.

But she and all that was hers would be left safe and untouchable. That was how it would be. If they won this. Her skin shivered. Untouchable. That was what she was, what she wanted to be.

That was what she would be, always, without him. Her wish. Her doom.

She put the thought aside. It was too strange, too frightening to deal with. What she wanted was the safety, for herself and Gifta. And this man, so full of strength, so foreign, so utterly unpredictable, was the key.

"Gifta saw my father's corpse."

It was said, the awfulness, just like that. He did not reply. Just sat down on the bench beside her. A perfectly ordinary movement. They were not even close enough to touch. But she felt it, his warmth. The sort of warmth that was made out of magic.

"I told you that my father was ambushed on the Hamwic road and killed. I told you…I said what Bulla Fire-Blind, the outlaw, sometimes does to… What they brought back, my father's body, had been so viciously mutilated that it could not be recognised except for the birthmark he had on his hand."

Her voice had an amazing steadiness. "I did not…" A small hesitation there. She picked up again. "It was such a shock. To me…to everyone. I wanted to keep Gifta away. I asked Cuthred, my husband, to keep her safe. But Cuthred seemed in a worse state than any of us and he let her…somehow she got back into the hall where the bodies were brought. Gifta saw him. She saw my father's body."

She did not say what happened afterwards, about the other death, because that belonged only to her. Her fault. Her grief. Not Gifta's. But it was suddenly so painfully in her thoughts. She was so deep in memory that the slight movement from the man next to her was enough to startle her.

Her gaze took in the present brightness of her own room at Healdsteda. But brightest of all were the slave's eyes. Though it was impossible to say more about Gifta, it was not necessary. He had seen Gifta's vagaries, how she mourned over anything that was hurt and now he understood what she was most vulnerable to.

Her throat burned with tears. He could do that to

her, the thrall. The first time she had mentioned her
father in his presence she had wanted to cry, to weep
out all the miserable agony of the last twelve months.
As though he could release her from the pain inside.
As though that would happen if she touched him, if
she felt his strength again.

It was like sorcery, the magic that lived somewhere
behind those deep grey eyes and found expression in
their liquid brightness. He must be a warlock to affect
her so. Some irresistible sort of enchantment seemed
to crackle in the air around him.

She remembered the strange feeling that had overwhelmed her when she had cut the rope that bound
his hands, the way the runes carved into the knife
blade had seemed to glow so that she had not been
able to tear her gaze away from them, just as she could
not tear her gaze from the glow of his eyes now.

It was so potent, the comfort of him, his warmth,
the elemental strength of his body, the understanding
in his mind. The need of it tore at her heart.

She could see how Gifta had surrendered herself to
that irresistible force.

And how much more potent it was to her as an
adult, who saw and felt things beyond a child's
thoughts. Who had a woman's desires, never yet fulfilled. Never truly wanted.

He was so beautiful, so dangerous. If she so much
as touched one shining hair on his head, if she so much
as breathed the clean scent of his skin she would be
bespelled. She would be his, never be free of his

power, never be master of her own fate again. And he would know all she lacked.

But she could not look away from him. Her body shivered with the need and the desire and the longing and all the pressure of her misery.

The hand, the large hand Gifta had held on to, stretched out towards her so that the sleeve of the tunic pulled back, showing the bandages round his wrist where he had been hurt.

Her heart lurched. The need, the desperate, separate needs of her body and her misery were so strong. They were the same need. A need of him.

But she could not take his hand. If she did the stone wall she had built to protect her feelings would come apart.

Such a hand. Such a strong hand and big. Too big. Her own would be lost in it. It was an *eten's* hand, a giant's. So dangerous. Too dangerous for her. And he would not want her. Not really.

Rowena jerked herself backwards, away from the thrall, the warlock. Her back flattened painfully against the wall.

The force of her recoil shocked him. She saw the brightness of his eyes give way to an instant of raw confusion. As though the spell worked in reverse, on him too, and he had as much trouble waking from its intensity as she did.

Her gaze fastened on the dangerous hand. It stopped in midmovement. She saw it happen.

And then he saw the direction of her gaze.

Wulf should have been prepared for her disgust. He was. Had been. It was just that she had spoken, at last, of what was so close to her heart. It was because she had looked at him as though she needed the strength he had too much of.

As though she needed him.

That was what had made him step across the divide that had been set for him by Hun, Osred's favoured thane. Set by himself.

But now he saw what she saw: the wood-scratched hand, the clumsy wadding of linen, the bandage that covered the evidence of having been tied up with rope and the marks made by iron fetters, new scars over old.

He saw it all for the first time exactly as someone like her would see it. He wanted to snatch his hand away, to hide the physical evidence of his humiliation. It would have been a greater relief to smash something.

He did not move his hand from view. He left it in the Lady Rowena's sight. Because she was right. So right, because even if the physical scars could have faded, they would never be gone from his heart.

That was how things were. Irretrievable.

But even as his mind formed the word, something else refused to accept it. Things might be irretrievable for him, but not for her.

That was what he was here for, to set her world to rights. That was what she had bought him for.

Yet it was not just that. There were some things that were beyond purchase. One was a person's fate. *Wyrd,* that shifting, mutable combination brought about both by your own decisions and the unfathomed workings of providence.

No one could know better than him what was at risk here. He had lived the dangers that now faced the Lady and her child from both sides.

He had the knowledge and the skills of the Lady Rowena's world and he had the hard-earned and less admissible skills of the world he inhabited now. The combination gave him an advantage and a freedom no other man could have.

Freedom. That word had been impossible to formulate until this moment, and yet there it was in his mind, just as though it had meaning. Perhaps it did. It was a thing scarce to be believed in. Yet the ill that had befallen him, the devastation of the world that he had built, no longer seemed so mind-destroyingly pointless, so utterly beyond redemption. Not if he could save this particular world, the small piece of Wessex land that lay as though sleeping under a curse, the beautiful hall, the frightened people.

And he had given his word, even if he had long lost the irrelevant concept of honour.

The patterns of the shifting brightness of the lamplight and the black shadows that were their other face, made up the web of *wyrd*. He knew it. He had never turned aside from fate's path in his life. He would not now.

"You should sleep," he said, "tomorrow will mean preparations for the harvest and the next day it will be

Lamas Eve." And soon he would be gone. With the beginning of the harvest, this would be over, one way or another.

After that would come whatever awaited him in the North.

He stood, as effortlessly as he did anything. The ache from the knife wound was fading already. Such things always did. He was quite sure control was back in place.

He drew down the sleeve of his borrowed tunic, to cover up the mess.

"Do not." The Lady's jewelled hand, which had withdrawn from him with such brutal honesty before, reached out to touch him.

The rasp of frozen breath in his throat could be heard. The black grip of memory obliterated sight.

"Do not," she said again.

"Why?" The sound of his voice, harsh as his indrawn breath, jeered at her. He could not help that. The memories which had been brought into this room were too strong. "Would you rather see it?" His voice, his whole body, vibrated with the brute implacable force learned in hell. It was not controlled, not controlled at all. She would sense that. She would know just how much blackness lay inside him and she would run screaming. There was naught he could do to stop it.

"Yes. I would rather see things as they are."

He had forgotten what she was truly like. He had

forgotten the quality of her that lay beneath what she chose to show to the world.

"Yes," she said. She had an Idess's heart. Her face swam into view, pale, made whiter by the floating mass of her veil. The eyes were wide. They must be frightened, but they watched his face as though she would have the soul out of him. She was so close that her scent, roses and the warmth of the South, wrapped itself around him. He could see the fine line of her throat beneath the neck of the dress meant to seduce the will of the King's representative. He could see the rise and fall of her breast, fast, heated. Her hands encircled his arm.

She was so very close.

"Lady, I asked you once before if you knew what you did."

"I know what I do." She did not move away. Her hand slid higher across the ridged muscles of his arm, pushing back the sleeve as though seeking the touch of his skin. The hardness of his arm tightened. But it did not stop the smooth, tender contact of a palm that had never known rough work in its life, the long, slender fingers splayed out across tightened cords of battle-scarred flesh.

An impossible combination.

Yet impossibility had no meaning. Just as it had not the first time their flesh had touched. In that moment seared in his mind forever, the vile background of the slave market, the dirt and the stench and the degradation, had lost their existence. Just because she had touched him.

"I know that before Lamas Tide is old you will be gone."

Her touch was as smoothly provocative as it had ever been, her voice pitched low with its cool Wessex drawl. Neither voice nor touch matched what was in her eyes.

It was need.

"I know that nothing I say to you can matter."

The hand on his arm was no longer steady.

"I know all that because you have told me so."

If he had not seen her eyes, if he had not seen that expression of frightening vulnerability, if so many months of total isolation had not given him the ability to recognise how desperate could be the need for contact with another human being. If she had not started to cry.

But she did.

He could not allow her to cry, not an Idess heart. His mouth took hers while the breath of shock was still on it.

He got everything. The shaken gasp of her breath. The single tear that escaped from the glittering eyes. The defenceless fall of her body against his in every soft and vulnerable curve. She had not the power left to stop it and then it was too late. The force of the physical attraction that pulled between them like a hunter's snare was too strong.

The sensuously curved lips melted into the heat of

his mouth, her hands clawed at his shoulders, her body cleaved to his and her head came to rest against his abused arm as though it belonged there.

But it did not.

There were no illusions for either of them. Only a moment of vulnerability that had coincided in time, strong enough to drive them to seek the release that came with the slaking of the body's need.

Their combined touch sent a jolt of sensation through him, so hard and strong he did not think he would be able to control it. Heat penetrated every part of his body in a burst of wrenching desire that hardened him and turned his blood to molten fire.

She must feel it, through the touch of his hands on her body. She must sense the wildness that was so tightly leashed inside him. She would be afraid, repulsed by it after all.

Yet her hands did not stop touching him. Her arms tightened round the solid planes of his back, her fingers found their way into the unruly mass of hair he hated, twisting in it as though they would never let go. Her breath moaned and that small involuntary sound told him more than her touch that her need was real.

His reaction to that was molten, piercing muscle and sinew and skin, straight to the core. The harsh swollen ache of his manhood was more than it was possible to bear. The flesh so tight, the surge of sensation so strong, that the slightest touch would bring the scorching instant burst of release.

There was nothing in the world except her. Her mouth melded to his. She tasted like summer, like life reborn. Her body, full and rich as earth's fruits clung to his with the elemental force of her need. He took it with all the passion there was.

ROWENA KNEW NOTHING, absolutely nothing, of what it would be like. She had only one spine-tingling memory of the feel of his mouth. Hot and dark and endlessly desirable.

She had thought she already knew the touch of his body, the hard contours of its shape. She had touched it and he had held her. But she had not known at all. It was nothing like this. That had been a passive touching, although latent with the charged awareness that lived in the very air wherever he was.

Not this. Not this breathing, living, moving, passionate flame that set her heart racing and brought the blood singing through her veins.

It was frightening, because at the edge of her awareness of him lay the humiliating shape of her failure, waiting for her. Yet she could not let him go, could not ease back by one hair's breadth from the potent drug of his body.

It was impossible to get enough of him even though his strength confounded her, that endless, fathomless strength that she had always wanted. She was nothing to that, insubstantial as gossamer. Yet he wanted her touch, sought it. It frightened her, because she did not know what to do, how to respond to the baring of that fierce passion. She would get it wrong. She always did. All she wanted was him.

She gasped as he took her small weight, swinging her feet off the ground, bedding her down on the cushioned window seat. His own body followed, lightly despite its size, but holding her there all the same, so that she felt his warmth, the touch of him: tightly leashed power, reined in by a thread.

Her hands slid round his shoulders, tightness and hard muscle and the soft fall of his hair. She was afraid of how much she wanted him.

The hands attached to the horribly scarred wrists traced the rounded curves of her breasts, slid inside her priceless silk-decorated dress, burning the softness of her skin, palming the heavily aching fullness. The work-hardened fingers found the terrifyingly sensitive peak, touching her. Her mind dizzied but he did not stop. Not even when she moaned against the tantalising warmth of his mouth. She could not stifle the soft, desperate noise deep in her throat. Even though it sounded pleading. Even though it made her sound like a wanton.

Cuthred would never have permitted his wife to sound like a wanton. Or to act like one. But in the end he had hated her for her coldness. *You are frozen as February snow.*

Her hands tightened on the strong body of the man who touched her, whose warmth enclosed her. She shut her mind on Cuthred, on what she was.

If his touch would not stop, if she could stay forever

like this in his arms, his mouth against hers, his moist heat, his lips. His tongue, inside her…

Her body writhed, as though it had a will and a hunger of its own, beyond her knowledge, beyond her power to control. The movement of her limbs was insuppressible, impossible to disguise. The thrall must have felt the reaction he had caused in her because all that warm lithe mass of muscle and sinew moved harder against her, pressing her back against the embroidered cushions.

Her hands clung helplessly to his shoulders. His body blocked out the light. She felt his knee slide itself between her legs, pushing upwards, rucking up her silk-decorated skirts, parting her thighs. As though she were some serving wench to be tumbled in the hay. And he was so assured.

She was no true match for that assurance. She could not permit such…the shape of his thigh. Just the feel of it between hers, the heavy fullness, the utterly captivating way it flared out from the tight knee. Indecent. An indecent shape. An indecent way, and indecent place to touch her. Her legs clamped round solid, swelling muscle like a vise. Her back arched, pressing herself closer, pressing *that* part of herself, the part that ached in unknown fire for release, against that thickened, solid warmth.

His body moved in an urgent, blood-tingling surge that had a rhythm of its own, and her own body followed by instinct. The sliding, tantalising pressure against that most intimate part of her was unbearably arousing, heightening the dizziness so that she felt she would swoon.

Her fingers slid round to grasp the back of his thigh, digging into the dense muscle, making it tense under her hand, moving upwards to the spare, tight curve of his buttock. She felt the shiver through his body, or perhaps it was through hers, she could no longer tell. It was as though they were one entity, hostage to the same need, breathing the same breath, sharing the same wildly beating heart.

She had never experienced such closeness, never felt such desperation, such longing beyond control. She was not prepared for it. It was not meant to be like this.

His body covered hers. Everywhere. She felt its weight. She felt everything. All of him in every male detail. The strong limbs, the broad chest, the compact power of his hips against hers. She felt the hardened, fiercely swollen contours of his manhood.

She gasped, her breath choking in the tightness of her throat, and the burning mouth released her. Only to fasten on the vulnerable skin of her throat. His dark hot lips were so tender. They should not/be. He should not be capable of being so tender.

Her eyes were tightly shut. So that she could not see. Only feel. The tenderness of his mouth and the shamelessness of his hands made her skin tingle, even through her clothes. And yet it was not through her clothes. The warmth of the work-roughened fingers was on the heated skin of her thigh, moving over her body, under her crushed and battered skirts.

The ache between her legs was like torture.

He would touch her there, with his slave's hands and his callused fingers. And not just his fingers, with the hard, pent-up force of his man's body and she would not be able to bear it. The whirling, dizzying mass of feelings he created inside her would be too strong.

If it was him who touched her like that she would die of it. She would never be the same again. He would do something, unloose something in her that would take away herself and leave her helpless.

And he would find out that she wasn't worth it. He would know and that would be like death, far worse than when Cuthred had spent himself on her and then left her aching in emptiness. Cuthred had killed pride and hope and unwanted affection. But this man would have the power to kill her heart.

She could not allow it, did not dare, could not.

She moved, with every ounce of force she had. She jerked herself backwards away from the thrall, away from longing, away from the terrifying heat of his touch, from the tenderness of his mouth.

She was no longer in danger. She took a breath of relief but she could not get air into her lungs. There was a moment frozen in ice. No movement. No life.

The silence, the deadness of it would stifle her. She wanted to move. She wanted to shatter it. She wanted to yell at her terrifying thrall never to touch her, never to come near her, never to so much as look on her again. No sound came out of her mouth.

She looked through the dead air and the ice cold towards the slave, the powerful shoulders, the tangled mess of his bright hair.

She had to explain. She had to tell him how wrong it had been. That it had been a terrible mistake. That he must never touch her again.

He looked up.

There were no words left in her head. There was nothing but his eyes. Somewhere inside her heart a hideous, crippling pain took root.

He spoke. He spoke, not her. Because he had so much more courage than she did. He was worth more. She saw him take breath, saw his lips shape themselves round words.

''You wish to tell me, do you not, Lady, that you have made a regrettable mistake.''

They must have been the words she was trying to say, because she felt her head nodding. Except the meaning of the words was now lost. All lost under the look in his eyes. The crippling pain inside her chest was going to break something.

''Yes,'' said her voice, ''thrall.''

''Then we shall have to see that you never make such a mistake again.''

Rowena straightened her sullied skirts round her ankles.

''Yes.''

It was finished. Over. She could go, unscathed.

Yet whatever it was inside her, the hideous pain that had been born in the moment she had seen in the slave's eyes the full and sordid measure of what she had done, was not finished. It had taken up a permanent place.

CHAPTER TWELVE

ROWENA SENT FOR her steward.

If you had done something you were ashamed of, you were supposed to atone for it. Even if you had meant, at the start, to assuage pain, not cause it.

"Ludda," enquired Rowena, "if I wanted to send someone to Iona to look for something, someone, could you arrange it for me?"

"Aye," agreed Ludda, as though this involved no more than an afternoon's ride up the Icknield Way.

"Thank you."

She didn't say anything else and neither did Ludda. He was not one to waste words, but she knew that he had guessed how important this was to her and so he had agreed. No questions. Loyalty. *Ludda would give his life for you.* Why had she not seen it?

She reached out a hand, and patted his arm. A thing she never did. Ludda grunted, which must be worth several hundred words, but then his look changed.

"Saw that thrall of yours today. Over at Alfred's farm."

"Alfred's farm?" Alfred's daughter. Freya's acolyte with the enormous quivering bosom. Impossible.

Churl Alfred's daughter giggling and…slavering. Over fine, marred skin. That wench would not have had the slightest difficulty in knowing how to please a man. She would not have had a weakness that…

"Someone is here."

She followed Ludda into the courtyard. Horsemen, riding fast. Eadward, come over to visit from Lindherst. She could see the bright madder-red slash of his cloak. But there were others, not just Eadward's men. She caught the flash of silver on leather harness fittings.

"They are racing," said Ludda. "Lackwits. They will ruin the best wheat field."

Ludda surged forward. She saw a huge black stallion goaded by its rider barge past Eadward, nearly unseating him. It was dangerous. Deadly. The other rider must know it. But he never even paused. She saw the wheat field obliterated. She rushed forward in Ludda's wake.

They would stop. But they did not. At least, not the black stallion. It came on, beyond control, its dark bulk filling her vision. She felt Ludda shove her sideways in the same instant that the killing hoofs slashed towards her. The mocking laughter of the rider rang in her ears, exultant, full of unclean pleasure. Ludda clutched her arm, swearing.

It was a face she had seen before, heavy featured, the eyes strangely colourless. They watched her with the same unclean pleasure that had been in the laugh-

ter, and she knew that the great black stallion had not
for one moment been beyond its rider's control.

She thought the shock and disbelief must be plain
to read on her face because the sick enjoyment in the
pale eyes deepened. Humiliation crawled through her,
like some monstrous worm eating at her vitals.

Eadward's grey skittered to a halt behind.

"Rowena!" He had not seen. How could he not
have seen what…she saw, his gaze slide from her to
the other man. She saw the consciousness in that look,
one part eagerness, two parts fear. Eadward had seen
all right. He knew what sort of man his companion
was. Eadward was frightened. But he was also at-
tracted.

Rowena's hands clenched themselves into fists. She
had been angry before but now the force of it was
doubled. Trebled. She was back in that sea of helpless
fury that had closed over her head the day her father's
body had been brought home and all her disasters had
begun.

She kept her eyes on Eadward. She did not even
look at the other.

"Eadward. I trust you're going to let me off some
of my taxes for ruining my valuable wheat."

"Lady Rowena, you jest—"

"Lady? *She* owns this. What a backward place is
this Wessex…" The voice of the other rider cut
straight across, rich, contemptuous. Northumbrian. She
recognised who he was. King Osred's ambassador.

"Rowena, I should introduce my guests. They come

from afar. From our country's allies against the Mercians. From Northumbria.''

"Really?" she said, transferring her attention to the wolf's-head at last, "Then you must sup with me. I have a great fondness for Northumbrians. I just bought one as a slave. For twelve mancuses. Eadward was convinced I paid too much, but I am sure your countrymen are worth every penny of that."

It was a hit. The pale, arrogant eyes narrowed.

"What does she mean?" But the question was fired at Eadward, just as though she was not there.

"Oh! She's joking again. Just some great ox of a fellow she bought at the market. Nothing you would even recognise. A criminal of some sort. Been flogged. I tried to tell her—"

"Flogged? A large man, you say?"

"Well, just—"

"I want to see him."

"I—Rowena?"

The consuming heat of her anger vanished, leaving behind a sudden coldness.

"You cannot," she said. "He is not here." Her heart began to race and she had the sensation of having taken a step into a changed landscape, full of hidden dangers she had no hope of understanding. The ghost of Eadward's fear of his Northern companion found its place inside her.

What had she done and what had she said? Why should it suddenly matter so desperately?

"Refreshments anyone?"

Rowena had no reason for surprise. Or concern. It was not as though she did not know where he was. It was a pleasant walk to Alfred's farm. She stepped past the empty cushion at her threshold and went out into the dawn light.

It was Lamas Eve. It was the commencement of the harvest. Tomorrow, loaves baked from the First Fruits would be offered at the church for the Loaf Mass. It had the makings of a good harvest. The weather might or might not hold. There was a lot to think about.

None of it mattered.

The future held nothing that could compare with the power of the past. If she had ever fooled herself into thinking otherwise, today had killed it with the force of a hammer blow.

She left the arrangements for the harvest to her loyal and competent steward. He smiled. She had forgotten how rare an occurrence that had become. But she could not be doing with smiles today. She hid, like the coward's spirit she was, until she could hide no longer.

Then she went down to the meadow. The first thing she saw was Dunn's brother with whom she had settled her dispute, reaping with ostentatious speed. The second thing was the slave.

He was stripped to the waist just as she had first seen him. He slid through the ripe sun-drenched corn, light on shadow, in a rhythm as old as the first harvest known to mankind. His skin glistened, burnished from the heat of the sun, slick with sweat, the muscles bunching underneath. His power was elemental, totally male, a strength that took all in its path. Like Frey come down from the heights to reap the earth's fruits and claim his sacrifice.

You would have thought he was perfect, a power and a vision with no limits. But even at this distance, her eyes could discern the healing gash of the knife wound and even the long swinging fall of his hair was not quite enough to hide the puckered threads of scarring across his back. Not if you knew what to look for.

The other Northumbrian had offered her fifteen mancuses for all that spoiled perfection.

Heaven knew why she should try and protect him. Thrall or not, he had as much contempt for her and what she was trying to do as the other Northumbrian. As Eadward. As the whole world probably had for a woman who had lost half her kindred and who thought she could hold on to three great estates, two in her name and one in the name of a six-year-old girl.

They all cheered when Ludda handed her the first sheaf of wheat bound with agrimony and tormentil. All except the slave. He just looked at her as though he could see straight through to the Nothing inside. The rest of them kept cheering the empty shell, pressing forward to touch her, jostling good naturedly to be the first. Because at that moment she was Freya, goddess of plenty, counterpart to Frey, Lord of the Harvest.

The sun beat down on their heads, the stillness of

the air, the very earth beneath their feet, was filled with life and the ripe heavy heat of summer fruitfulness. They touched her, men and women, the shy and the eager, laughing or silent, all with the same complete belief in what they did. They believed that she, Lady of the land, would give them luck and prosperity and the same fruitfulness symbolised by the wheat sheaf in her arms. She kept smiling.

The slave came last. As befitted his station. Or his reluctance to come anywhere near her. She kept her gaze on the golden heads of the wheat in her arms. But beyond them, her eyes saw skin the same colour, with the heat and the life of the sun trapped in it. Her gaze was at the level of the tight flexible line of his abdomen, she saw nothing but the burnished skin, the dark gold hairs dampened with sweat, the taut suggestion of hip-bones.

She felt the heat of the fertile fields of Healdsteda, the heat of *him* touch inside her, as though she was part of this after all.

But that was untrue, the cruelest untruth of all. She was no symbol of life renewing itself, of the world around her, no part of the elemental strength of the slave. She was nothing. A woman with a bitter heart who had no father, no husband.

And no son.

She wrenched herself away from his touch. She had naught but the fleeting impression of the warmth of callused fingers on her arm, and then she fled.

THE MOON WAS FULL. But its brilliant radiance was swallowed up by the oak trees, heavy with summer foliage. The shadows were black. Shadows you could get lost in. Rowena did not know where she was going. Only that she could not stay this night of all nights, sleepless in her great lonely bed. Tormented by shades.

She had gone out, with only her cloak to cover her shift, treading silently on cold, bare feet. She did not have to run the gauntlet of passing her watchdog across the doorway because he had not been there. She hoped the strapping wench exhausted him.

Instead she had found, of all people, her steward propped in a chair. She had returned to her chamber and climbed out of her window.

She did not court sleep tonight. Tonight belonged to Beornred.

She pressed forward, holding poor Beornred's spirit in her mind and the tears she could not shed at home dropped cold and unheeded from her eyes. The air was pure as glass. She stepped through it and let it touch her, cold and clear and untrammelled by the hot misery of human feelings.

She stopped only when the moonlight struck her night-blind, tear-blind eyes. She was no longer amongst the trees but in a clearing. Bright silver radiance reflected off still water, washed everything in its other-worldly glow. It was eerie. The grass beneath her feet was a smooth shadow studded with small bright shapes that were flowers. She thought it was enchanter's nightshade. She tried not to tread on it.

The breeze was lost here. There was such silence. Just the silence and herself.

The grove which had belonged to Nerthus, the earth mother. The pool where they used to drown people.

Her skin prickled and the small hairs rose on the nape of her neck.

The sheet of water, moonlit, disintegrated under her sight into a thousand shards of dancing light. A shape, sleek and darkly shadowed, broke through the water in one powerful surge, arms outstretched, bathed in moving liquid fire.

Her bones froze. She stared.

The shape, the terrifying light-dark shape…it was human, a man. No, it could not be a mortal man. Not here, not swimming in Nerthus's pool.

Moonlight gleamed on his pale skin and the dark swirling mass of his hair, it glittered from tiny points of reflected light that were small moving droplets of water. He was half-turned away, so that she saw him obliquely. The long powerful line of his side, the broad back glimpsed through the sliding mass of soaking hair, the swell of buttock and thigh and calf, the strongly arched foot.

Shivers took her skin. Her eyes stayed, wide, fixed. She wanted to flee, but movement was impossible, just as it was impossible to look away.

The sleek creation of solid muscle flexed and moved. It was not mortal, that beauty. It was Frey. His hands caught lake water that was ice water, dragged through it, catching it in his cupped fingers. The shadowed face tipped upwards to the white moon, the heavy mass of his hair fell in cascades down his back, every muscle of the powerful body tightened in what she suddenly knew was anticipation of sensual pleasure. She knew it because she could feel that tingling expectation in her own flesh, in every part of her body, inside and out. Just from watching him.

The water hit in a glittering frozen arc, droplets that would be cold as ice striking head and chest, face and belly and sex and legs.

She heard the gasp that came with that freezing, pin-sharp contact, whether from his throat or hers, she could not tell. It was a sound of absolute abandonment. It knifed through her, as though she could feel what he felt. Her own flesh tingled. Her mind dizzied. Her hands clutched at the rough bark of the tree at her back. To stop her from falling.

"Thrall…"

But it only came out as a whisper. Borne away on the wakening northern breeze. He did not hear. She watched him bend his head, wringing the water from his dripping hair, shaking it out and teasing the tangled weight apart with his fingers.

He did not know she was there. His world was his own. It always had been.

Yet why had he come here tonight? To this of all places? It was not an ordinary lake for bathing. This was not an ordinary grove of trees. Tonight was not ordinary. Ghosts walked.

But they were only her ghosts and perhaps the only magic was in her mind and the hopeless dazzlement of her senses.

She should never have come to a dangerous place like this. After all that had happened, the last thing she should be doing was spying on the naked body of her slave, with heaven knew what madness in her bitter heart.

She straightened her spine. But even as she moved, something changed in the uncanny air, in him. He looked up, as though he had seen or heard something. But not at her. It must be some small animal or some night bird that he had heard and she had not. Yet relief that she was safe from his gaze died on a spurt of fear. He was staring, transfixed. There was a tension of quite a different kind now in every brutal muscle.

The fear leapt, the hideous, primitive fear of the unknown. The silver-dark creature spoke. Just one word, a name, *Athelbrand,* sharp and fast, like a shout of warning. So intense, so real, that she fully expected the name's owner to come bursting out of the blackness of the watching trees, like a *hellthane.* But there was nothing, only silence filled by her fear and the insane idea that there was something else there. The thrall saw it. She knew he did. She knew that to him it was real.

His voice split the silence, "The shield!" His own

left arm came up, with the swift unthinking sureness of the trained.

He actually felt the blow. She sensed the echo of it through the spellbound air. She saw him fall to his knees at the edge of the lake where they used to drown slaves.

She ran.

Her feet slid on grass, crushed flowers, tree roots, moss. Freezing, blood-numbing cold closed over her ankles. Lake water splashed. She stumbled. Liquid ice closed on her skin, dragging at her cloak and her skirt. She lurched forward through cold.

She touched him. Her arms closed round damp, solid flesh. His shoulders. He was not alive. The coldness of the lake had taken him. Her hands tightened like claws.

"Thrall…"

She touched his face, fingers slippery with water, shaking. He did not know she was there. She turned his head to face her. She did it, not him. His eyes were blank.

Her gut crawled with the terror of losing him to something she could not understand. She could not bear that.

She begged. There was nothing else left.

"Please…"

Her voice was like the rawest of whispers. But he heard it. The eyes, wide and black, seemed to struggle to see her. He touched her. One large rough-palmed hand cupped her arm.

''Rowena.''

He said that. Not *Lady*. Just her name. She buried her face against his neck and clung. The hand around her arm tightened.

''Lady, what are you doing here? What—''

She looked up.

''Never mind me. What about you? You have to get out of this water. It is enchanted.''

''Enchanted?''

''Yes. It is Nerthus's lake. They used to drown slaves in this lake. They would make the slaves draw her chariot. Then they would drown them. Just because they had seen her.''

He said nothing. He looked at the black water as though it fascinated him.

''Just move. You have to.'' She had to get him out of the lake.

He did not seem to know he was naked. She knew. His thigh flexed as he stood. Her belly clenched, despite her fear. Her head pounded. She tried not to look at a thing so sense-maddening. Or at anything else, darkly shadowed and intimately fascinating, that was near it.

Droplets of ice water splashed through the thin linen of her shift as he got to his feet. The lower half of her cloak was soaking. She tried to concentrate on that and on getting him away from the dangerous lake.

His feet were supple. And the ankles, the swell of muscle above and the neatly tapering knee. She tried not to remember that she had held that leg between her own.

His skin was ice.

"Do you not have any clothes?"

"Any…oh. Yes. Over there somewhere." He looked at her and the awareness flared between them, overbright, knife sharp.

Her heart beat with a force that sent the blood rushing to her face. He would see it, despite the shadows. He would know that despite the humiliation of what she had done with him, she still desired him. More than ever. Panic seized her. She could not let him see that she still wanted him. She could not offer herself up for disaster a second time.

She tore her gaze away but that only brought it into contact with a wide expanse of taut, glistening, darkly shadowed flesh. There was nowhere to look that did not make her breath catch. She took refuge behind the shield of her anger.

"What on earth did you think you were doing, bathing in Nerthus's pool? Do you have a death wish?"

He did not say anything.

The heart that had been beating so fast seemed to stop in the silence.

Her hands tightened on ice. The urge to cover that death-cold flesh with her own warmth was visceral. She wanted to hold him until that coldness melted and she was lost again under the lifegiving force that was uniquely his, until she understood him, until all the words he could not say flowed from that fine-chiselled mouth into her ears alone.

Madness.

He was a dangerous stranger. He cared nothing for her.

No, worse than madness. Enchantment. The silver-black air crawled with it. She was spellbound in this grove of otherworld. Helpless. Fettered by magic. Fear writhed inside.

She would stop it. She must.

"Why do you have to be so much trouble? Why would you come to a place full of enchantments on Lamas Eve?"

The massive shoulders shrugged under her hand.

"Why should it make any difference to me? I am descended from Woden, after all." His voice was rich with irony, but distracted, as though he were not even thinking of what he said. As though he was still caught in whatever strangeness had held him in the lake.

"Woden?" she snapped, out of her fear. "Hardly." Ludicrous. You had to be of royal blood to be descended of the chief of the sky gods. Besides, it was not long-gone sky gods like Woden with their cold, unfathomable thoughts that came to mind when she looked at her naked slave. It was a creature of legend quite different.

"Frey, more like," she muttered, her gaze raking the white, moon-washed length of his side. Tiny silver droplets clung to the smooth taut skin across his ribs, nestled in the small dark hairs across his thigh like trapped starlight. Frey. Beauty, fruitfulness, untamed life and maleness.

Her belly tightened. Inside was a primitive longing for life and for the hope of it, and for everything that had been killed. She tried not to let it be there.

"Frey? Hardly." Her own words struck back at her with the force of arrows. "What a fertile imagination you have, Lady. Like one of Freya's acolytes?"

Her own words. He would taunt her with them, with the shaming, miserable jealousy that had made her say them. Her slave and Alfred's comely daughter. The well-endowed bedwarmer. The one that quickened men's blood. The young and fresh, the one who was not a miserable frigid failure of twenty-three winters.

She stopped. Which made him stop, too, because she was right in front of him. She had to show him. She had to show him that he did not have the power to see straight through her, that he did not have the right to find her wanting. As everyone else had. Not him. Oh, not him.

He had believed from the start that she was shallow, spoilt and heartless. All she had to do was perform her part.

She allowed her gaze to travel downwards, beginning at the top of the gleaming wet head, skipping the dangerous face, taking in the wide shoulders, the way the broad chest tapered to the flat tight belly and compact hips, lingering on the erotically shadowed bulk of his sex, moving only when he had seen her look at him, down the strong glistening legs, to finish at the beautifully shaped feet.

"Nay," she said at last, "not me. I found I had no taste for that."

The lie had an ugliness of its own. But it was all that could be said. It would be a relief for both of them to have things so clear, although she was prepared for some anger. She looked up.

Her heart slammed against her ribs with force enough to break them. Her breath choked on a long sharp-drawn gasp that was shockingly audible. The sound registered on a stone-cold face, on the thinned predatory curve of a fine mouth, in the harsh silver glitter of fierce eyes. It was not just anger. His eyes held a fathomless well of emotion she could not guess at.

She was suddenly aware that she was alone in the depths of the night forest with a trapped criminal who must hate her. Because she had treated him badly.

Her spine banged against the hard trunk of an oak tree.

The burning wildness of that wolf's gaze held her as though the cold moonlit distance between them did not exist. It bored straight through her.

"Thrall…" She did not know what to say. How to redress what she had already said. Only that she must speak. The raw, tearing emotion in him forced a response out of her, out of some deep, hard-suppressed part of her that had nothing to do with the lies she had just spoken.

The power of that drove her forward, despite the numbing fingers of fear coiled inside. Half a step and then another across the cold moon-blanched grass.

But she was too late. For whatever it was she could possibly do.

He had already turned away, with that ruthless strength that held everything enclosed, under his control, unreachable.

She watched him bend down to gather up the dark shape of his discarded cloak. Blackness covered the pale gleam of his skin, eerie and consuming. The uncanny prickling on her half-clothed flesh was unbearable. She should go. Back to the warmth and safety of her bower. Now. Before he could so much as get to his beautifully shaped feet. But he did not get to his feet. He remained where he was, a large menacing lump of denser blackness. Unmoving. She might not have been there.

"Thrall?"

"Why are you here? Lady?"

She swallowed. *I am looking for the dead.*

"I…I could not sleep. I had to get outside, it was so stifling. I just…" she collected her voice, "I have every right to—"

"Why did Ludda not stop you?"

"Ludda? How did you know he was…he would have. I had to go back into my chamber and climb out of the window."

A small amount of tension seemed to leave the bunched black shoulders.

"I do not believe it."

She pulled her cloak tighter round her shift. "Why are you here?"

"I could not sleep," he quoted, "I wanted to get outside." The coldness of his voice made her want to recoil and yet at the same time, the bitterness underneath drove her forward. He was still on his knees, a black rock in the shadows.

"I should not have left it to Ludda, this night, should I?"

Left it to Ludda?

"Do you still sleep... I did not see you this morning." It had been just past dawn.

"It was the beginning of the harvest. I believe I rise earlier than you."

She asked the one question she should not.

"Why did you visit Alfred's farm this afternoon?"

"Alfred? What has...because I believe he will help me, and you, in the matter of the King's Reeve."

It was impossible not to believe the impatience in his voice. Her heart thudded, wrongly and against all reason. He had not gone to see the wench. It had not so much as occurred to him that she might have thought so.

Because he did not care at all about her.

Just as she did not, could not, care about him.

She should still go. She had no reason to be here with him.

She knelt down with him among the shadows. He

did not move. Did not draw away from her. Did not straighten up.

Could not.

Whatever had happened to him in the lake had been more terrible to him than it was possible to express. She knew it just by the shape of his shoulders. It was quite unknown to her, what had happened to him. She did not truly understand at all. Except, he needed her.

It did not seem possible that any other adult in the world could need her. But perhaps he did. She reached out with her hand. Perhaps—he moved away from her touch.

But that was just how he was. He did not take anything from anyone. He only gave. Even when he did not want to.

This time she would make him take.

CHAPTER THIRTEEN

SHE SLID on damp grass. Her foot caught in the wet hem of her cloak. If she used all of her weight, she just might be able to knock him over. He was not expecting this. He collapsed underneath her with a most satisfying grunt. Success.

Except…he was, as always, so much more than she expected. He seemed to cover an extraordinary amount of ground and she had not counted on the disabling strength of her reaction to him. Everywhere she put her hand it landed somewhere it should not, sending shocks of heat through her body. She gasped, twisting inelegantly in a tangle of male flesh. That only made it worse. She felt more of him. Everything. His hands caught her.

"Will you stop thrashing about, woman. You will do yourself an—"

"Ouch," she said as her knee slid away into an unexpected blackthorn.

"—injury. What have you done—"

"Nothing," she gasped trying to remove her hand from a dangerous and fascinating location on the inside of his thigh. His arms closed round her, pulling her free of the offending blackthorn tree, securing her tightly against him. So there was only him and the male rough-smooth contours of his body. Nothing else. Her hand remained trapped where it was. Her head was pillowed against the silk-damp length of his hair.

She could feel him breathe.

"You are so cold." It frightened her. Her other hand slid experimentally across the wide expanse of his back, up underneath the heavy cold wet hair. Freezing. She found the curve of his neck. Ice. She felt him move under her touch, the way the curve of his neck fitted into her hand. She had not quite counted on this, not on the way he could make her feel.

He sat up, taking her with him, every shred of his flesh pressed against her through the thinness of her shift. His strength took her weight. She had to allow it. She had committed herself to this. She let every scarcely concealed curve of her body rest against his. He must not think that what she did might be deliberate. He must believe she was quite helpless and he was in control.

Or he would never admit what was wrong.

She lay quite still, but her heart beat so fast. Did he feel it? Did he know?

Oh, he must. He knew what was unfinished between them, what she could control and what she could not. Her throat closed at the thought of finishing it here and now, at the terrifying thought of that beautiful moon-washed body over hers, of all that leashed strength moving without control on her body. Her breath sobbed as though it was real, as though it happened now, at this moment.

His hands tightened. "What is the matter? Lady, what have you done?"

She opened her eyes. Tactics. She was not in this for herself. She was in it for him, the impossible thrall with the will of iron and the eyes full of mind-wounds.

Tactics.

"I hit my knee." It was half true at least. She had got tangled with the blackthorn. But she had hardly felt it.

"Let me see." His hand grasped the hem of her shift. She had to let him. She had asked for this. She thought her breath would choke as she watched his strong scarred hand take the fragile expensive silk, move upwards, brushing the silk aside, touching her skin, sliding across it. Her flesh tingled. Sensation writhed down her spine.

"You will have a bruise."

Her knee bent into the hollow of his hand. She watched his hand on her flesh, huge, its strength unbreakable on the small bones of her knee.

"How you ever climbed out of a window unaided…"

"Oh, I always manage what I want." Her voice was breathless and she lied. The shades of her past crowded round her, like her own personal reflections of the sorrows that lived in her thrall's eyes.

"And what is it you want?"

He knew. He knew it was all subterfuge, what she did, that she was provoking him just as she had before. When it had all ended in disaster. Her heart thundered.

His hand, large, male, so unbearably exciting, slid round to cup the sensitive skin of her inner thigh, mirroring the gesture of her own hand on his flesh. And that which was unfinished between them, the sweet fierceness of it scorched the air.

"I want what I wanted before."

He was all she had ever wanted, all she had been looking for, without realising it, for all of her life.

"I was wrong before," she said, her voice stumbled over such unfamiliar words. But she was desperate. Her subterfuge, her plan to wrest the secrets out of that lethal, self-contained, vulnerable heart was swallowed up by the depth of her need for him. "I was wrong to push you away when…" Her voice stopped under the soul-stripping scrutiny of those eyes.

"No." His eyes would drag her inside out. "You were not." His hand slid round her leg, feather-light for all its rough strength, completely controlled while her own body shook, just from his nearness and the look in his eyes. He would take his hand away. He would withdraw from her the way everyone had. She waited, with her soul stretched to the point where it must break.

He did not withdraw his hand, not straight away and her heart leapt, and then the shadows shifted. The frost-clear moonlight showed her what he wanted her to see, silver trapped on silver, the thin twisting scar threads on the inside of his wrist where the skin was thinner. The marks of slavery, the old scars twisting through the dark, half-healed mass of the new.

She felt suddenly sick, as though the hot life-blood leached from her limbs. He saw it. The intelligent eyes measured her reaction. In his eyes she could see a trapped savage anger and a loss that was raw and unspeakable. But no blame. The deadly anger was glossed over by acceptance, like the black killing depths of the North Sea under ice.

"Nothing has changed," he said. "Nothing can change."

But she could not allow that. She might be worthless, but he was not.

"Do not," she said, as she had once before. But what she said was just as doomed. She tried to hold on to his arm. Her nails scored his skin but she could not hold him. Her hand clutched empty moonlight. He turned away. Left her.

"Wait—"

"Lady, you should go from here. I will take you back." The voice held nothing of the force of emotion between them. It was utterly blank, as much of a stone wall as his back, as his utter isolation scarce two handspans distant from her.

She sat on the carpet of crushed flowers, utterly alone. She looked at the solid back, half-exposed where the cloak had slipped showing the mutilated flesh beneath.

She could not bear it. She could not bear the sight of that stone wall. She could not bear him to be alone.

She moved one hand to touch his shoulder. It was as hard and cold as ice. You could break your fingers on it.

Her hand faltered despite all the resolution of her will, and then she felt it. A faint movement, a shudder somewhere deep inside. Coldness. Such utter coldness that you could sicken and die of it.

Do you have a death wish? She had asked, and he had not answered.

But he was not going to sicken and die. Not on the inside or the out. She had bought him to save him from death and she would do it.

In one sudden movement, she pulled the cloak across the exposed shoulder. She seized the entire unruly mass of freezing-damp hair and dragged it out from under the cloak, away from his skin.

She thought for one instant that he would murder her. His eyes were completely wild. She could not breathe and she had hold of his hair. She forced all the strength she had into her voice. Men slew monsters with swords. Women did it with words.

"I shall not let you go. You will have to make me." The words sliced through the tingling air between them the way the rune blade had sliced through rope when she had first set him free of his bonds. And just like then, she did not know whether she would win, or be destroyed.

He did not move. But the eyes gave nothing away. The frightening power of his muscles bunched.

"There is naught I would be able to do to save myself from you," she said and the words cut through her mind in the way they cut through the air. "You could do anything you wanted right now. You could murder me."

The feral wildness, the wolf's look, left his eyes, exposing what lived beneath.

She buried her face in his neck. Her hands held him and they were far, far stronger than his. She could feel the shudder in his breath, the wild beating of his heart.

"You have to tell me," she said. "You have to tell me what happened in the lake. It is like dreams. If you tell someone, they lose their power."

She could also feel the hardened flexible sheet of muscle under her hands and her mind knew what it could do.

"You have to tell me what you saw."

"How do you know I saw anything?"

Her hand was still buried in his hair. Its cold length spilled down her arm, winding round her tingling flesh as though it had a will of its own. She fixed her gaze on it. It seemed to attract and reflect every tiny gleam of light in the enchantment-filled glade.

"Why did you go in the lake?" Her hand twisted in his hair. Brightness dazzled her aching eyes. Tiny silver sparks flew from it, striking her bare arm like small frozen needles. Ice water. Lake water.

The muscles tensed. "It was clean."

"Clean? But you do not need—you are always clean...." It was true. She took that for granted. She...she had not always taken it for granted. She had not expected it. Because he was...her hands clenched, dragging on his hair, digging into his scarred skin.

"This cannot go on. You must tell me what you saw."

"No, it cannot go on." He had stopped breathing. She knew because she held him so tight.

"Please..." she sobbed at him, because she felt so utterly defeated, and then he breathed and he spoke.

She had to be told, the woman with the Idess heart. There was no more room for pretence.

She had to know what there was: emptiness. Nothing more. All the fathomless anger and all the bitter effort had been for naught. He had seen the proof of that before his eyes.

If he had seen it.

Mayhap it was not the bond he had shared with Athelbrand since they were children. Mayhap it was just madness, the crazed insanity of a trapped beast.

He could feel the Idess tugging on his hair. He could feel the small animal warmth of her body, the lush female flesh separated from his skin by only a thin sheath of silk. He ached for that. But it was not his.

She knew that.

Why did she have to choose tonight of all nights to indulge in her dangerous game of teasing the savage thrall to see whether she could get it to bite? One day he would bite and then she would regret it. Bitterly. But so would he.

He opened his eyes and looked on the pure, cold light of the stars and the vastness of the night sky.

He had never felt so trapped, so finally defeated.

"Thrall, you must tell me," commanded the Idess.

But even though the decision was made, it was impossible to know where to start. He kept his gaze on the stars and sought with his mind for the gift of clear thought that never failed him. It was not there. There were no words. Or at least none that did not sound moon-witted. He said nothing.

"Tell me," asked the woman in his arms. "Tell me about Athelbrand?"

The stars went out.

"I heard you," she said. "You said his name. That is what you saw, is it not?"

There was nothing except her breath and the soft rise and fall of her breast against his chest, tender and inexpressibly sweet.

"Yes." He made himself go on so that she would know he was finally mad. "I could not sleep, like you. I had to get outside. I was thinking about my brother and when I was in the lake…I thought I saw him. Athelbrand."

She stayed where she was, her warm body entwined with his, holding him with all her small strength, one hand still lost in the wild tangle of his hair. Just as though she cared what became of him.

He tried to imagine what it would be like if that

were so. If it were possible to break the complete isolation of what he had become; to give voice and shape to all the things that pressed against his heart, even such things as were inadmissible to himself.

It was not possible.

The woman's hand smoothed damp hair out of his face, her touch delicate. As though he were made of Rhenish glass and might break under her fingers.

Ridiculous.

But that was how he felt. Just as brittle and finely stretched. As though something inside would shatter.

"It is all right," said Rowena's voice, like the clear breath of the wind. "Such things can happen. You were concerned for your brother and so you saw him in your mind. You care about him so much that—"

"If I cared about him so much, I would have been with him. What I saw," he yelled, so there could be no mistake, "was an axe-wielding mercenary trying to take his head off from behind with a double-handed down stroke. And I was not with him."

The words split the night and bounced off the trees and then were lost in silence.

"Yes, you were."

"What?"

He was still yelling like a savage, further proof he was mad. She would leave him. But all she did was twist her head round so she could look at him with eyes deeper than Nerthus's accursed pool.

"You were with him. I heard you telling him what to do."

He was suddenly aware that his left arm, his shield arm, ached. "That is insane. *I* am insane."

"Only if it is insane to care about someone and have them care about you. Of course that would make me completely sane." But she clung to him as though she was quite as crazy as he was.

"How did you know it was a mercenary?"

"They were King's men," he said helplessly. "Norsemen. His bodyguard. Paid."

Her arms closed round his rib-cage in what seemed to be some sort of death hold.

"These King's men, were they something to do with you becoming…a thrall? How…"

How. The whole of his life seemed to burn through his eyes. His home with the hills behind it rising to eternity, the light and the warmth in the hall. The fine tapestries and the glass goblets and the young goshawk in its first plumage. The paved path and the well-stocked barns. The horses from Francia. The particular room beside the chapel where no one went except for him. The room full of things more precious than the finest steed or the costliest sword. Books. Copied out in Rome and Francia, York and Monkwearmouth and Jarrow. The copy of Boethius that had once belonged to Benedict Biscop. The thought-hoard of the entire world.

Lost.

Nothing but ashes and bitterness and now the thought of Brand dying alone.

The arms clamped round his body nearly took his

breath. They crushed his flesh like the jaws of a trap. But the Lady had not the strength to hold him so. And she would never want to.

Yet she did and the force of her arms was no longer like a trap but the only thing that kept him from disintegrating where he lay.

"Athelbrand is alive," she said, "and so are you."

"Aye. I did not expect to survive. Not even as a thrall. I expected them to kill me."

The fine strength of her arms slid across his skin and he could feel the rapid beat of her heart. She made a faint choking noise.

"Rowena?"

The last thing he wanted was to force unwelcome pity from her. The thought made the tightness inside unbearable.

"There are no regrets," he said against the blinding dark. "It was my choice to do as I did and if it were to be done over again, I would make the same decision."

"Yes. Yes, I can see…" The movement of her arms became more agitated. He tried to stop them but she managed to slide under the clumsiness of his left arm and her fingers fastened painfully into the top of his shoulder.

"And this?" she said.

There was a certain completeness to the cycle of humiliation that had begun in the fire-shot dark of Northumbria, had continued through stupidity and now ended in the heathen madness of this place.

Her fingers slid over the uneven surface of his back.

"I would have chosen death over that. Except…"
The decision was there in his mind all over again. He
could have taken death. But in the end he had not.
"Except Athelbrand was still alive, somewhere, and
so was his enemy. And mine."

He stopped himself because there was nothing else
that was fit to say to her. Not the blackness and the
rage and the ruthless unslaked desire for revenge. He
would put none of that on her.

"Lady, you know all there is to know. There is
nothing more I can say. You must go. You must—"

There was something wet and faintly warm against
the pain in his shoulder and the slowly thawing ache
in his arm.

She was crying.

ROWENA CHOKED back a gasp. She was not crying.
She never cried. It was only the crushed breath inside
her that made her feel as though she would die of pity
for him. And anger for what had been so cruelly done
to him. And admiration for what he was.

She must not cry. Because then she would no longer
be able to help him. She would never be able to undo
all the damage that had been done.

And tears of pity were not something he would either expect or welcome in her.

Besides, if she cried, all those dreadful, tearing emotions, the ones that took apart your very soul, would
find their way out from where they were gathered like

ravening beasts on the inside. They would take her for their own and she would be helpless, crippled by grief and loss.

She swallowed the frightening pain in her throat. She must say something, and then he would not notice.

"Rowena, what is the matter?"

Her fingers dug into his shoulders with enough force to add to the scars across his skin. She tried to move herself away, to put some slight distance between them so that she could work out what to say. But she could not do it. She could not, at this moment, survive without him.

If she could think. But she could not. She could only feel. All the things she never wanted to feel again. It would kill her.

There was silence. Nothing but breath. The same breath shared by both of them. The same pain.

If he did not realise. If he did not say anything that—

"Why are you weeping?"

"I am not. I do not." Tears squeezed out of her eyes, found their way onto his bare skin, oozed like the drops of moonlight into his hair.

"Rowena, look at me." There was that dark, heated tenderness, now, in the mysterious foreign depths of his voice. The voice, the hidden promise of heat that had undone her before.

"No."

She watched his shoulders, white ice in blackness,

hard as stone. Except that she felt his warmth, felt the
pliable mutability of living flesh.

His hands cupped her face. Her head turned. She
looked.

His face was clear sculptured bone and shadow,
beautiful to her, framed by the fateful mass of his hair.
The shadowed hair glittered: moonlight, magic lake
water and tears. His eyes, in the stark face, burned
with all the fire that must be walled in by that clever,
ruthlessly disciplined mind.

Those eyes were fixed on hers. His body touched
her, and somewhere in the back of her mind, ready to
spring out and take her if she let it, was the thought
that it might not be at this moment that she could not
do without him. It might be for as long as she lived.

"Rowena, why?"

Because of you. Because you have the most coura-
geous mind and the highest heart of anyone I have
ever known. Because you are what you are, and what
happened to you should not have happened. She
wanted to yell it. Just like he had. Because her feelings
were so strong. She wanted the words to bounce off
the magic trees and fill the accursed lake and echo as
far as barbaric cold-hearted Northumbria.

But she could not. He had been yelling for his
brother. For his home.

She had nothing. Just the frightening feelings
trapped in the back of her mind. The ones that would
overwhelm all that she was.

"Tell me. Rowena."

Because I need you.

Words like that, words even more terrifying, were in her mind, in her mouth, pressing against her lips.

His eyes on hers would have the very soul out of her.

And then what? And then what would he do with her soul? He would not want it. No man ever had.

She could not say the words. She was too frightened. Her lips parted, as though forced, and what escaped from the prison of her mouth was the last thing she expected.

"Because of Beornred."

CHAPTER FOURTEEN

BEORNRED. It was a name Rowena had never said out loud into the living air of the world. It existed only in her thought-hoard. Until now.

"Beornred?" The unused word took shape in the warm breath of the man whose body enfolded hers. His eyes, the glittering slate-grey eyes, really would take nothing less than her soul. She felt every finely tuned muscle in the body touching hers tense.

"Who is Beornred?"

"Beornred is...was..." Nothing. An insubstantial spirit. Perhaps not even that.

The eyes never left hers.

"Beornred was my son," she said and her soul was finally lost with the words.

"Your *son?*"

No more than one heartbeat until he said those words. She could count it, because she held the restless beat of that wild Northumbrian heart under her own. One beat of his heart and hers and it seemed as though a whole eternity had passed and the shell of the Lady Rowena had disintegrated, and all that was left was a lonely, terrified girl.

"I did not know you had a son."

"I do not. I did not. I was with child," said the terrified girl, "but I lost him."

"The child miscarried?"

"Yes. It was when..." Her voice gave out but it did not matter because he knew without having to be told. It was such a relief that he knew *when*. Without her having to put it into words. The dead bodies and the smell of blood, her blood, were obliterated by his touch.

He would break every bone in her body. It hurt, the way he held her, because he did not know his own strength. But she did not care. It was better than the pain inside. The feel of the completeness of his strength at last was the only thing that would stop her from disintegrating further. The last of her breath died against his skin.

He was stroking her hair. The crushing pressure of his arms was gone. Just his warmth, quite open and without stint. Heaven could not hold that much warmth. And the tenderness that had been in his voice was now in his hands.

"I..."

"Hush. It is all right—"

"No, it is not. It was my fault." The words she had never said came out under the soft touch of his hand.

"Rowena..."

"It was the shock. Just seeing the bodies when they brought them in. My father...I could not even recognise his face. Gifta having to see it and nobody would do anything. Not even Cuthred—''

''How could he have done nothing to help you?''

She could feel the anger through his skin, through every tight, lethal curve of muscle, through the strength that in two more seconds would have crushed every rib in her chest. It frightened, except…it was on her behalf, all that fierce fury. For her. Even though she had done nothing for him. Even though she did not deserve it.

''How could he not help you?''

''I… He did try but… He was my father's friend. They were like brothers. No-one closer. My father saved his life once when they were fighting together in Mercia. Cuthred felt guilty because…he had wanted to go with my father. Cuthred had heard the rumours about outlaws. About Bulla Fire-Blind. He did not go because I wanted him to stay at home. With me.''

Rowena swallowed tears, thousands of them as yet unshed, waiting ready to drown her after twelve months of bitterness.

''I was not well, you see. It was not like the first time with Gifta. I was well all the time then, and so very strong with it. But not this time. There were always aches and pains and dizziness and swellings and no one could explain why, or what to do. I wanted Cuthred to be with me. I made him stay. It was my fault.''

''Your fault? He chose to stay. What kind of man would not stick by his own decisions?''

It was my choice to do as I did and if it were to be done over again, I would make the same decision.

One who has not your heart. The conviction was unstoppable.

"Besides," said the voice, so utterly full of conviction, "were there not enough others to go?"

"My father's men were all busy with the harvest and those we had brought, Cuthred's, I do not know why they did not—"

"Really?"

That single word held not the vibrating passion of his earlier anger, but pure Northumbrian ice. But he had to face the truth about her. The words that had been suppressed for so long would come out.

"Yes, but if I had not been so weak it would not have happened. Cuthred knew that, as well as I." She felt the muscular mass underneath her move and she clung to it in desperation. Because even though he should, would, leave her, she could not face it yet.

"I lost my head. Everyone thought I was so brave giving orders about what to do with the bodies and sending to the Ealdorman and looking after Gifta. But I was not. I was not brave at all inside, and something went wrong with the baby. Because I was so upset."

The thrall's arms round her were the only solid thing left in the world.

"When the pains started, and the blood, Cuthred said…he was angry. He said I must not lose his son. I had always been convinced it was a boy I was carrying. That was what he wanted. Not a girl.'' As my father had wanted a son, not me.

"I got angry because I was so frightened and I asked him if he only cared about the child and not me. I knew he had married me because my father wanted it. I said he did not care about me at all. Only about the fact that my family was rich. I know that is an acceptable reason for marrying but he…he had made out that he cared for me.''

She choked and the night sky and the sight of her thrall's face blurred beyond recognition. She could only feel his touch and smell the clean dampness of his hair.

"Why did he have to pretend?''

That was what had killed her heart. Because it had such unacceptable echoes. That she could not be loved. That she was never good enough. That what lay behind Cuthred's careless charm and her father's hearty smiles was the fact that she was not good enough. An unsatisfactory wife. A daughter and not a son.

"I accused him. I said he had just been pretending. To make it easier. To be sure he could gain my wealth, my father's influence. I wanted him to deny it. But of course he did not. He said that there was no other reason he would have married me. Because I would not have been worth it. He said I was as cold as February snow. It is true.''

"It is not true,'' said his voice against her hair,

"Cuthred was a fool and wrong. Very wrong. He did not know what he had."

"Yes he did. A spoilt, naïve girl who thought everyone had to love her and that life would always give her whatever she wanted. But not this time. I had lost my father and now I lost the baby. They would not even let me see the baby. They said I should just think about getting well. They talked as though it was just an illness and the baby, my son, was not real. He was real to me."

"Of course he was real."

It was just because his voice always held such conviction whenever he said what he thought. That was why the tears started again.

She cried. Even though she had heard the words she wanted to hear from someone else more than anything in the world.

"It is my fault. I could not protect my child."

"Nay. It must have been *fæg*. No one can turn that aside."

Fated. You could believe that voice. Or perhaps it was because of this place. Perhaps she had been meant to come here. Just like him.

"It is a year to this very day since Beornred died. That's why I could not sleep. That's why I came here."

His hands on her hair and her shoulders were like magic.

"Rowena, I wish I knew what I could say to you.

But I can't begin to imagine how a mother would feel.''

Mother. Not woman. Mother. She swallowed tears and let his hands slide through her hair. ''You know what it is to lose all you have.'' Her hands touched him, mirroring his own gesture, burying themselves in magic. ''You know it can happen. Cuthred never forgave me. Not even when he died.''

He stopped stroking her hair.

''How?''

It was not so much the single word that shocked her as the sudden coldness in his voice, the sliding tightness of his muscles.

''How did your husband die?''

''He…it was the flux. We tried every kind of cure. Father Bertric said masses. Gifta would not leave him. Eadward got me medicines… What is it?''

''Naught.''

His voice was ice again. She understood why. ''You know what I am, now, and you know what I have become. I told myself after Cuthred's death, after…after I lost Beornred, that I would never be weak again and I have not been. But it has not changed what I have done, what I am like inside. All the failures— to my father, to my husband, to my son. Even Gifta. I cannot help her out of her sadness.''

''Gifta could not do without you—''

''But—''

''Rowena, why do you think I stayed here?''

''Why? You are a—'' the word *slave* got stuck in

her throat. Her fingers dug into him just to make sure he was there. "I made you stay," she said.

"Lady, you have a very exaggerated idea of what you can make people do."

"But you could hardly escape—"

"You left me so free I could have escaped at any time I decided to."

"But even if you had they would have stoned you to death when they caught you."

"*If* they caught me. I would still have gone."

I expected them to kill me.... There are no regrets....

She closed her aching eyes and tried not to think about the way her thrall looked upon decisions.

"I stopped you going back to your brother. I kept you here because it was what I wanted and I—" she swallowed a lump of shame "—insulted you and treated you badly...."

"Treated me badly?"

"...made you sleep on the floor and said things that—"

"Cuthbert's bones, woman, you have not the slightest idea what treated badly means."

She shut up and what was left of the tears landed on the scars on his skin.

"I did not stay for untouchable *hægtesse*—"

"*Hægtesse?*"

"Or for the spoilt maiden. I stayed because you cared about things, your father, your daughter. I stayed because under all that endless bravado I thought you had a heart that was worth it. I was right.''

''No, you are not,'' she said, ''you always think you are right when you are not. You are so…''

''Right?''

Somehow she was looking at him. Looking into those slate-grey eyes that were no longer opaque as ice, but open to her to see all the fire that burned beneath. She lost her breath and the heart he was talking about felt as though it would break in two. He could do that, break what was left of her heart. He could do that to her now so easily.

He was so beautiful and she wanted him so much. He made her head spin and the blood pound in her veins and her body ache for him. He was the only solace her mind understood. He could make her die with need just from looking at him.

And looking into those eyes could make her believe he desired her. She wanted to believe that more than anything in the world but…she was terrified by his power.

''No,'' she said, ''not right. Arrogant. Infuriating—''

His mouth obliterated hers.

WULF CAME FULLY HARD in the instant his mouth touched hers. The force of it was like lightning striking through him. So that he could have taken her in that moment, with one single thrust to the final annihilation.

He gasped with the red-hot shock of it and Rowena's mouth opened under his, taking the breath from his lungs. She did not reject him. The lush softness of her body opened to him in just the same way as her mouth. Her arms fastened across the width of his back, pulling him closer, as though she wanted him with the same desperation he felt for her.

There was no restraint, no preliminary movement. The smooth fullness of her thighs tightened round his hips. The thin barrier of her shift was pushed aside so that the first thing that he felt was wholly her: wet heat, the tingling rasp of her woman's hair. The touch of her against the bursting, painfully engorged skin of his shaft would send him mad. All his body knew was the slick promise of the blood-swollen folds of tender flesh beneath that would take his heat and quench it as none other.

"Rowena…" It was not a word, no more than his breath against the endless inviting darkness of her mouth. He could not speak, but the moan that followed was hers, against his mouth, like shared breath.

He tried to still the fierce uncontrolled movement of his body against hers. He had not meant to take her like this, to batter the life out of her in one primitive moment. The kiss, what he had done, had been meant out of all the feelings that pressed against his heart. The sort of feelings he could not express and had no right to.

He could not bear to think of the way those who should have loved her had used her, to an extent she still did not realise. It filled him with a rage that would find its mark though it took until the end of the world. But running through that was the need to take away her pain. Not to leave her in the wasteland of bitterness and loss. He knew how it blighted like frost, how it kept people alone. How it killed.

He had meant, by his touch, all that it was impossible to say.

He moved his hopelessly roughened hands down the delicate line of her side, the curve of her waist, soothing. He tried to twist his weight away from her, to put some of the coolness of the night between the rampant heat of his flesh and hers.

The small sharp fingers dug into his back, fingernails scoring the raw edge of scarring across his shoulders.

''Do not let me go. Do not stop touching me this time.''

Her voice held her need. Her flushed face was wet with tears. Her hands tangled in his hair again, trying to drag his head towards her.

''Kiss me. Let me believe you want me. You must want me.''

Her eyes were wide and dark as the night sky. A darkness he would not have understood only moments ago.

Her lips were shaking. He bent his head and his mouth came down on hers, covering it. He caught her half-clad body into his arms, taking her balance, swinging her slight weight against him without effort.

She cried out. He choked it off, taking the sweetness of her lips with his mouth, the satin softness of every vulnerable curve of her body with his hands.

Rowena thought she would die. No one had ever touched her with such intimate hunger. Because no one had ever truly wanted her.

This man's touch wanted, demanded, a response. It knew no compromise and no mercy. It made her afraid. But she wanted it.

She wanted someone to want her that much. Out of control. No thoughts. Only need. She had wanted him from first sight and she had to know that she could arouse that primitive, savage, all-consuming need in him. The need that would obliterate all that had been in the past. The power of all that was to come.

The same need that was in her.

She wanted the untameable savage of the market-place and she wanted the man she now knew: the one who gave, even when it was not deserved.

She wanted him so much. Her hands almost tore at him, snagging at the wildness of his hair, seeking every dangerously bunched muscle, every tough male line of his body. He was so strong. There was nothing that had to be held back. The relief of that was unspeakable.

She held him while her own body seemed to melt under his heat, the touch of his skin, his lips, his hands underneath her crumpled shift, the sound of his breath.

The scorching heat of his mouth found her breast. The flick of his tongue across her nipple brought sensation so sharp that it made her body arch towards him. He caught her hips, the strong hands moulding over her buttocks, holding her, suspended against him. He moved. For one agonising instant of slowness, so that she felt him. Hot, damp, slick, pulsing, metal-hard underneath that smoothness, touching her, sliding across that most intimate part of her, so that her body would have spasmed again except that he held her with his strength. Held her and touched her so, kept on touching her until her body was screaming inside.

The sound of her need beat at her lips, finding its way out in a low animal noise that had no words and needed none. His fingers touched her, sliding inside, making her ready, touching some part of her that made the blood sing in her head. It went on, softly, until she arched against him in a movement that had no softness at all and his body entered hers, meshed with it in one writhing endless streak of fire.

The feel of him inside, the moment when his hips crushed against hers was enough to send her spiralling over the edge. Every thought, everything she was, disintegrated. Her hands, clutching at his maltreated shoulders, were the only things real. The rest was a dizzying rush of light and dark that wiped out consciousness.

There was nothing else but him, the warm alive feel of him. She clung, still wanting him, shaking, wanting him closer, craving the hard thrust of his body, the almost painful feel of him inside her oversensitised flesh. Her hands slid down his heated skin, greedy, abandoned in their touch, unable to care what was right or what was wrong.

Her touch was as possessive as his. Her body cleaved to him, seeking out the long line of his back, the small dip at the base of his spine. Her fingers found the thick springy flesh of his buttocks, dug in, spread out over taut globes of muscle. She felt him tighten under her touch, the powerful surge of his body meeting hers, filling it.

She heard him gasp, knew the measure of his desire because it was hers. Her hands forced him closer. But she could not. He slid away from her, his hands loosening their hold on her, the tangled softness of his hair feather-light against her shoulders, her breasts.

''Do not...'' But even as the shock of denial dawned through her clamouring senses, her mind understood why, that he would not risk on her what the consequences might be.

All the reasons why he was right pressed ready-formed in the back of her mind. But something far stronger refused to accept them. The overwhelming awareness of him, now, the completeness with which she wanted him, all of him, swept away everything else. The driving need shared between them was deeper yet. It seemed to pulse in the air of the magic grove on Lamas Eve with a force of its own.

Her body surged towards his, with a strength it did not have, meeting his power and merging with it in one white-hot moment.

She felt his body convulse in her arms, heard the

raw sound deep in his throat, felt the release as wrenching as hers. Its echo shuddered through her as though it was her own. She fell against him into the silent dark, her flesh pressed against his, her head buried against his warmth and the raging beat of his heart.

CHAPTER FIFTEEN

HERE IS IT MADE KNOWN in this Gospel that Rowena of Healdsteada and Acleah has bought Wulf Longhair for twelve mancuses to eternal— The quill blotted. Rowena swore under her breath, *freedom* she scrawled, the ink scoring through the high-gloss vellum. The morning sun beat through the window of her chamber.

Whosoever perverts this and robs her soul of this, may Christ blind him… She dipped the quill in the ink again, *and St Birinus…* She gave her favourite saint his full name, *unleash wrath on his head, dead or alive, ever into eternity.* Her hand shook…*and St Cuthbert,* she added, just to make sure. The ink blotted over the name of the Northumbrian saint.

She left a space on the flyleaf of her gold bound bible for Father Bertric to witness. Father Bertric had told her from the start that this was what she should do.

And the thrall had shown her. Not by any deliberate act, but by what he was.

He had made her whole. She had told him everything, all the things she had never been able to say out loud and he had not turned away from her. He had taken her in his arms and he had...wanted her. Just for that one night.

He had said she had a heart and he had shown her, at last, what was meant between man and woman. Even now, her body ached for him. His touch. She would never stop needing him.

But she had seen inside him, just as he had seen inside her. She knew what his heart wept for. It was not for her. Her hand closed over the gold filigree edges of the book.

He wanted to go home. He wanted his brother and his own life and his own kindred. So much that he could conjure visions of them out of the dangerous air of some terrible half-forgotten goddess's grove.

She did not know how she would go on living without him.

She turned her face to the Wessex sun. She felt so tired and...strange. The tears, now begun after the gap of a year, seemed inexhaustible.

THE TROLLOP was in her chamber. Alone. Which was good. He kicked the door shut. She did not stir, the Lady of Healdsteda. Perhaps she was weary after a night of lusts.

He crossed the room to where she sat, leaned over her, hands on either side of her body. His shadow blocked out the sun, except for one stray gleam that caught the ripe golden yellow of her hair. She was not wearing a veil because despite the fine touch-me-not nobility, she was a wanton.

Her eyelids fluttered. That was a trick of hers. She must have heard him. Her lips moved in a half-formed whisper, like someone in unquiet dreams. He leaned closer.

"Thrall... Hold me...kiss me again..."

He did.

The moment when she realised was exquisite. He was completely prepared.

"Eadward..."

She could hardly get it out because his hand was at her throat and his body pinned hers. He savoured shock, crushed flesh, the puny movements of hope-lessly small muscles.

"So how long have you been squandering on your slave what you never gave your husband? I have come to tell you it is over, Rowena. I am here to take your plaything away and I would say he is dead flesh. But then, he always was."

"What—"

But he had grown bored with waiting.

She tried breaking his grip but it was useless, of course. She was nothing. Just a woman. But he liked the struggle. He liked the way her mouth moved. His weight flattened her. He would hurt her quite as much as he needed to. As much as she deserved. He would enjoy it.

She must have sensed that. She must have realised, finally, what he liked. Her soft, infuriating, volup-tuous mouth opened under his. Her hands skimmed his body, his thigh, his...oh, she would know what a real man was.

The breath left his throat the instant he felt the blood.

Os. BREATH. Rune of the mind. It flashed before Rowena's eyes in the sunlight. It was all she could see. That and the blood oozing from the black, formless shape on her floor.

She had killed him. The *seax* in her hand shook.

"You filthy slattern. You—"

She did not hear the rest of it. Her head was a pounding chaos. She would be sick. The instinct to run was like pain. But she could not. She had spoken of her thrall as she should not, before the King's Reeve. And he had said—

"Get up," she spat.

There was blood on the side of his neck where the blade had bitten. But not much. Not dangerous. It was just the way he had screamed. She could not look at his eyes.

"Shall we talk?" She smiled with bruised lips. She would have toyed with the knife but then he would see how her hands were shaking. Eadward...

He bared his teeth. "You impetuous...wench. I came to Healdsteda to do you a favour." She realised the baring of teeth was meant to be a smile. He sat up. The expression in his overbright eyes made her shudder.

She licked suddenly dry lips, wanting to rid herself

of the memory of his mouth on hers. His eyes watched her. His tongue, pink and sharp as some predatory animal's, touched his own lips in taunting parody, deliberate, obscene.

"Do you have any idea how you taste?"

"Ice crystals? Perhaps you should have discussed that with my husband, too."

"Poor Cuthred. To think he got the frigid treatment. Yes, there were no secrets between Cuthred and me. And now you are lusting on that piece of meat you bought in the market. I have come to relieve you of your embarrassment."

"What…what do you mean?"

"The thrall. I am offering to buy it."

"I will not sell."

Eadward got to his feet. "You fool. You do not know, do you? Your precious thrall is a traitor. He has so infuriated the King of Northumbria that the King's ambassador, my guest at Lindherst, would pay dearly for the slave's blood."

"The King of Northumbria?"

"Osred the Merciful. The one who has people murdered, exiled, forcibly tonsured and walled up in monasteries—"

"You cannot be a traitor to someone who murders people—"

"Ah, but murder. That is what your lover has done. Did he tell you who it was he killed? A boy, a mere stripling, and simple to boot. An idiot. Defenceless.

An innocent. A fellow prisoner. The King's men saw it."

They were King's men.

These King's men, were they something to do with you becoming…a thrall? How…

I killed someone who was completely helpless….
Broke his neck with my bare hands.

She dropped the *seax*.

Eadward lunged. It did not matter. It did not matter whether he picked up the *seax* and used it on her or not. She was already dead.

She had bought her slave for his power and his single-mindedness. She had bought him because he had made her dream of things that might be possible. She had lain with him in the enchanted forest because she had fallen in love with him.

Eadward's foot was poised to step over the *seax*. Sunlight flashed on the blade. *Os* the rune that loosed fetters.

"I will not let you have him."

"You witless child. Do you think that I, or you, will refuse an emissary from the King of Northumbria, one who is here to prop up an increasingly shaky alliance with Wessex? Do you know who else will be arriving here any day? King Ine. Believe me, you would be better to take your chances with Bulla Fire-Blind on a moonless night. He only puts your eyes out for hire and then beats you to death. So. What do you say now? A deal, sweeting? I will even give you the full twelve mancuses, though you should only have paid eight.''

Her life seemed to flow out with her breath. ''Fifteen,'' she said. ''You can collect him tomorrow.''

Eadward smiled.

HE HAD TO DIE. It was the only way.

Ludda fetched him.

''You should see how well the harvest's going,'' said Ludda, obviously unable to conceive that she could not care. ''Be finished in the best time ever. Wulf, here, had this idea about the barley field that…'' Ludda explained.

Wulf, here. She kept forgetting the so-called name he went by. Wulf the incredibly dangerous Northumbrian. The one who had King Osred's thane prepared to pay to get him back. She looked past Ludda's enthusiastic face.

Her thrall looked just as he had yesterday, before they had lain together in the forest. He was wearing only an old and faded pair of trousers. His hair hung loose round his shoulders. His skin glowed in the light like something luminous, heated by the sun and the bright morning air, by hard work in the fields of Healdsteda.

He was like the light itself, like life.

Dead flesh, Eadward had said, *dead flesh*.

''…and then we could…''

''Yes, of course we could. Thank you, Ludda. Would you…would you leave us? Just for a moment.''

''Oh. Aye. But remember he has got a bet on with Dunn's brother. The most wheatsheafs by…''

She was alone with him and she was afraid. Just as she had been on that first morning at Hamwic.

Just like then, she did not look at his face.

Just like then, she had to make him do what she wanted and she did not know how.

But it was not like then. Everything had changed. He moved towards her and she saw that his hair was a shade lighter because of the sun. The glowing skin was bronze. The ribs were no longer quite so visible. He was all tight pads of muscle, sleek and perfectly balanced, the way he ought to look, the way things ought to be.

But they were not.

''Last night…'' and there her voice failed her. Because after last night, she knew him. She knew how his body reacted when he touched her, when she touched him. She knew every last inch of that sun-warmed flesh and she knew, just something, of what was in his mind.

And he knew her.

She had to persuade him that he did not.

She looked at him and the grey eyes that she had once thought as hard as slate held all the unconditional acceptance of what she was and what she had done. The sort of acceptance that she had wanted all her life to see in her father's eyes and Cuthred's. The thing her soul craved more than any other. It was like finding the light after twenty-three years of crawling around in the darkness. It was just there, like a gift. Something that did not have to be deserved.

She wanted that. She wanted it so much that it ate the heart out of her. Without it she would never be whole again. She would be back, in the dark, like some *helgefangene,* trapped for eternity.

But she could not take his gift. She had to break it. She had to break whatever was or was not between them. She had to kill all that she wanted, or she would kill him.

She had already betrayed him. It had been her words that had led the emissary of Northumbria, the one who looked like a wolf's head, the man who took such pleasure in others' harm, to her thrall.

She had spoken those fatal, damning words out of anger and fear and ignorance. Out of her own inadequacies.

"Last night," she drawled, "I made the biggest mistake of my life. I am sure I do not have to tell you why. You are quite bright for a thrall and you have always known how things stood. We both have."

There was silence, so deep you could suffocate in it. She tried to breathe and kept on speaking.

"Oh, I know I got upset about other things," she said into the unbreathable air, "but underneath all that it was a game, really, with you. And I won. I got what I wanted. It was definitely worth twelve mancuses…" She waited for the sky to fall in on her head. It did not. There was only the silence. She could no longer

look at him now. Only at the scuffed rushes round
her feet.

"Eadward came to visit me today—"

"Eadward?"

She looked up again and it was entirely possible to
believe her thrall had done murder.

A boy, a mere stripling and simple to boot.

*I took the life from someone who was completely
helpless.*

She wanted to look away again but she could not.
The grey eyes held her pinned.

Oh, thrall, she thought, who are you? What have
you done? We have lain together in love. You have
taken all of me that there is and I have heard your
voice and had the touch of your body over mine, and
I know nothing of who you are.

She took a breath and said the words that would
finally end it.

"Yes," she said. "We had a good talk, Eadward
and I. Straightened a lot of things out. He gave me
some good advice and…I think it is time to call a
halt."

She produced one of her famous smiles. It seemed
to shatter against his eyes. Her chest was heaving and
the dizziness, the strangeness, was loud in her head.
She hoped he did not notice, could not see such weakness.

"Eadward said all this to you?"

He did not believe a word she had said. She would

never convince him. Never get him to do what she wanted. What he *must* do.

"Yes, Eadward. I have no quarrel with him anymore so you see I really do not need your…services. In any way at all. It was all a bit foolish of me, I will admit. And as Eadward pointed out, I could damage my reputation for nothing. For some silly lewd fancy. Suppose people got to know and…and…" The next bit would be unforgivable. It was just that she would never break the force of those eyes and she had to. There was no other way. For any of them.

"I have my child to consider. Suppose this got back to Gifta. She really loved her father. He had a spotless reputation."

Something did change in the eyes then. Something deep inside, on another level. Something hidden, in that part of him she had never yet seen fully, only glimpsed beside Nerthus's lake. But the ice-cold Northumbrian eyes never wavered from hers and she had to look away, because she could not sustain this.

"Ludda will take you to my estate at Acleah. After that we will work out something for you. I will still pay you as I promised and I will…" Pretend you have died, she finished silently. Here in Nerthus's lake so I will not have to produce a corpse. If I could tell you that, if I could say what was in my heart, you would appreciate the irony. But she could not go on.

He was no longer looking at her. It was as though she had ceased to exist. She felt as though everything that had happened to her in the last day and night, everything she was had ceased to exist.

"Will you go?" It should have been a command and it came out like the most wretched plea.

He did not so much as glance at her. "Aye," he said, as though it was completely irrelevant.

There was only one thing left to ask, what she should have asked before, on that first day: the question that would break the enchantment. She looked at the peerlessly clear grey eyes.

"Before you go, will you tell me your true name?"

"Athelwulf of Bernicia."

CHAPTER SIXTEEN

"WHAT DO YOU MEAN, you have lost him?"

Rowena stared in fascinated horror at Ludda's black eye.

"I mean that he did not wish to go to Acleah."

"Wish? It was not a question of what he wished. There is someone out to kill him!" She resisted the urge to blacken her steward's other eye. "Ludda, there were four of you."

"Aye."

She should scream at him. She should give vent to her anger and to the terrible fear that lay behind it. Ludda expected it. It was plain on his face.

She groped blindly for her steward's hand.

"He does not know," she said. "He does not know he is supposed to be dead."

WULF LOOKED at the sleeping face. It would be so easy to snuff the life out of that. He wanted to. Because of what the King's Reeve had done to Rowena. Because of the lives Eadward had taken without thought.

He leaned over the bed and the darkness of

Lindherst covered him. He made no noise. He was a master at that. He watched the closed eyes, the slack jaw, the shadowed throat. So easy. It was not as though he had not done murder before. One hand across mouth and nose, the other…the wave of sickness washed through him, tensing muscles already stretched to breaking, rousing cold sweat on his skin. It was too close to that other murder. Far too close.

Besides, justice on the King's Reeve belonged only to Rowena. He would give it to her. It needed only a matter of hours to achieve, and there could be no danger to her in that time. It would be some while before the King's Reeve discovered he had been robbed. He had guests from afar to keep him occupied, so they said. They could not matter, the Reeve's guests. What would matter to Rowena was the guest of the Ealdorman. He would have to take Alfred with him. No one would believe the word of a runaway slave.

ROWENA WAS READY when they came the next day. But the dizziness still hit her when she stood. It was strain. She could not afford to be ill. Or weak. She went outside.

It was not Eadward and the Northumbrian. It looked like an invading army from Mercia. Horsemen filled her courtyard, their mounts wheeling, sending servants and milk pails flying. Their leader pulled to a stop before her.

He was beautiful. The hair was shorter and tended

more towards gold, the eyes were tawny. But otherwise the likeness was shocking.

"You have hurt your arm."

He dismounted and walked towards her. His good hand moved in a blur of gold armrings and unsheathed a gold-hilted sword. He looked rich enough to buy and sell King Ine. He looked furious enough to ravage the entire kingdom of Wessex. Ludda stepped in front of her.

"Athelbrand," she said.

The next thing she knew she was lying on cushions. In her hall. It was full of people. And then she forgot them. She looked into a pair of terrible amber eyes.

"Where is my brother?"

I do not know. She could not get the words out.

"Lady, I will have my brother if I have to kill every person in this room to get him. Where is Athelwulf?"

"Do you mean Wulf?" the voice was not hers. It was thin and childish. Her heart thudded against her ribs. "He will be back this afternoon. He promised to mend my badger cage."

"Gifta! Not now. Sweetheart, do not—"

"Mother why were you asleep?"

"Badger cage?"

A gold inlaid sword hit the floor. She heard it strike. She swallowed. "Ludda, will you get the Lord Athelbrand a drink. He is going to need it."

"…AND SO I TRIED to send him to Acleah. Only he gave Ludda a black eye and escaped. Now no one

knows where he is and Eadward and your King Osred's favourite thane will be here at any minute.''

"King Osred is dead. Somebody gave him what was
coming to him. Two days ago. South of the Mercian
border. But I'm looking forward to meeting his favourite thane.''

She had only seen one other person whose face
could take on that expression.

"You know I would never have believed a word
you said, Lady, if I had not met your messenger on
the Icknield Way.''

"The Icknield Way? What were you doing in the
south?''

But she knew. Fighting. King's men.

"No need to look so. It was not me who dealt to
Osred, more's the pity. All I did was tangle with the
remnants of his retreating guard. No, I was looking for
someone else.''

"Athelwulf.'' The word, strange, stumbled over her
tongue. It seemed to have nothing to do with the man
she had loved.

"No. I thought Athelwulf was dead. At least I did
until two days ago. I was looking for two people. One
was the man I believed had killed him, the man who
in fact, flogged him and sold him into slavery.''

"The Northumbrian ambassador?''

"Hun. Ex-ambassador. Ex-thane. Aye.''

She remembered the colourless eyes, the brutal undisguised pleasure in others' pain. The sickness of it

filled her veins. But it was followed by a frightening strength. Her heart burned. She sat up.

"Easy, Lady. That was a strange fainting fit." There was speculation in the world-weary amber eyes. She ignored it.

"Your ambassador will not live," she said.

"No," said Athelbrand. He did not understand. He thought that the right to revenge was only his. It was not.

"And who was the other person you were looking for?"

"Hun's intended bride, the Pictish princess. I had eloped with her. Only she left me."

"You…you made off with that man's bride?"

"Aye. No one took it well. Athelwulf and I are related to the rival royal house of Cenred."

I am descended from Woden….

"I had paid Hun off and he had accepted. But he must have decided that was not enough. It was meant to be my punishment, what happened. But it fell on my brother."

It was impossible to be filled with such rage and still live and breathe. She fixed her eyes on the selfish, arrogant barbarian who had so nearly killed his own brother. She thought of what had happened to her former thrall. She thought of everything he had done for her and a household of foreigners in Wessex. She thought of how much the oblivious, self-willed barbarian meant to him.

"You idiot," she spat. "You ignorant, half-witted

abortion of a rational being. You had someone who cared enough about you to risk life, maiming and dispossession, to sacrifice everything he had to preserve your worthless hide and you put it all on the line for wilfulness. You do not know. You just do not know what love like that is worth...."

She was shaking. She would have given everything she had, Healdsteda, Acleah and every last ounce of useless gold for someone to care that much about what happened to her.

"Lady, if you wish to use that blade on behalf of my brother, you have a right."

She was on her feet. The rune blade was in her hand. Athelbrand did not move a muscle.

She saw what was in his eyes. Guilt, the guilt of unwitting betrayal. She recognised it because it was what was in her heart, too. The blade dropped from her hand.

"I am at fault as much as you."

"How disappointing." She started. The alien voice seemed to come from the back of the hall, chilling, utterly confident. Northumbrian. "I really thought you were going to save me the trouble of killing this unruly lecher."

Her head shot round. She had not heard. No one had. They had all been too engrossed by her antics with the *seax*.

It was Hun, once Northumbrian ambassador, and behind him Eadward looking as green as rotting lampreys. Behind them were so many men. Her hand reached out instinctively to find Gifta and hold her close to her side. The light in Athelbrand's eyes turned savage. But then his large jewelled hand withdrew from the fallen sword. She saw why.

They had Ludda. Blood welled from a slashing cut in his arm. She buried Gifta's face in her skirts. Her gaze moved to the face of the man who held her steward and she saw her nightmare, scars, a blackened hole where one eye should be. Bulla Fire-Blind. He had a knife that dripped blood.

"I see it is as well I was advised to bring my hired…my friends. Eadward also told me of your reluctance to sell, Lady, and now I find you with the criminal slave's brother."

Hired. Bulla Fire-Blind only puts your eyes out for hire and then beats you to death. Eadward had told her… The connection was made at last. Eadward had known to hire Bulla Fire-Blind before. To kill her father. Eadward would do anything to save himself.

She thought of his sympathy over her father's death. Over Cuthred's. *There were no secrets between Cuthred and me.* The thought jarred her, so badly that she must have relaxed her grip on Gifta. The child squirmed free. Heading for Ludda.

"Gifta!" Her cry bounced off the rafters but the other voice drowned it.

"Wench, if you move, Bulla will have to blind your steward. Someone catch that child and shut it up."

"No!" but someone already had her. "Gifta…" She tried to hold the child's terrified gaze with her own, tried to keep the crippling fear out of her own voice. "Hush. Stay still. It will be all right soon. I promise." If they harmed Gifta, she would die. She took a breath. They had not hurt her yet. The man who had her did not hold her hard.

"I want the lecher and I want the slave. Otherwise Bulla will take this man's eyes out, one at a time."

Her blood froze. She knew what Ludda would do for her. She must say something. Gain time. If Athelbrand had half a chance—but something erupted at the door of her crowded hall.

"Wait. Lady, we have caught him, the slave…"

It was like having the breath punched out of her body. She stared, helpless. The press of people by the door melted away. A group of men, her own men of Healdsteda were driving something forward, packed around it in a circle with spears and a pitch fork as though it was a wild boar.

It was her thrall. Her eyes, Athelbrand's eyes, the eyes of everyone on the hall fixed on him. His clothes were torn and filthied. There was a cut across his cheekbone, swollen and oozing blood. They had bound his hands. He was out of breath. His powerful chest heaved and his eyes held all the trapped wild fury she had first seen in her bower at Hamwic.

First of the boar baiters were Dunn and his brother. Dunn, seemingly quite recovered from his illness, held the pitchfork. Dunn. His brother grinned. Eagerness.

She thought she would be sick. That the dizziness inside would overcome her and she would fall again into that strange half-darkness that blocked out sight and sense. She wished she would. Then she would not have to see this. The man who had meant everything to her being driven to some hideous death like a beast to the slaughter.

"The thrall is yours," said Dunn. He was addressing Hun, the Northumbrian, not her. "Yours to do with as you will."

Hun threw back his head and laughed.

She thought Athelbrand would run berserk. That the slaughter would be for them all at that moment, starting with Gifta.

Frozen grey clashed for one instant with the molten heat of gold, then her thrall's gaze swept on, past Athelbrand. Found her.

What was in his eyes was not frozen at all. She felt the trapped power of his anger through her skin. It was terrifying. She tried to meet the force of it, to put all that she felt into her eyes.

One glance, that was all she was allowed, one fleeting instant into which to fit the unsayable. That she did not want him to die from this, through her fault, at any price she herself could pay. That she loved him. It was true. She knew it in that one searing instant between longing and terror. The love that she felt for him was the centre of all that she was. And she had no right to it.

She had betrayed this man that she loved. She would cause his death. Right now, in her own hall.

But there were no words to say anything that was

in her heart, and an instant was just that. A fragment between one moment and the next that scarcely existed. The frightening gaze swept past her, taking in everything in the hall. Hun, Bulla Fire-Blind, Ludda, Athelbrand, Eadward, the place of every man and every weapon. Gifta. It stopped at Gifta and the entire world seemed to change. He smiled. It was the most extraordinary thing in the vile atmosphere of her crowded hall. It lasted no more than an instant. But it elicited a miracle. Gifta smiled back.

"The bondsman." Hun's voice snapped the moment.

They drove him forward, all the way down the length of the hall to stand before the man who had enslaved him.

Nothing happened. Rowena's heart seemed to beat faster and faster until it would choke her. Waiting, just waiting for someone to take him, to deal with him as Ludda had been dealt with.

She could not understand why Hun did not move, did not just kill his prize on the spot. There was nothing anyone could have done to prevent him. Not Athelbrand. Not her.

She looked across at the malicious face, even though she did not want to. She saw the pale eyes fixed on the trapped man and she understood. The anticipation was part of the pleasure. He was so confident of having his will that he could afford to indulge that pleasure.

"Leave him be."

One wave of a jewelled hand and Dunn and his fellow hunters of men moved back. Just a pace. Perhaps in case the quarry bolted. It was unnecessary. What could they do compared to Hun? They had no idea of what they had delivered their captive to. But she had. She had had one glimpse herself and had seen just something of the damage that had already been done to her thrall. She had seen only the physical evidence and the rest she could not begin to guess.

Her thrall just stood, silent and still, powerless as when he had stood in bonds before her. He had been just as confined to helplessness then, and yet she had been afraid of him.

She had not been able to work out why, then. Now she could. She could see it, completely and unexpectedly.

It was the way he stood, perfectly balanced, unmoving and yet each thickened flexible muscle disciplined into one cohesive, frightening mass of latent force.

It seemed so obvious. It was enough to shift the balance of power in that tension-packed hall just slightly off centre.

She wondered that Hun could not feel the force and the strength of the will that underlay all that trapped fury. It was something apart, something controlled. Something quite deadly.

Her throat tightened but Hun seemed oblivious. There was nothing in his eyes except an obscene anticipation.

"Kneel, slave."

The slave took a step and then another, backwards and sideways, away from Hun, the feet, so carefully aligned when he stood, shuffling clumsily in the rushes as though he was afraid. He was so utterly alone.

"Kneel."

He took one more step before he complied and when he did, the solid wall of his body obscured Gifta from view.

"Good. Now the lecher."

Athelbrand moved. There was no choice, after all.

"So. Observe how the mighty are fallen. Is everyone looking?" Hun's gaze took in the strained faces fixed on the captives, on him. He smiled. "Look carefully at what happens to those who defy me, who defy their king."

Rowena stopped the small betraying movement before it was made. King. Hun did not know yet that his king was dead. Somewhere in Mercia. Hun was smiling, openly.

"Let the slave's tunic be removed. I want everyone to see how I have used him already."

But this time she must have moved because their tormentor's head turned towards her

"Did I detect a protest?"

The world narrowed to the compass of those savage, colourless eyes. He could kill her. He could do it easily and not care. Or he would hurt Ludda because of what she had done. Or Gifta. Not Gifta...

"Not from her."

Rowena flinched. Not so much from the words as from the harsh contempt with which they were said. Waves of coldness blossomed out from the pit of her stomach.

Her former slave was right. She deserved that bitterness for what she had done. Besides, that contempt for her was what she had wanted him to feel. The assessment of her that lay behind those three simple words were what she had wanted him to believe, for his own sake, so that he would leave her and be safe.

Yet for all that, she had not been prepared for what it was like to hear it from his mouth, the mouth that had cleaved to hers and had shown her what love might have been. There was nothing she could say, nothing in this packed hall full of enemies that she could do to save him. Nothing.

He did not so much as cast a glance in her direction and neither did Hun. His attention was back where it should be, on his quarry.

Laughter rang in her ears, loud, full of triumph and anticipation. No more than half sane.

"Do I hear a certain resentment in that? Do I hear the recriminations of something used and cast aside? You pathetic fool. What an animal I have reduced you to, have I not? Grovelling for the favours of those now so far above you. Even this little Wessex whore… wench!"

The malicious attention was focussed back on her. "You can do this *nithing* one last favour. Remove his clothes for him. I am sure you will both enjoy it," and when she could not move her shaking legs, "now." She saw out of the corner of her eye Bulla's blade move towards Ludda's face. She took a step forwards.

Somewhere on the edge of her senses she was aware of the eyes of so many people on them. But they did not exist, those other people, only the few of them locked here in this small hell of torment. Herself and the man who had been her thrall. Ludda and Athelbrand.

Gifta.

She took one last look at her child and then knelt on the hard floor among the rushes beside her slave. She could smell meadowsweet and comfrey and feel the sharp pricking of the rushes through the fabric of her skirts.

She could feel Athelbrand's eyes on her burning like coals. But not his brother's. The big body was so close to hers, filling her vision, the folds of his tunic sleeve ruffled over his bent arms, the stray strand of ash-brown hair. His solidness.

She could not touch him. Not with the weight of guilt in her heart, not with the knowledge of what was to come. She could not do it. Her throat burned.

"Get on with it. I think you can safely untie his hands. He is not going anywhere. Yet."

She swallowed bile. "Athelwulf…" it stuck on her tongue, a stranger's name that could mean nothing to what they had shared over the last few days, the most intensely felt days of her life. The unfamiliar sound made scarce even a whisper and she did not know what she could say. Only that she must have some response from him, something that would anchor her back in reality out of this nightmare.

"You can at least untie my hands," he spat. She moved instantly, as though he had struck her. His voice was low, savage, meant only for her, but she knew Hun must hear every word. And Athelbrand. She got his shoulder, the broad back and the tied hands, anything but his face, a glance from his eyes. "Go on, do it."

She touched his hands. Warm, so warm and strong. The rope...she remembered blood, the way Eadward had damaged his skin, the way *she* had done. Her hands fumbled, numb with horror, useless.

"It cannot be that hard. You managed enough feats of strength the other night in the glade did you not?" Her hands shook. How could he say that? Here? Speak now, in this place, of what had been between them?

But why should he not? She had killed what they had had, just as she would kill him.

Her fingers would scarce move. She could still hear the savage whisper in her ears.

"...Nothing stopped you then, you would climb through a window, if you remember..." A gust of wind from the half-open window of her hall lifted the soft threads of his hair, obscuring her view. She thought she heard some strange noise outside. She felt the thick muscles under her hands stiffen. She thought she must have hurt him but the rope parted. It was impossible. She had hardly touched it and then so clumsily. It could scarce have been tied.

She knelt on the wooden floorboards, the rope in her hands, unable to move. There was silence. The man next to her, half a breath away, seemed hardly aware of her. His mind focussed elsewhere, head angled away from her, the breeze against his face.

"Do you stop, wench?"

She jumped at the sound of Hun's voice, rich with anticipation. Cold fear stabbed its way through her guts. She could feel the attention of the packed hall on her, on what she did next. On her thrall. To be turned on the indelible marks across his flesh that witnessed what he had suffered from this man.

She could not move her hands. She could not touch his clothes, go through with one more step along the path that would lead first to humiliation, then to pain, and then to death.

"Do you wish Bulla to provide you with some encouragement?

"She will need no encouragement." It was Eadward's voice, close. Not to save her or Ludda from punishment but because he could not help himself. She heard eagerness, the same unclean fascination that had held him and made him watch her in the marketplace.

Her hands would not work. It was like a nightmare that robbed all feeling and sense.

The averted head turned back to look at her. The eyes were slate, frozen. She could not look away from them.

"Just do it," he said, "or do you lack the courage?"

Her hands moved, towards the cheap, clumsy iron buckle that held the thin strap of leather at his waist. Her fingers touched metal, hard, sharp-edged, warmed through by contact with his body. She pulled the leather tighter against the taut narrow hips. His body moved fractionally towards her, the coarse folds of his tunic sliding over her skin. She brushed the folds aside, the back of her hand pressed against him. She felt the firm line of his belly tighten beneath the torn and dirtied material.

Her own stomach muscles clenched in instant response. She tried not to touch him so. She tried to keep hands suddenly slippery with sweat on the sharp iron and the worn leather. She tried to work the strap through the buckle as deftly and smoothly as possible but her hands were stiff, her whole body taut as a bowstring.

The leather parted. She set it aside among the rushes she had had laid fresh. The buckle landed on meadowsweet, bruising it. She smelt the sweet scent.

Her shaking hands were empty. She felt every man's gaze on her. Her head pounded. Her breath came hard and her throat ached.

"…she will not do it—"

"Nay, watch her…"

She moved. Not because of Hun's voice, Eadward's, but because of the one closer. The ice-clear voice of the North. The ice that burned with a heat that would take all that she was.

"You have not the courage…"

She moved as she should. As she had to. Her hands buried themselves in the fabric of the woollen tunic, ripped, dirtied by whatever struggle it had taken to bring him here. Her fingers fastened on its torn folds.

"You will have to move your arms."

She could scarce believe that was her voice. Speaking to him.

The noise came again from outside, borne on the breeze, distracting, out of place. He was free. She felt the muscles of his arms tighten. She felt the power she had sensed beneath all that trapped fury take shape and strength. The breeze against her heated skin quickened. There was something outside. There was—

"Does that bring back memories? Would you climb through a window now?"

Hun laughed.

The window, open right beside her. The *window.* Her heart leapt, with impossible hope, with anticipation. With terror. Gifta. He must know she would not go without her child. He did know. He had smiled at Gifta. In the midst of all the horror. Yet what could he do, now?

She noticed Athelbrand had chosen to kneel on the side closest to the sword. If only she still had her *seax.* If only…she saw it. She saw the sunlight touch something hidden in the rushes with gold. It glowed so that she wondered the whole hall could not see it. She could read the runes. *Tir*. Victory.

"You will get what is coming to you," she muttered sulkily. She shook out the rope. "As for that filthy tunic…" she leaned back and stumbled over her skirts. Her foot touched something hard, slid it through the rushes under her skirts. She wanted to take the blade herself, with all that she had. But something stayed her hand.

He was closer to Gifta than she was. He had more skill. He would not let her down. Whatever she had done, whatever he now thought of her, he would get her and Gifta out of this nightmare. He would do it. Because that was who he was.

The blade touched his leg. She staggered to her feet, brushing rushes off her skirts.

"Let all see," said Hun, "what happens to those who defy King Osred—"

"King Osred," said the Northumbrian Athelwulf, "is dead."

In the instant of shock that distorted Hun's face, the world changed. She did not see him pick up the *seax* beside him. It seemed to skim through the air of its own accord, inexorable, deadly. She heard the gasp of expelled breath as the rune blade buried itself to the hilt through the heart of her father's murderer, the murderer of so many others. She saw Ludda dragged clear of Bulla Fire-Blind's lifeless grasp by Dunn. She was running, running the few steps towards Gifta.

But Gifta was already free. It had happened while

every eye had been on Bulla, on Ludda, on Hun. She
had not even seen it though she had expected it. Gifta
was running towards her, the man who had held her
buried under her thrall's weight.

Gifta crashed into her. She caught her daughter and
swung her high, towards the window.

There were people in the courtyard. Men. Everywhere. The bright links of chain mail reflecting sparks
in the sun. In the midst was a furiously impatient man,
with a sword in one hand and what looked like a roll
of parchment in the other. He flashed gold in the light.
Someone took the child out of her arms.

It was Alfred.

''She is safe. Lady. Give me your hand. I will help
you through.''

He put Gifta down. She saw, amongst all the armed
men, the surprisingly calm figure of Gifta's nurse. The
child vanished in a flurry of female clothing. Gifta was
safe.

She dragged her hand out of Alfred's.

''No,'' she said and plunged back into the hell of
her hall.

CHAPTER SEVENTEEN

HE HAD TO BE ALIVE. He had to. Her desperate eyes could not see him. She tried to shove her way through the press but someone else brushed past her in a blur of gold. Followed by what looked like the entire army of Wessex, pouring in through the windows, the door.

The gold bedecked man was standing right in front of her. He belted someone over the head one-handed with the hilt of his sword. A Northumbrian dropped like a stone. The hilt had a lot of gold leaf and a little blood.

"Drop your weapons," bellowed the man in a voice that would have deafened a town the size of Hamwic. "If any man breaks the peace of the King of Wessex he will be hanged." The cry, like the roar of waves against a cliff, was taken up by dozens of voices.

The silence that came after stunned the senses.

She saw him. In the sea of shocked faces and fallen weapons there was only one figure she could focus on. Her heart felt as though it would burst. He was safe. He was bent over something heavy but he lived and moved. He looked up and saw her. His gaze had picked her out before King Ine had stopped speaking.

He made no move towards her. He stood up, shoulder to shoulder with his brother, as he should.

But his gaze…it was as though he had touched her. The heat of it scorched every part of her like a brand of possession. To know that she was there. That she was safe. She let it take her and possess her completely for that instant because the look in those grey eyes was all that her soul craved.

It was not something that rightly belonged to her. But her response to it was pure unconquerable instinct and he knew it. She saw it in his eyes. He smiled. But she could not bear that. She could not take that from him and she looked away, turning her gaze to the man with the bright gold hair and the bright gold decorated corselet.

"I will have order," bellowed King Ine, southern descendant of Woden. "Where is the man Hun of Northumbria?"

She saw Athelbrand step over something prone on the floor.

"He is dead, Lord."

A steel-blue gaze flicked over Wulf's brother. "I see. An unfortunate accident. I hope my northern allies will not take it too hard."

"Not," said Athelbrand, his large chest heaving, "those who are loyal to the house of King Cenred."

"You relieve my mind greatly," said the gold-bedecked one, "as I do not believe there is anyone in this hall who is not a loyal supporter of my noble ally King Cenred. Or am I mistaken?"

Athelbrand nearly self-ignited. She saw his brother reach up to place a hand on his arm. Her thrall's eyes were watching King Ine in fascination. There was silence in the hall.

The most cunning king in all the isles of Britain permitted himself a smile. "Everyone is loyal to the new king of the North. How very satisfactory. And now where is my Reeve?"

She saw what her thrall was holding.

It was the King's Reeve. Blood streamed from his nose. Her thrall hauled him upright.

"Ah. Eadward. Fetch him here."

Her thrall crossed the small space between them. He dropped his burden at the King of Wessex's gold buckled feet. Eadward's breath sobbed.

"Lady?" The King beckoned her towards him with the hand that still held rolls of parchment. "I hear you are learned and know right well how to read?" The steel-blue gaze move first to her thrall's face and then to hers. She watched in astonishment.

"But…yes, Lord."

"Take this and read aloud. We all wish to hear."

She looked at the parchment thrust into her shaking hands. "They are lists, Lord, lists of…taxes? Taxes received from…from Healdsteda? And others. Alfred's farm…"

"Yes. How diligent of my Reeve to have been able to fill out the amount of taxes received from all of you and due to me before the harvest is in. By the way, you are going to have a bad year and you are short."

The thing on the floor that had once been Eadward cringed. She looked from the trembling heap of fine clothing towards the torn and battered shape of her escaped slave.

"You?" It was not a word, it had no sound because there was so little breath in her lungs and it was needed to support the wild beating of her heart. That single word was nothing at all, just a shape in the air, but he read it. As he could read all there was to read about her.

His eyes were quite steady and they never wavered from hers and she knew that he had done it somehow. He had freed himself from Ludda and the escort she had sent with him and he had got the proof from Lindherst. The proof that she needed. The proof that freed her from Eadward forever and vindicated what her father had tried to do.

She wanted to speak to him. To rush across the floor and cast herself into his arms and say all the things that made her heart burst. But she could not. She had no right. And besides, the eyes, though they wanted her to hear all that the King said, though they wanted her to be free of Eadward's shadow, held her back.

"Read the next," ordered King Ine.

She tore her gaze back to the crinkled parchment. She tried to focus her eyes on the writing but her vision blurred and her mind would not take it in. At last the ink marks, neatly written by somebody's scribe, took shape.

"In the name of Almighty God, I stand in true witness, unbidden and unbought, as I saw with my eyes and heard with my ears that which I pronounce…'' Her hands shook. "It's an oath, of 120 shillings. It is from the Ealdorman.'' Her voice began to shake, but she made it sound across to the far end of her hall. "It says that the King's Reeve of Lindherst arranged the death of my father through Bulla Fire-Blind.''

The parchment fell out of her hand. Something white and bloodied shot through the rushes, quick as a snake. King Ine was quicker. He stood on his Reeve's hand. Eadward screamed.

"The crime of compassing death by secret means is bootless and you will not get one man in my kingdom to swear on your behalf. Your property is forfeit. It must be your death. Or exile. Lady, this man has committed crimes against us both. I would kill him, what would you?''

Somewhere around their feet she could hear Eadward whimpering. There should be blood for blood. It was only right. But it already sullied her hall. Bulla Fire-Blind. Her father's ghost had had his revenge through the rune blade and Bulla was dead for his sins. For the deaths of her father and all of his companions, for the deaths of all the other unwary travellers he had killed in the forest. It was enough.

"Exile,'' she said. "Let every man's hand be turned against him. Let him have nothing—no rights, no privileges, no possessions. Let us see what he can make of that.'' But her gaze was not on Eadward. It rested

for one burning instant on her thrall who had created
magic out of exactly that. And then she looked away.

"Then hear that this man is outlawed from my
realm. Let him be removed from this place and set on
the road. Let every man know he bears a wolf's head.
Let every man's hand be turned against him and any
who dare to harbour him know the penalty of the
King...."

It was over. She heard King Ine's voice, still speaking. People began moving about in the hall and it was
over and done. Finished.

There was something different in her hall, something clean, something that meant the world had
changed and would start anew. Something indefinable
yet full of purpose, that had not happened just at this
moment but had begun some time ago, and was now
fulfilled.

Something that had begun the moment her thrall had
set foot in Healdsteda.

Her ex-thrall. He was the only person in the
crowded hall she could see. Not all the people who
kept asking her what should be done with this and that,
and how everyone was going to be fed. Not even King
Ine himself. Just him. She saw and marked every turn
of his powerful shoulders, the gleam of his hair, the
smooth gold of his skin, the angle of his head, every
expression of his face. But he did not see her.

There was so much she wanted to say. So much she
had to say.

She began to move through the press. It was like

struggling through quicksand. Anxious servants. Dunn's brother wearing a huge grin and explaining the cleverness of his part in the events to anyone who would listen. Northumbrians. Officious King's men. The King. He kept getting in the way, soothing Athelbrand now that all unnecessary international complications had been avoided, talking, of all people, to her thrall. Laughing. Heartily. As though he had known her Northumbrian thrall all his life.

The King turned. "Ah, the Lady." The laughter in the eyes that missed nothing was turned on her. "The very lady for whose sake I am now short of a Reeve. Nay, do not look so struck when you have the means to atone for all the trouble you have caused me."

"*I*, Lord?" she said with a wary eye on the man who could beat the whole of Mercia into submission.

"You, Lady. You must add your superior persuasion to mine. I have a fancy for a new Reeve who knows how to count, even if he does count in Northumbrian. Someone who has done me some service and may expect a fair reward."

There was a noise around the hall like a hundred indrawn breaths. One was hers. Every eye fixed on the two Northumbrians standing before the King. She saw the same surprise on Athelbrand's face that must be on hers, on everyone's, but on her thrall's face was a quite different expression, deeper. It was shock.

She clenched her fists. It was a generous and unexpected offer from the King to a foreigner but it was not impossible. It was a position of some standing but

in no way extraordinary for a senior thane. That was
what, in truth, her ex-thrall was. Yet what she could
see in his eyes, in that small unguarded moment, was
a disbelief that brought home to her what damage Hun
had done. She thought the burning ache inside, made
out of all her love for him and her helpless anger,
would choke her.

She must have made some involuntary movement
because he looked at her. The slate-grey eyes held not
the mask of contempt and fury that had been meant
only to protect her. They held no mask at all and they
were so bright. They were full of all that she had ever
wished from him. They held the brightness that was
so strong it could drag her out of the past into a world
of different possibilities. His eyes were so clear, at
once as clear as Northumbrian ice and as heated as
the sun of a Wessex summer.

It was all there in that one unguarded instant between shock and the inevitable return of self control.
All that she longed for to make her whole. Just one
step towards it and she would be in the light forever.

The urge to do that was strong beyond compare.
But it was the very clearness of his eyes that made it
impossible. She had understood his look because she
alone had the knowledge to recognise that one moment
of vulnerability. And he only looked so, at her, because he did not know what she had done.

She had failed him at every turn since she had met
him and at the last she had betrayed him. There was
only one thing in which she could not fail now.

The King was looking at her. They were all looking at her. She must say some word that would take Athelwulf the Northumbrian thane out of the disaster that Wessex had been for him and set him free. She tried to breathe, to speak, to force the necessary words through the swollen heat of her throat. She could not get a sound out of her mouth. She had no need to. It must be in her face. She saw his eyes turn impenetrable grey.

The King asked again whether she would add her persuasion to his extraordinarily generous offer to a foreigner, whether his offer would be taken.

She had not the strength to say it. But she was not forced to. It was said for her. They all turned their heads towards her thrall. He looked, even marked and half naked, more formidable, more full of power, more real than any man there arrayed in jewels and chain mail.

"No."

For tact, for political astuteness, it was an answer that would not have disgraced Athelbrand. She would not have been surprised if every barbarian from the north had been annihilated on the spot.

Instead, they became enmeshed in some interminable feast which involved every last ounce of available meat and every single barrel of imported Frankish wine.

They were all very polite to King Ine.

"Open it," she said, glaring at the last barrel. The

smell of it was like to make her sick. She stumbled out into the night.

The air was like the breath of heaven. The stars were achingly bright and the harvest moon, just past the full, cast uncanny shadows. She thought of the moon on the lake in the forest glade.

The thought of that would kill her.

She turned her steps away.

It was hot in Ludda's room. It was hot everywhere that was not outside in the moonlight. Ludda looked feverish but Father Bertric had said he was going to live. He would even be able to use his arm again. Father Bertric knew how to stitch things.

She watched the sleeping, restless face. It looked pitiable. This was something else that would not have happened but for her.

She sank down on the bench beside the bed.

"I am sorry," she said into the stifling dark of the sickroom. "Ludda, you had better live. I am such an idiot. I do not deserve a steward as loyal as you have been. But I do need you."

"If I agreed to that, I would probably be dismissed."

"Ludda! You are supposed to be asleep."

"I would be if people did not keep coming in to check up on me."

"I am sorry. Who—"

"The Atheling."

"The…the *Atheling?*"

"Aye. So it seems. Throne-worthy up north, apparently. Not everyone gets a black eye from a prince. Or their life saved, I suppose.''

"No.'' She tried not to think of the horrors in the hall and what the consequences would have been but for the thrall…Atheling. "Throne-worthy?''

"Aye. Same grandfather as the new King Cenred.''

"Woden?''

"Eh? No, Cuthwine or something. Anyway, it must have been enough to put the wind up Osred. Enough to put the wind up most people, your slave.''

"Atheling.''

"Aye. Or Reeve.''

She clutched the edge of the wooden bench so hard that it hurt. "Ludda, he is not going to be the Reeve.''

"Yes, he is. Nay, do not look like that. He really is. He said when he came to see me. Changed his mind. Thought he would once he knew…well always was the sort to do the right thing. You will see.''

Ludda was delirious. She got up because the sick feeling was worse and she had to get back outside. She would find Father Bertric and tell him to attend to his patient properly.

At least Gifta was safely asleep. She had checked at least five times. She hesitated beside the door to her daughter's room. She did not want to risk waking the child, because sleep was what she needed after what she had witnessed today. They had been adult horrors. Too cruel and too bewildering for a child to see.

But just to look in on her again and make sure that…she stopped in disbelief at the shrill squeaking that came to her on the clear night air. It came again. She shoved open the door. Gifta and the nurse were giggling.

"Mother—"

"Lady, you gave me such a fright. It is…she wouldn't sleep properly for being scared and then—"

"I was not scared."

"No, dearling, of course not, but…he came in and put it right, you see. Explained what happened, about everyone pretending that, oh he just said it in such a way that…well, it was funny."

Gifta began giggling again, which set the idiot nurse off once more.

"Who," she enquired with the last shreds of her patience, "came in and said what?"

"The thrall. I mean the Atheling."

"Wulf," squeaked Gifta, "Wulf."

Rowena stared at the bright-eyed mischievous face, which was how Gifta used to look. So long ago she had forgotten. Bright-eyed and bouncy and full of herself and a frequent nuisance and… It would break her heart, the sight of that face.

"It was ever so funny," repeated Gifta. "Only Wulf said I had to be nice to you in case you were scared and…Mother, you are not going to cry are you?"

"Me? Why should I cry?"

She caught the small body in her arms and buried her face in sleep-tangled russet curls so that Gifta could not see.

"I was not scared one little bit," said Gifta smugly.

Rowena closed her eyes and held on to her daughter and thought that of all the various miracles the Atheling had wrought at Healdsteda, this was the greatest.

"Neither was I," she lied.

ROWENA STOOD BESIDE the open window of her bower and looked at the bright moon and imagined climbing through that small space again and finding her way into a place of magic.

It was impossible.

The magic did not exist in the night forest glade. It existed in Wulf. Everything good that had happened in the glade had happened because of his heart and his spirit, and when he went, the magic would go with him.

She closed her aching eyelids against the moon, against the thought of surviving in the wasteland without Athelwulf of Bernicia. She could hear the sound of feasting in her mead-hall floating towards her across the courtyard. They would celebrate all night. Everything had turned out right. Even she, in the end, had done right.

The aloneness tore through her like the claws of some savage beast of prey. It would kill her if she let it. And then she would be no use to Gifta, or to Ludda, or to anyone at Healdsteda. The aloneness would kill her from the inside.

She did not know whether she could stop it.

Someone barged into her chamber without asking.

She did not turn round. "Get out," she said. "I will see no one."

The door of her room hit the wall with a smack that would break it.

"You will see me."

"Wulf…"

She turned round. It was not Wulf the thrall. It was the Atheling.

She looked at the tall figure in its fine tunic of madder-red splashed with gold, the thick twisted gold arm ring, the dark trousers held in below the knee with decorated leather. He had cut his hair.

Only the eyes were the same. Impenetrable grey. They were filled with cold fury.

"How could you not tell me?"

Her back jarred against the wall before she was aware she had moved.

"Tell you what?"

"That I would be leaving behind some poor nameless bastard."

The room went black. But she could not actually have swooned because she was sitting on the cushioned window seat, still talking.

Her voice, high-pitched and breathless said, "What…how…what do you mean? I am not—"

"You would deny it? To me? When everyone here knows it, Athelbrand, your King Ine, even the lowest serving wench knows you are with child."

"Knows I am *what?* That is ridiculous. It is not true."

"Brand said you fainted."

Athelbrand was the world's bane. She remembered the look of speculation those amber eyes had given her. She had ignored it. It had not occurred to her that— "But that was not why I…that was just the shock of him arriving like that and yelling all hell because you were not here and—" not knowing where you were and thinking you might be dead or prey to Hun "—and I had not slept and I was not feeling well—"

"You were not feeling well—"

"No, but I told you that is just…" her voice wavered. She did not feel well. At least, she did not feel ill. Nothing that sleep would not cure but she felt…different. She had felt different since—

"It is just…it is not because…" She looked at his eyes and she was back in the cold moonlight of the glade. With him. Just him, his body the only source of warmth in the coldness. She remembered how he had felt, covering her, touching her flesh, the heat of him between her thighs, inside her, urgent, demanding, and then…he would have pulled back.

Because he had had no desire to risk the consequences. And she had stopped him. Out of selfishness. Because she could not let him go. Because she wanted him too much. Because the pain and the emptiness in her heart had been too great.

Selfishness.

"It is not true," she said. "You cannot possibly tell

after two days. I am not…'' But she could not get the
words out.

He just looked at her. That was all it took and her
lie was exposed in its malformed shape between them.
She knew what was true. Beyond reason and beyond
reckoning. They both did.

Her mind was filled with the awareness of the power
that had been in the moonlit air of the glade on Lamas
Eve, the power that was in him.

She knew what was true and she also knew that it
had been her fault. Her actions had destroyed the only
way she had to redeem all that had happened.

Ludda's words that she had dismissed as feverish
ramblings burned in her head. *Once he knew…well
always was the sort to do the right thing.*

She had trapped the man who had been her thrall
more surely than she could ever have done with
chains.

She could not let it happen.

She sat up straighter and said in her old self-assured
way, ''Even if it is true, it does not matter—''

''Does not *matter?*''

''No. Not to me. You forget. I do not need you. I
want you to go back where you came from. To Northumbria. I have all that I need here, position, wealth.''
She wished she had not said that. She would have
given anything to call the words back. But she could
not afford to. She had to go on. She dredged up one
of her false smiles. ''I am a woman of consequence.
I am sure my reputation will survive, and as for the

child, lots of people are illegitimate. It is hardly unusual.''

But that made the eyes harden again into stone.

''Not my child. I will not allow that to happen.''

Her hands, buried in the cushions had balled themselves into fists.

''You will not have a choice.'' She could feel her
palms damp with sweat. The Atheling took a step towards her. His fine shoes made no sound in the rushes.
Torchlight glowed on the unfamiliar red tunic, flashed
on gold. She felt the stranger's shadow fall over her,
just as Eadward's had. There seemed to be no air in
the room at all. She shut her eyes.

When she opened them again, he was simply watching her. The width of his shoulders was a black wall
against the torchlight behind him. His face was shadows. But she thought the fury was gone. No, not gone,
banked down, and in front of it an intense attention
that took her apart in small pieces. She lowered her
head because she could not bear that clear-eyed scrutiny.

He sat down. Deep red cloth filled the entire span
of her vision. *Eten* size. She could not see his face
anymore because she refused to raise her head. Between the masking edges of her veil was nothing but
the endless expanse of finely woven red wool. She
could not move. There was nowhere to go. She saw
the bright cloth swell with the force of his breath. She
waited for him to speak. He did not. There was a blur
of bright gold on the edge of her vision. Then her hand

was dragged out from the cushions despite the total resistance of her rigid arm. His *eten* hand swallowed hers.

His flesh was warm and unmoving, achingly secure. It was terrible because he would know she was shaking.

"Rowena."

She would not look at him. She would retain that much control. Deep red cloth stretched over thick muscle. She stared at it.

"I will not leave you on your own."

"But—"

"And I will not leave a son without a father's love."

A son. That was all he said. But it meant he knew. Everything. That in the forest glade she had been thinking about her losses. The father who had not really loved her. The husband who had betrayed her. Her dead son, the cruelest loss of all.

It was her fault that she was with child again. It had been through her choice and her act of will in the power-charged air of that place. She had used that, used him, to fulfil her own needs. To redeem what had been lost.

Except it had not been just that. Even though her thoughts had been so confused and so painful, she had never lost her awareness of him and who he was and what he meant. It had been him and only him she had wanted through everything. What she had truly wanted was the final and ultimate act of closeness with him.

And now he would never believe that.

He knew too much.

"Rowena, it is all right."

He always acted to get other people out of their own mess. Whatever the cost.

"It is not all right."

"Rowena—"

She ripped her hand out of his with a strength that was greater. She looked at him in all the wildness of her desperation. She felt as though the oppression around her heart would kill her. But there was nothing that would break her will in this.

"It can never be made right."

"It can. We can make it right. Rowena, I am asking you to marry me."

CHAPTER EIGHTEEN

SHE STARTED WEEPING.

It was the last thing Wulf expected in the face of her anger. The terrible keening sound of it went through his shocked mind like a knife blade.

It was not the way she had wept before, with such passionate defiance in the midst of all her hurt. It was simply hopelessness, as though that small spark of defiance had finally been extinguished.

He could not bear that thought. Or the consciousness that he had been the means of bringing that about. The fierce, primitive response to that, the urge to protect her somehow from such pain was far stronger than the knowledge that she would not wish it. He had moved before thought was possible.

She fought him with all the strength that she had, tearing herself away from his touch as though the very contact of his body were poison.

Her tears doubled. He had never seen anybody cry so. Doubled up and gasping, as though in some terrible physical pain.

"Rowena…"

The sound of his voice made her flinch, her hunched

body shrinking away from him as though he had offered to strike her, not to help her. That hurt more than it was possible to imagine. He would rather Hun had ripped his guts out and left him to die. Nay, Hun should just have killed him outright when the chance had first been his on that long ago day in Northumbria, and then none of this would have happened. He would not have been here to inflict such misery on someone else through his own unquenchable arrogance.

He had always believed he knew better. That he could arrange other people's lives for them far better than they could do it for themselves. And now he had brought pain and ruin and humiliation on the one person above all others whom he had wanted to save. He had wanted to put the Lady Rowena's world right for her.

He had wanted to free that bright spirit from the shadows that oppressed it. So that she could be as blithe and happy and secure and just slightly heedless as she was meant to be. He had wanted so much for her, and he had wanted her so much. He had been dazzled right from the start by how beautiful she was, how passionate and wilful. And then he had got to know that she had a heart. One which could be broken.

He watched the helpless angle of the bent head in its drooping fall of white linen. He heard the painful sound of her sorrow. And he knew that he had caused it. And for once in his life there was nothing he could do to stop someone suffering.

She wept without hope or remedy. He could not

touch her, could not so much as speak without increasing the force of her sorrow. She had asked him to go. He was not what she wished. He knew that right well. Borrowed clothes no longer made an Atheling.

Nothing could wipe out what he had been, what he still was.

He should leave her as she wished and it would be better for her. Except that he could not. It was not in him. Whether he was right or wrong he no longer knew. It had no significance compared to the way she wept at this moment. Nothing in his life had any meaning compared to that.

He slid off her extravagantly cushioned window seat with one knee amongst the straw at her feet because he was such an awkwardly intimidating size compared to her. He took her hand. At least, not quite that. He just let her fingertips rest against his palm so that his roughened fingers did not enclose hers. So she could escape his touch if she wished.

"Rowena."

She did not tear away from him this time.

"Rowena," he said, with the sort of voice he had always used to steady his impulsive family, "you must stop this or you will make yourself ill."

The sobs abated and he could see the slim straight shoulders steel themselves for the last confrontation. He ignored the savagery of the urge to crush that small frame into his arms.

His heart beat as it never had before a battle. "Rowena, listen to me," he said in the same clear voice.

She had stopped crying and if she did not raise her head, neither did she take her fingers away from his hand and she listened.

He had no idea what to say.

He had come in with the one single-minded idea of what was the right and honourable thing to do. Now he did not know what was right. He looked at the delicate fingers resting against his skin, his hand roughened, freshly scratched and blistered from the harvest. Just below Athelbrand's gold arm ring which was not quite wide enough to hide all the scars. He pulled down Athelbrand's sleeve.

If there had been any mercy in the world he would know what to say to her.

What came out, not quite as steadily as before, were fragments of truth.

"Rowena, I know I am not what you would have wished for the father of your child. I know—" He felt the fingertips move against his skin. He did not know how he stopped himself from catching them. From trying to preserve that one tiny source of contact between them. But he could not do it to her.

"I would not try and force you into anything that you do not wish but—"

"You are an Atheling, a prince." Her voice, tight and expressionless said, "How could any woman wish for more?"

He swallowed what rose to his tongue and tried to look as though Athelbrand's best spare tunic and Athelbrand's sword belt and Athelbrand's jewellery fitted him. Anything that would make her feel even marginally less distressed.

"Yes," he said, "I am, and I wish that could have been how you had met me, that you had never had to see me as anything else that would bring you shame. I cannot change the past. I would for your sake that I could. But if you could think of things as they are now and not of that...I do not know whether you can. But if you could, my offer is still there. All that I have. I wish it could have been different for us."

"Do you? Is that what you think?" Her voice had gone hoarse. It would be from such weeping.

"Of course." It was only putting words to the obvious, what he had said, but the fingers on his palm had begun to shake.

"I see." Just those two words. But her voice was no longer expressionless. It held all the hopelessness of her tears. Even the truth had not been enough. There seemed nothing left that he could say.

The fingers withdrew. He watched them. And that was the end. He, both of them, were lost. He knew, he had been taught it well enough, that there was no mercy and no justice on middle earth.

But she spoke. He sensed her breath rather than heard it. It had no sound. And if he had not been looking at her he would not have caught the faint movement of her veil. He would not have heard her voice because her words were so faint.

"Do you know what I would change?"

He waited, the movement to get at least to his feet

suspended. But he could not answer. Could not speak, because the despair of everything that had happened had taken his voice. He just sat in the rushes and she began to talk.

"I would change nothing. Can you possibly understand that? I do not expect you to believe me. I have given you no reason to believe anything that I could now say to you. But it is true." The hand reached back towards him. It did not touch him. It lighted on Athelbrand's arm ring. "I would not have wanted to meet some perfect Northumbrian Atheling full of false pride and arrogance." The fingers wrapped themselves around the torqued gold, pushing it up his arm, rumpling Athelbrand's silk-embroidered tunic sleeve as it moved. "It would have been worth nothing to me."

The veil fluttered. "Instead I met you. I would change nothing about you, unless I could have taken away your pain. But I would not change one thing about what you are and what you think and what you do. About what you have done." Her fingers touched his flesh at last, at his wrist, featherlight and elegant against its distorted ugliness. "I would not change one breath of you. What I would change is myself. Because then I might deserve you."

"I do not understand," said something rough and grating that had once been an arrogant thane's voice.

Her hand closed over his wrist. The shock of her touch penetrated every muscle in his body, making the dead flesh alive with feeling. He felt as though his head would burst.

"You have done nothing wrong," said the rough voice and the small fingers dug into his wrist. They were trembling. His hand moved instinctively to cover hers, to stop it shaking.

The last of the truth came out of him. The truth that existed of itself, even though he had never put it into words, not even to himself.

"You have my heart. You must have known that through everything that I did. I just could not say it. Because of what I was, what I am…" his chest felt as though it was on fire. He could not see her face.

"Do not," she said, "do not say such things. You will kill me. You have done all for me. All that I wanted, vindicated my father's death, saved me from all danger, given me, given Healdsteda, new life. You risked everything, without stint, for me, and you gave me kindness."

She looked up.

"But you do not know what I have done in return. I betrayed you."

A small cold space found its place just beneath Wulf's heart. He could feel his face freeze into the expression that gave away nothing. His mind, obedient to long years of training, began the process of assessing the problem that confronted it. While all the time, the cold patch was growing.

"How?" asked the voice that was harsher than the face. Then he added carefully, "Tell me what you mean," because a single word spoken like that was far too ruthless to get a response out of the horrified eyes locked on his own.

"He would not have known you were here, he would not have guessed, but for me. I told him, Hun, the man who wanted to kill you, who had already…"

Fortunately for his self-control, she stopped there.

"Will you tell me why?" The coldness under his heart seemed to be seeping through his limbs, like death.

"Because I am worthless."

He frowned, and on the level of thought his mind tried to grapple with a response that had no logic. She started crying again. At least, it was only stray tears that escaped from the haunted eyes. She was still talking.

"You were right you see. You knew from the beginning. When we first made this terrible bargain and I thought I was so clever. You just looked at me as though I was some empty, shallow, spoiled brat who was not worth the dust under your feet. Someone who was utterly ignorant of what life was about."

The source of coldness at his heart seemed to have turned into a murderous tightness, so that it was hard even to draw breath. The world was going black round the edges, narrowed to the pale oval of her face in its white veil, the deep pools of her eyes. The fine, thin skin of her face was flushed with heat and streaked with tears. Her eyes looked wild, hunted, and he was certain in some region far beyond the thought-hoard of his mind that she could feel the darkness closing in on her, too. The darkness that killed everything.

It would kill her. He knew it so well.

But he could not permit that. Whatever she had or had not done, the darkness could not be allowed to win her.

He leaned back and clasped his hands loosely around his bent knees in a grim mockery of ease. He turned his face towards the rich tapestry on the opposite wall. Some hunting scene with a white hart. He positioned his head so that he could still see her eyes but she would not know he was looking at her.

"You had better tell me. What did you do, sell me at a profit for fifteen mancuses?" His voice, under perfect control, came out with all the apparent off-handedness of his pose.

He saw the startled look that crossed the tortured eyes. Such a small and ordinary and steadying reaction out of such anguish. She might even begin to think again. But then the eyes went dark.

"Yes," she said.

It was blunt. But at least she had said it. Not a muscle of his body moved. Slave's training was useful for something.

"You could not get any more?"

The small startled look appeared again, like a bright-scaled fish surfacing out of a dark pool.

"I did not care how much. I just wanted to shut

Eadward up to…'' She stopped. Whatever it was she had wanted to say about the exiled reeve, she would not.

He took a breath. There was fresh night air in the room. It had always been there. He just had not been able to feel it. It was the cold blessing of the North, the source of his strength, a power insubstantial.

"Eadward?" he inquired, with his face towards the tapestry, "you sold me twice? You were double dealing. That was why Hun was quite so put out."

"No!" The eyes became intolerably confused. "It was not…Eadward was only acting for Hun. It was…the point is what I did before. I told Hun."

"Ah. I suppose he offered you twenty."

The confusion deepened. She had to think, so that what was in her mind could come out. The effort caused a small spark in the deadness of her eyes. Infinitely small, but more precious than gold.

"It was not the price," she said at last. "It was because I was so angry with him, so angry with *you*."

He took a breath of ice-clear air and said stonily, "I never make you angry."

The small spark almost took on a life of its own. "You do. At least you did. All the time. You made me dissatisfied with myself. That was what the problem was. Me. You made me see things I did not want to see. You made me want you."

The pause between them was as fragile and breakable as the touch of ice in the air. Perhaps as strong and as life-giving if he did not speak.

"That was what it was. I did not want to want anyone's regard, anyone's *friendship* again,'' she said, and the word she had chosen, that her voice had stumbled over, *freonscip,* had a hidden double meaning between men and women. Despite every last ounce of resolve, his large scratched hands clenched themselves into fists.

''It was when you…after the first time you kissed me and I turned you away. I turned you away because I knew how much I wanted you in spite of everything I had done to show the contrary. I was afraid of you and I was afraid of what I felt and I was selfish enough to be afraid of the future.''

''It was not selfish. It was quite natural,'' he said and his gaze suddenly became focussed on the solid scratched lump of his fists.

''That is what I told myself. It was quite natural and justified. It was the way things were and it fitted in with the person I wanted to become. Independent and self-sufficient and invulnerable and nobody's fool. But I never stopped wanting you and it made me so angry. I tried to think I was angry with you but it was not just that. I was angry with myself and I did not like myself. That is when I got Ludda to send someone to look for Athelbrand.''

''You—''

''I paid a small fortune in silver for a messenger to find your brother. It was conscience money. But then Ludda told me he had seen you over at Alfred's farm with his daughter.''

''With his…that silly benighted wench who…''

"Looks like Freya's acolyte. Yes. So that meant I could be really angry with you."

He suddenly felt as though the intolerable confusion had burst into his mind, not hers.

"But you could not—"

"Be jealous of the thought of my thrall disporting himself with a *churl's* daughter? Oh, yes I could. The Lady Rowena had been slighted and although she should not care, she did. It hurt. And it made me even more frightened I was out of control. And then when Hun came and infuriated me further I struck back and I reasserted myself as who I was. Hun insulted me. Oh, it does not matter how and he did me no injury. Besides, you and Athelbrand have made him pay with his life."

Wulf made himself sit back down. He straightened out his hands. He heard her breath. It was not steady.

He knew what Hun had been like. He knew what Hun did to people, even if he did not touch them. "Rowena, you do not have to—"

"Yes, I do. I have to tell you what I did. It was obvious what kind of a man he was but I still said it. To put him in his place. To put you back in your place. I knew he was Northumbrian. Like you. So I said I had just bought a Northumbrian as a slave and Eadward...Eadward mentioned that you had been flogged. And that was it. I had done it."

Her voice paused and then said, "So all the time you were with me in the forest glade, all the time you made me feel for once that I was really worthwhile and exactly what somebody wanted, without having to wish I was different, it was all a lie. I had killed all that we had together, all that we could ever have. I had as good as killed you. I did not understand what I had done until Hun sent Eadward to buy you.

"You said, that night, that you thought I had a heart that was worth saving. But it was the selfishness that won in the end, and do you know what the most terrible thing is? I would never have said anything to Hun if you had not meant so much to me."

Those last few words were the ones he had most wanted to hear from her in all the world. But not like this, not at such a cost to her.

The clenched tightness of his hands buried itself for an instant in his newly shortened hair. How could anyone who could arrange people's lives for them so much better than they could do it for themselves have created such a mess?

But he knew how, deep inside. The fault was in him. He had arranged everyone else's life while his own had spun far beyond his control. It was something he had refused to admit, out of pride and arrogance and self-protection. Out of the necessity to shore up something from the wreckage of what he had been. He had used the pride and the conscious layer of invulnerability like a shield for the mind in the same way that the hard steel skin of chain mail protected the body. It hid the fact that anything could be hurt underneath. He had kept it in place because he did not know what would happen if he let it go.

He still did not know what would happen. But there was no other choice to be made.

"Rowena, it was not your fault. It was mine."

"But..."

He took a breath that had all the self-possession and well-practiced steadiness that a thane would have shown before battle. His voice fell into the smoothly strong, perfectly balanced pattern of someone who had been expensively trained in both the art of command and the art of rhetoric.

"You did not know who I was. You could not have known, whatever you may now think looking back with the knowledge you have now. You did not know because I did not tell you. I should have."

"But you could not." Her voice still trembled but it sounded stronger. "I know that you were still in danger until the moment King Osred died. Just because of who you are. It was your secret and your burden. Besides, I never gave you any reason to suppose that I would help you the way you helped me."

"And I did not give you the opportunity. I shut you out even when I should not. I shut everyone out. Everything." Or perhaps that was not the way of it. Perhaps something had been shut in. Trapped and locked up like a prisoner. He did not want to let whatever it was out. Not even now.

But he could not leave her alone in the wilderness. And that was what he had done, although he had not meant it, had not even seen what he had done.

"You said that I helped you that night in the forest

glade. That was what I wanted to do more than anything. You told me about yourself, about who you
were and all the terrible things that had happened to
you." There was a pause, even in the strong thane's
voice, but he made it go on.

"I wanted to take all that pain away from you. I
wanted to show you how much I cared, to show you
how much there was in you to love. You told me all
your grief but I said nothing. It was all there, in my
heart, but I decided it was not necessary for me to say
it. I thought I would be embroiling you in something
sordid and dangerous and utterly without hope. But I
had already brought you danger, just by being there."

"But you could not have known that. If I had not
spoken when I should not—"

"You mean if I had spoken when I should. There
were other reasons why I should have…" How did he
put such reasons into words? They were reasons that
did not admit themselves into mere words. They did
not live in the ruthlessly ordered pathways of his mind.
They lived in his heart.

"You deserved my confidence," he said, "as you
gave me yours."

"No. I deserved nothing, and there is nothing that
you need to say to me now. I know there are things
you do not wish to speak of. I may be selfish but I
can see that much. There is naught that you need to
explain to me."

And there it was. The opportunity to withdraw from
the field of such difficult ground intact. The with-

drawal inside was immediate and so strong. Impregnable. But her voice had returned to the deadness of despair and he could not allow that. Besides, the defence was no longer impregnable. The prisoner inside would no longer be contained and was already storming the gates.

"I must tell you."

The prisoner bound and left for dead, the one abandoned in the darkness for so long broke free.

"It began," said Athelwulf, "in Bernicia."

ROWENA WATCHED from the protective concealment of her veil. He had changed. Even through the grey mist of her own pain she could see it. It was not just the fine clothes and the shortened hair. It was him.

It was inside, coming out through his eyes and the way he moved and above all, through his voice. It had been scarce there at first but now on that last fatal word, it was so strong. There, not just in his accent, but in the very tone of his voice. *Bernicia,* northernmost half of the vast kingdom of Northumbria. The one thing, that even if she had done every thing right, even if she was a better person, she could not have competed with.

"It began with my home," said Athelwulf the stranger, restored Northumbrian thane, Atheling of the house of Cenred. "Everything is so different in the North. The country is different. Beautiful, wilder, not so fertile, so that one's lands are wider, at least ours were. But it was not just because our home was so beautiful, it's because of where it is. Just north of Jarrow and Wearmouth.''

''Jarrow?'' she said, so lost, so ignorant of what he meant, she could have wept for it.

''There are monasteries there you see, with manuscripts. I used to go there, whenever I could, so I could know what was in the books. I started learning Latin so that I could read everything. Do you know, there is even a monk there who is writing a book on how to calculate time? Can you imagine that? Having a system to bring something as elemental as time into order. I was no more than a boy and I was dazzled. But the wonder of it stayed with me, until…for a long time.''

Just a slight pause in that perfect foreign voice, but she heard it and the pain that caused it coiled like a waiting serpent in her own breast.

''That was the first step on the road and once my feet were on it, I could not turn back. I went south, into Deira, to York where there is a cathedral and a library with books from Rome. My father let me have some of them copied. The *Dialogues* of Gregory the Great so that I should know how to lead other men and Boethius' book on philosophy so that I would know how to think, and life seemed so very easy. But then my parents died.''

''What happened?'' She thought of the mother she had never known, the hideous corpse of her father. Of being suddenly alone.

''Sickness. It is a common happening.''

"But…" she felt the serpent inside coil one notch tighter.

"Of course there were rumours it was poison. Because of who we are. But no one knew. I still do not know."

"Wulf…" *Because of who we are.* "Athelwulf…" she corrected herself. But he went on speaking, the voice as clear, as relentlessly firm as ever.

"I went home. It was all down to me. I was the eldest. I was determined that no one would ever harm my family. I had no interest in going to court, except to see where danger might lie. I fulfilled every service we owed but the court, the kind of court that gathered around Osred, did not form part of my world. What I wanted was somewhere that reflected all the good that I had learned. And so it did."

She watched his face, the slate-grey eyes that hid so much, the ruthless lines of his bones. He would not see her looking at him. She did not think he even saw the room that they were in. Perhaps he saw only his home as it had been, a thing of beauty that had nothing to do with landscapes and riches and everything to do with the strength of his will.

"How old were you when your parents died?"

She saw a faint frown cross the sculpted line of his brow, as though she had said something totally irrelevant.

"Just entering my sixteenth winter."

"I see." Not quite sixteen and creating a world all by yourself because there was no one else to do it.

Her hand slid across the embroidered cushions. She did not quite dare to touch him, but her fingers found the edge of his fine tunic sleeve and fastened on it like an eagle's claws. She touched only material, not him, and she did not think he would notice. But he did. And that was when she realised his attention was not on Bernicia at all, but solely and utterly founded on her.

The awareness between them was wound as tight as a bow's string before the arrow flies. Her breath caught and her hand shook.

"Tell me," she said, "tell me what happened." Because it was the key. She knew it. She did not know why or what he would say but only that he must.

"We prospered. We prospered and none touched us. My sisters married well. Athelbrand…" His voice broke off in response to some movement transmitted through the fingers that did not even touch him and that she had not meant to make.

"Yes, I was angry. I was so angry with Brand for what he did, for what he destroyed, that I could have taken him apart with my bare hands. I did not understand how he could have done it. How he could have put everything at risk for the sake of passion. But I did not know then how much it is possible to feel."

A sudden heat flooded through her veins, burning white hot. If it were only possible that… If it were possible that he might feel such a thing for her. The heat burned through her skin even though she did not touch him. But deep inside was still the coiled serpent, fell and monstrous and waiting to strike.

"Athelbrand told me what he did," she said. "I know why—"

"Why all came to ruin? What Brand did was not the only reason. I think the real reason was that we prospered too much for Osred's comfort; and for all my care he, his advisers, could not believe I had no wish for the kind of power that they wielded. My kind of power was something quite other."

She knew that. She could see it now, as clearly as day. But she did not know whether she had seen it at first. She had seen the strength and the edge of danger, and the force of will that let others who had less taste the cold breath of panic. She could imagine what a king, overyoung and full of greed and unease and the lust for power over others, would have seen.

One slender finger moved, like some small creature fascinated by the beast of prey that could kill it, towards the thick muscle of his neck. It tightened against her hand and her breath froze because she did not know if he still wanted her touch. Her finger looked ridiculously small. She felt his warmth. Just for an instant. And then that heavy, smoothly flexible power slid away from her grasp so that he leaned forward. The shortened length of his hair slid across his face, hiding it from her sight.

"It was all so well planned," said his perfect voice, "and far too quick. Brand had come home with his prize only long enough to get what he needed for the journey and then he was off to the coast, and a boat to Francia. But even that time was long enough for Hun, and Osred's men.''

''And you went back,'' she said, ''and saved his skin.''

The powerful shoulders shrugged, as they tended to do at something he viewed as irrelevant.

''He would do the same for me.''

He stopped speaking.

It was so self-evident to him, that statement, so incapable of being refuted. That was how he loved, and that was how his family must love him. Her hands, empty of him and clenched in her lap, twisted in a painful grip she did not feel through her abused fingers, but through her heart. That love was what she had wanted all her life. What she wanted from him. What she had wanted to give, even though she had been too clumsy and too inept, too afraid to do it.

She wanted to give it now. To make things right for him somehow. Even if it meant that he was never hers. Even if it meant that he should go where his heart was at ease. To his home.

She had to know what was best to do, how to help him. She tried to think. To work things out clearly, the way he did. But she did not know. She did not know what was locked into that blank, averted head.

Which meant he had to tell her.

He had said that he should have told her about himself when they had been together in the forest glade. He had said it...he had used such a tone of voice, and she began to see, now, the extent of all he had lost. But it was not just that. It was something else. She had to find out what it was.

She looked at him and it was like looking at a stranger, a shape shifter who had taken on someone else's form that was completely familiar and at the same time subtly changed. Because you no longer knew what was inside.

Her gaze followed the sheer size of his back, the stark, uncompromising set of lines that made up the terrifying whole of him. Nay, it was not so much that which terrified, but what she could not see. What was in the even stronger citadel of his mind.

She had to make him speak.

She swallowed.

"You said there were things that you had wished to say to me…things that you thought you should have said that…" There was no reaction in him at all and her voice dried up on a strange rasping noise. There was a silence that seemed to her to stretch for hours but could have lasted no longer than seconds. She had to fill it. To gain his attention. To say something that…anything.

"Athelwulf…" she began and she realised what had been staring her in the face. It was not some shape shifter who had taken over the body of Wulf the thrall. The rightful owner had come back to reclaim what was his.

It was someone she did not know.

Then as if in answer to some spellword bound in that foreign name, the stranger spoke.

CHAPTER NINETEEN

"IT WOULD HAVE BEEN so much better," said Athelwulf, "if I had died when I was supposed to. But I
did not. At least, not in the way you would think."

That was a stupid beginning. She would think he
was moon-mad. She might be right.

"I went back to throw Hun off the scent, to give
Brand time to get himself and everyone else away. I
got caught. That was not so much a risk as almost a
certainty, and since I had no intention of being caught
alive that should have been that. But it was not. You
see there was somebody else there. I had not intended—" He stopped, because from being so quiet
she had made the sort of wordless sound people utter
when something suddenly makes sense to them.

But he had not even begun yet.

He tried again.

"It was just the stable boy, but—"

"But that would not have mattered, would it?"

He frowned. "No, but—"

"There was someone else so you had to help him."

He paused and looked at the choices that had been

before him. "Yes. He was scarce sixteen and simple with it. He—"

"He was someone who was helpless?"

"Aye—" He suddenly remembered he had told her that much before and what he had done. But not why, or how it happened. Because of the horror of it. Because the rawness of it had been too recent. Because there had been no way to redeem his past and she had had to know even then that he was not fit for her.

And now he had to tell her. For all the same reasons.

And because he cared too much about her.

"I had thought I was alone but the boy went back there. Because of me. He used to follow me like a shadow when he could. I could not just abandon him."

"Of course not. You did not have a choice did you? Because you are you," she said, which was totally confusing. Besides, she did not know who or what he was. He had to tell her. He fixed his eyes on the comfortable room in Wessex and the tapestry on the wall. But inside his head was the long slow twilight of Northumbria and the cold bite of the wind cutting against the hot sweat on his skin.

"I had tried to make an escape for him. They were not interested in him compared to me, but he would not leave me. He did not understand. So I fought on even though it was pointless until someone did the sensible thing and knocked me out."

The darkness behind his open eyes was almost complete now, apart from the bright edge of fire. Rowena was quite silent.

"When I woke, I heard the screaming. They had left the boy next to me, pinned to the ground with a spear through his guts. His life was gone but…it takes a long time to die like that. He was begging them for help. It made them laugh. Poor lad. He did not even know who they were or why they were there."

Athelwulf could smell the wet earth under his face, taste the bitter smoke of burning thatch borne on the wind. He had been able to tell which part of his home burned without looking. They had left the hall to the east because it was of value and still had such treasure as he and Brand had not been able to carry away. What they had burned was of no value to them. The chapel he had just begun to build and the room beside it that held his books.

"They were so sure of the kill, so careless, they did not see the moment when I woke, and a moment was quite enough. I broke the boy's neck. It was quite simple. He was only small." Athelwulf looked at the size of his hands. He could still feel the helpless crack of young bones.

"I will never forget what I did but I could not leave him like that and…it was done. No going back, and that was the moment Hun and I came to the same decision. I would live."

There was a sudden rustling noise and a small thud in some other place and time. He forced his mind to take it in. He caught the bright splash of blue wool and many-coloured embroidery spilling over the rushes in the comfortable room. He blinked in the darkness. Rowena's skirts. She had slid down from the bench beside him. He stared at the fine edge of her dress but he could not look at her. Neither could he move. He was still too far in the dark. The dark that had nothing to do with her brightness.

He stayed where he was. Speechless. If she did not touch him. Let her not touch him. Not now with the darkness all round him and so much unaccounted for. It should not touch her brightness. The whole force of his will was bent on that. There was silence, and she did not touch him. She sat amongst the rushes, just as he did.

"I cannot tell you too much of the rest," he said, with his eyes on the jewelled brightness of her. "I do not remember it all and what I do remember is not fit for you."

"Anything that has happened to you is fit for me to hear."

Her voice startled him. It was no longer choked with tears. It was as strong as steel and as clear as the bell at Prime.

She was such a mass of contradictions that you could forget, if you were not careful, just how great her courage was. He had to force himself not to look at her.

But there was no doubt of those things he would not burden her with.

"Then let us just say that there are some memories I would not care to rekindle," he said out of respect for that extraordinary courage. "Besides, I came out of it still breathing. I made myself survive it because I knew it was not really the end. Hun would not rest until he had caught the one he really wanted, Athelbrand. And I was not going to die while Brand was still alive and that creature walked the same earth. But…''

He took a breath. It was pointless reliving that rage so that it burned through his veins, hotter than the fire that had consumed the world he had created. Hun was dead, and by Athelbrand's hand not his. He had thought that achieving vengeance, some form of justice on the man who had destroyed so much had been the only way out. But when it had come to the point he had not given spit for taking revenge, even when it had been within a sword's length of him. The only thing he had cared about was Rowena. And that was all that mattered now.

"What I am trying to explain is what happened later, when I came to myself, in chains, on a ship bound for Frisia. I was then what you first saw me as—a slave.'' He paused, choosing his words. ''A thane, worse still, an Atheling with the arrogance to try and remake an entire world over to the way he wants it, does not make a good slave.''

He looked at the rich cloth under his eyes in the room in Wessex.

"I buried Athelwulf and became the thing you bought. I survived when they all thought I was going to die, and there I was: a thrall with a mind full of fury who could outlive anything. But I was not easy to manage, deliberately so. I could not stay where I was, and by the time I had been resold four times I was given to a trader who was making for England. I was on the road back to find Athelbrand at last.''

"But then I bought you at Hamwic for twelve man-cuses, and I kept you here in the South for my own ends, so you could be useful to me. I kept you a prisoner when you wanted to be free. I treated you so badly—''

"You? I have told you. You would not know where to start.''

"But the things I said and did…I prevented you from leaving.'' Her voice, so clear and strong before, had taken back some of the tremor and the sadness. He could not stand her sadness.

"Prevented me? You could not have prevented Brocc the three legged badger from leaving this place. I could have been half-way back to Bernicia on the first day. I stayed because…'' *Because of your heart.* He had said that once before, just before he had brought this disaster on her. He stopped over what passion had nearly led him into. This was the most difficult part, the one that tore the holes in the pieces of his heart that remained.

"It was the very ease of this place that was the problem. It could make me forget sometimes what I was.''

Not to mention falling in love with the owner. With such wildness and unstoppable force. Even now, just sitting next to her, not even touching, designedly not touching, he could still feel the deep desire for her. It was like the ache of some unhealable wound, like a hunger that only increased the more the senses fed on her. He wanted her more than the power of reason, more than he had ever wanted his perfect world.

But he could not be what she wanted, what she deserved. She deserved happiness after so much sorrow. Not some creature like him dressed up in thane's clothing that no longer fitted and tarnished forever by the past.

In that first moment of shock when he had learned about the child, it had seemed so right, buoyed up by the sort of anger that hid pain, to demand that she marry him.

The way to put everything right. But it was not. Her first reaction had been the clearest. She had looked sick at the thought. Horrified. She had said that she did not need him. She was right. She could still marry well. Any man in his right mind would have her, child or none.

She would be happier. She would. But whoever it was, even if he was the patron saint of Wessex, he could not love her as much as he did.

Suppose the patron saint of Wessex did not know how to value her? And then there was the small maiden who boiled butter and looked after badgers. Suppose he did not realise how very careful you had to be with her?

But that was just the kind of arrogance that had got him into this mess. Whoever had the blessing of mar-

rying the Lady Rowena would surely have a whole
heart. Not the damage inside that he carried.

She did not know what he was. She would be happier with someone else.

He took off his brother's arm ring. She watched
him. He knew she did even though he did not look at
her. He knew what she saw. What had filled her with
such repugnance despite her pity.

"There is no pretence possible between us, is there?
You know what I have been, what I am still despite
an Atheling's clothing. The marks that are on me will
be there all my life, not to be hidden by overlong hair,
or by clothing, so that no one asks any awkward questions. They will always be there and even if they were
not, even if it were possible to be rid of them it would
not matter. Because they are nothing to what is on the
inside."

He paused and then said, "I had thought that if I
ever regained what was mine, all would be as before.
But it is not. I said I killed off Athelwulf when I became a slave. But it was not true. He was still there
underneath, and in the same way I will never be able
to kill Wulf the slave. He will always be there in part
of me. I do not think the way I used to, the way I am
supposed to. I'm changed and I can never be what I
was, what I should be. What you would wish."

His hands tightened on the twisted gold so that the
torqued strands dug into palms ruined both by wood-
cutting and weapon fighting.

"I would not try and force you into something you

cannot want. What was between us is…I cannot say what it is to me but it was something that…there was too much sorrow in both of us but I would not bind you to that forever. I am neither what you wish nor what you should have but…I will still do all in my power to ease things for you, for the child. I am not a pauper anymore, or powerless. But above all other things I would have you free."

The last step had to be taken for her sake.

"I am going back to Northumbria."

The silence between them had the quality of stretched wire. She did not move.

"Rowena, you do understand what I have said, why I—"

"I wish it had been me who killed Hun."

"What? You…*you*…why…" It was bizarre. It had nothing to do with what he had been saying. It…he nearly choked on the black rage and the underlying terror that flooded through him. "What have you not told me? What did he do when he came here first?"

He was shouting. He saw her narrow shoulders flinch but he could not stop himself for the fear that the defiling evil that was Hun had touched her. "What else happened when you first saw him?"

"Nothing! There was nothing that happened that…it has nothing to do with me." Her voice gathered strength and the hunched shoulders suddenly went straight. "I would kill him for what he had done to you."

He was dumbstruck. It was insane. He had spent his

life driven by the need to protect other people. It had not occurred to him that anyone could feel that way about him. It was crazed. Women did not say things like that about men. Not unless…unless, perhaps, where they loved.

He did not think she could have meant what she said. He did not think he could have heard her right.

He turned his head and saw her eyes.

He no longer thought at all. Her lips were hot, hot and soft and swollen from the force of her tears, her taste deep and rich so that his senses swam in the first second. Her mouth opened on a small helpless gasp of surprise and he took it with his own mouth. Her slender form tightened under his weight. Her mouth cleaved to his, drawing him in, deeper. Her hands caught his shoulders, tangling in the wool of Athelbrand's tunic, raking at the flesh beneath.

Her breath, her lips, melted into his and her body strained against the width of his chest, his thighs, the desperate, rock-hard lust at his loins.

He touched her and control was impossible. He was terrified of hurting her but she did not seem to care. She clung to him as though she wanted him, as though nothing that had been said in this room had any meaning compared to how much they wanted each other. She clawed at him, her body twisting round him. The fine material of her skirts ripped under the force of their combined hands. He touched the soft slick wetness of her woman's core. But that he would not take with force.

He held her still, effortlessly, while his mouth gentled against hers, tasted the full sweetness of her. He held her body weightless against his, one hand cupping the moist heat of her sex. He waited until she was quite still. Her breath fast, every small muscle in her body stretched tight enough to break.

He moved his hand and found what he sought and knew from the wild glazed look in her eyes what he could do. His touch on her wet pulsing skin, so soft as to be on the edge of sensation, made her writhe. Her head tossed and he could almost feel the heat rush through her body.

But her flushed face sought his and he felt the warmth of her breath against the sweat on his skin.

"Wulf," she said, as though he was still the wild savage she had bought, "I want you. All of you. I want to feel you inside me.

"No," she said before a sound could cross his lips, "you will not harm what I carry, our son."

Her arms, tight round him, dragged him closer.

"Please." Her voice was no more than a ragged whisper, her breath was felt against his skin as much as heard. "I need this. I need to show you how much I want you. Just you. Only you. In everything. Let me do this."

Their bodies moved together, their combined hands released the last restriction of clothing.

"Wulf," she said to the savage, and then, "mine."

He took her in one thrust. The scorching heat of her body surrounded him and there was nothing in all the kingdoms of the world except her.

SHAKING HANDS straightened clothing. Hers. His. Rowena could not tell which. She had scratched one of his hands. Her tunic was torn.

"I did that. I have ripped your dress. I am sorry."

"It is my second best," she said, with a satisfaction that was almost frighteningly perverse.

"Your…not the one you used for impressing the Ealdorman."

"Yes. Only he had not got the guts to rip it."

"Just as well. I would have killed him."

The satisfaction really was perverse.

"I…I am not sorry at all. Are you?" Her hands were shaking so badly she did not have the strength to move a featherlight piece of material over her legs.

"No. Yes. At least, I meant to convince you I was no good for you."

"I think you unconvinced me."

"Rowena, you cannot mean it."

"Do not tell me what I can and cannot mean, you impudent thrall." Her voice was shaking as much as her hands. She… "All right," she said, when she could speak again, "ex-thrall. Thane. Atheling—" He kissed like a savage, like… "Bernician Barbarian—" No, not like a savage. As soft as heaven. Like…if he touched her again she really would die. "But you cannot stay here."

"I beg your pardon. Did I hear you attempting to

countermand the wishes of the King's Reeve? I have a certain position in Wessex, you know, which is not to be treated lightly.''

''No,'' she said, giving away the pretence of being able to hide her deadly earnestness from his sight, just as she had no longer the strength to cover her nakedness. ''You cannot stay here. It would break your heart.''

''No. You are the only one who could do that.''

She buried her head in the creased red tunic and if there had been any tears left, she would have cried them.

''Do you not understand,'' she said, ''how much you are to me? What I wanted, what I have wanted for a long time, even when I was too stubborn and miserable to admit it, was for you to be happy again. I might have strutted round like the lady of the manor in front of her thrall. I was so scared of you and what you might mean to me that that was how I wanted you to see me. But all the time, like it or not, from the first time I touched you, from the moment I paid twelve grubby mancuses, I was lost.

''Do you not see?'' she said to the tunic, ''I could not bear to see you as you were not because it was something shameful,'' she felt the sharp breath of the man underneath the tunic and her voice, pitched as strong and true as she could make it, said, ''It was because I knew it was wrong.''

But the man moved, underneath her light weight

that could not contain him and she was still afraid. Because the future still hung on a knife edge.

The knife.

"The runes told me what to do."

"The *what?*"

"The runes. On my father's *seax*. They spoke to me. They gave me the courage to cut your bonds even when I was afraid of your strength. Just like my heart tells me now what I must do, even though I am afraid I do not have the courage. But you know what an Idess does. I have told you: picks apart the chains. That is what I wanted to do. More than anything."

She moved, then, of her own accord and regardless of her ruined clothes, walked away and found what she sought. She held it out.

"But it is a bible. It—"

"Read what is inside the cover."

He read it, her Northern barbarian who would not have the wit to make out the letters.

"I like the curse. That is very good. You even added Cuthbert. He is Northumbrian."

Yes, she thought, from Jarrow. All-powerful Jarrow.

"Yes," she said aloud, in the bright-edged voice they both used to cover what lay beneath. "I wanted to be prepared for all eventualities. My kingdom and yours."

"When did you write it?"

"After that night, our night, in the glade. I would have done anything after that to free you of your burdens the way you had freed me. I know what my dead

husband did. I know he must have conspired with Eadward because he was part of Eadward's schemes to
gain wealth. But I do not think he intended my father's
death and he felt guilty and I think…perhaps Eadward
killed him, with poison.

"It is all right," she said when he would have
moved to touch her, for that inexpressible sense of
comfort only he could give. "I have worked it all out
and I know how things were. I know how much my
father did and did not love me. I know the extent of
Eadward's treachery. I know how much I loved my
dead son. I know all that and the only reason I can
live with it is because of what you showed me. That
someone could care about me selflessly and with no
regard for whether I deserved it or not. I will not fail
that selflessness. I will be worth it. And you will go
home and be proud of me," her lip curled, "deserved
or not."

"I am staying here."

"Please do not say any more, because I am not quite
as selfless as you and there is only so much I can
bear."

"Rowena—"

"You hate it here. You cannot deny that. You could
not even bear to be in my hall."

"No. I could not."

"You see—"

"The creature I was could not bear to be in your
hall because even though it was different, it reminded
me of my home. Because it was so beautiful and I still

coveted that. You see, my reasons for staying here are not selfless at all. I cannot go back to Bernicia, to what I left. It is not in me. I endured because of Athelbrand and because of the measure of my rage. I have a very bad temper.''

"I know. On the whole, it is just as well.'' But she should not have said that because her voice broke on the words.

"I cannot go back to being what I was. It…it did not all survive. I cannot be Athelwulf the thane just as he was. I can only be myself, as I am now. A mixture of all that has happened. Athelwulf has his place, but it is not a place that is fixed on earth, not even in Northumbria, it is just one part of me, wherever I am. I have no place if it is not here. And I have no future if it is not with you. Because without you I would have no heart.''

He meant it. She saw him get up. She knew he would touch her and she should turn away before he did. But she could not move. He touched her, so gently, his hands just resting at her waist.

"Anyway. You do need me. You have not finished the harvest yet and I have got a bet on with Dunn's brother. Think of the time wasted already.'' His hands were shaking. If it had not been for that she might never have believed what she wanted to believe so desperately. Her hands caught his arms.

"Besides,'' he said, "I still have not had time to mend the badger cage. Do you think…Gifta would like me to stay and do that?''

She knew what he was asking, with that utterly un-characteristic hesitation, and she knew beyond any possibility of doubt what the answer was.

"She would like that above anything in the world."

"But if I stayed, it would be for always. Would she want that?"

"If you had gone I did not know how I was going to console her. Yes. Yes, she would want that."

"And would you?"

Her heart thundered, as though it would choke her.

"Yes, yes, I would."

"I suppose I had better stay then, since nobody south of the Humber seems capable of managing any-thing."

She looked at his eyes and there it was, all that she had ever wanted, regardless of what anyone, either he or she, deserved.

"Stupid Northumbrian blockhead," she whispered against his short hair.

"I knew you would be overwhelmed. That was a proposal of marriage, by the way. Again."

His hands slid up to her shoulders, found the curve of her neck, caressed her skin so that it shivered. His fingers touched her face. His eyes were on hers. Slate-grey. Indomitable.

"So what do you say?"

She considered her answer. She put all the provo-cation she could into the look she gave back to him.

Her fingers dug into the hard muscles of his arms just to make sure he was real. Tears spilled out of her eyes.

"All right then," she said, "thrall."

It was the last thing she said for a very long time.

* * * * *

HISTORICAL NOTE ON THE YEAR 716

History gave King Osred of Northumbria a bad reputation, from Saint Boniface who called him a worthless youth leading an evil life, to a ninth-century poem recording him as murdering his nobles or banishing them to monasteries.

The *Anglo Saxon Chronicles* sparingly remark that he was killed in 716 south of the border, i.e. in Mercia, the kingdom which lay between Northumbria and Wessex.

It is known for certain that Northumbria was plagued by faction fights. The tragedy for the great Northern Kingdom was that this happened at the same time as the greatest flowering of its cultural life.

Wessex, by contrast, flourished under the resourceful and enterprising King Ine. He was often involved in border disputes with Mercia, but found time to establish the luxurious trading town of Hamwic (Southampton) and to develop a law code which was preserved by his more famous descendant, King Alfred the Great. Ine finished his life as adventurously as he lived it, making the arduous and dangerous pilgrimage to Rome where he lived out the last of his days.

Apart from these two kings, the characters in my book did not exist. Their lives are imagined against the wildly differing backgrounds of the lands they came from.

Author Note

What would you do if the price of love was too high, yet you could not stop loving?

Athelbrand of Bernicia broke the rules and the consequences were as unexpected as they were devastating. Brand, Wulf's brother, is a man with debts to pay: to the past and to the future. My next story is his.

For Brand the risks are high. He must find the woman for whom he once sacrificed everything before his enemy does; before his country is plunged into war. But the road to redemption is not what he expects. He must open his heart once more, and this time the sacrifice demanded of him is the deepest part of himself.

Alina's duty lies between her Celtic homeland and the Saxon warrior she loves. Her passion once came close to destroying him. She will not let it do so again.

The honouring of obligations was the foundation stone of life in the early middle ages. Conflicts between duty and emotion held a special fascination for the Anglo-Saxons. Their stories still touch us over the distance of a thousand years with the drama of impossible choices and the courage to triumph over the odds.

Brand and Alina's story is written in the spirit of this long tradition. I hope you will join me to share with them the next journey into the colourful Saxon world. Please enjoy the following preview of *Embers*, available 2006.

Helen

Helen Kirkman

CHAPTER ONE

HE HAD COME FOR HER, her wild-souled Northumbrian, and he would take: not love, but vengeance.

Her betrayal of him had been absolute. He had no reason for forgiveness. She would give him none. Not if it meant her life.

She stepped forward, out of the press of shivering strangers clustered round her.

"Brand," she said. It was the Saxon word for fire. Living fire.

He moved. Just the tread of one heavy warrior's foot, and the cold empty space round her gaped wide in the sudden rustling retreat of a dozen people. She stood her ground in front of them, just as she had come in from the orchard, her rough plain tunic and kirtle stained with purple sloe juice, streaks of wild dark hair escaping from the uncomfortable restriction of her coarse veil.

A nun's wimple in front of the finest, the best, the highest-hearted man in all the lands of England, of Britain.

"You remembered."

He strode forward. Sunlight from the open window

glinted on his flame-bright hair, dazzled on the gold twisted round his wrists, on the sword hilt, on the buckle of his leather belt. Her aching eyes stared in disbelief.

But it was there: all she had robbed him of by reason of who she was. Wealth, position, riches, all the very foundation of his life had been restored.

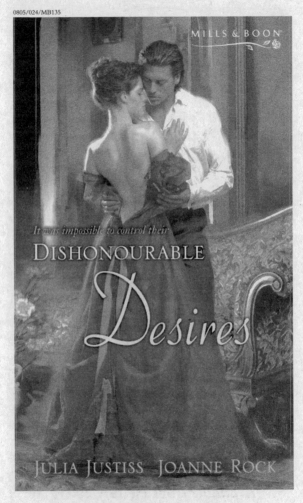

MILLS & BOON

It was impossible to control their

DISHONOURABLE

Desires

JULIA JUSTISS JOANNE ROCK

On sale 5th August 2005

Available at most branches of WHSmith, Tesco, ASDA, Martins, Borders, Eason, Sainsbury's and all good paperback bookshops.